Windmill Hill

Windmill Hill

MICHAEL JACOBSON

HODDER

A Mark Macleod Book

Published in Australia and New Zealand in 2002
by Hodder Headline Australia Pty Limited
(A member of the Hodder Headline Group)
Level 22, 201 Kent Street, Sydney NSW 2000
Website: www.hha.com.au

Copyright © Michael Jacobson 2002

This book is copyright. Apart from any fair dealing for
the purposes of private study, research, criticism or
review permitted under the *Copyright Act 1968*,
no part may be stored or reproduced by any process
without prior written permission. Enquiries should
be made to the publisher.

**National Library of Australia
Cataloguing-in-Publication data**

Jacobson, Michael, 1961- .
   Windmill Hill.

   ISBN 0 7336 1595 3.

   1. Men - Fiction. 2. Grandfathers - Tasmania - Fiction.
   3. Reminiscing in old age - Fiction. I. Title.

A823.4

Cover design by Ellie Exarchos
Cover image © Ellie Exarchos
Text design and typesetting by Bookhouse, Sydney
Printed in Australia by Griffin Press, Adelaide

For my family

chapter 1

I'm looking back, remembering everything, because now that I know how it ends I want to be clear about the journey.

When I arrive at Pleasant View, Lisa is on the reception desk. I make small talk.

'How's Dave?' I ask. Dave is fine.

'Getting chilly, isn't it?' Yes, it is.

I nod hello to the orderlies and cleaners as I walk down the tiled corridor to Blink's room. The sweet smell of antiseptic makes me gag.

My father calls nursing homes "Heaven's holding pens" but, unlike some of the places I've heard horror stories about, Pleasant View Home for the Aged seems clean, friendly and functional.

And for a place of supposed rest, Pleasant View is always alive with activity.

There's carpet bowls, sing-alongs and dancing, and cards or chess. Someone is always mopping or sweeping, carrying shiny metal trays, pushing a wheelchair, folding linen or entering a ward armed with a smile, a chirpy voice, a syringe or tablet container.

Every television is set to a glaring brightness, like you get when you wake up and look straight into the sun, and the volume is always as loud as it can go.

I can hear phlegmy coughs and moans from some of the patients—the management calls them residents—and the shuffle and swish of the staff walking up and down.

Weaving through all of this is the maddening soundtrack provided by a string ensemble bowing and plucking love songs over the PA. There's a speaker right outside Blink's room.

Blink is my grandfather and he has a room-mate, Stan McLaughlin. They don't get on and when I round the door-way I can tell that Blink is agitated.

I place the overnight bag on the corner chair near the wardrobe. Blink is grimacing and pointing towards Stan's bed.

As in the children's rhyme, the old man is snoring. Stan's pink and scabby bald head is poking out from under the sheets. His teeth are in a glass of milky water.

The stench in the room is overpowering.

'Can you smell that, Angus?' asks Blink. 'Can you smell that? Dirty bastard. Dirty, filthy bastard. Shat himself. Everywhere.'

'The orderlies will see to it,' I tell him, taking a handkerchief and holding it over my nose. I press the Call button. Jesus, it stinks in here.

'You're a good fellow, Angus,' says Blink.

He reaches out to hug me and a fresh wave of stench rises from his bed. I see that Blink's hands are covered in a foul, runny, brown–green slime.

Incredulous, he holds his hands in front of his face and they drip with muck.

'Dirty, filthy bastard. Shat in my bed. What kind of person shits in another bloke's bed?'

I try to avoid being smeared as I pull back the bedclothes. I hold my head away, trying to escape both the smell and how awful it feels to see Blink this way. His pyjamas are stained.

Still waiting for an orderly, I remove the blanket and bedspread and then yank the soiled bottom sheet from under Blink, leaving him on the plastic-covered mattress.

'Don't worry, Mr Johns,' says Max, who is suddenly there. 'We'll have you fixed up in no time.'

I can't think of anything to say as the orderly takes over. He slides on a pair of slick surgical gloves and begins to mix soap and warm water in a basin.

Max removes Blink's pyjamas and, turning him this way and that, washes the muttering old man.

'There's fresh bedding and clean clothes in the cupboard,' says Max, and it takes a few seconds for me to realise he is speaking to me.

I pull out underpants, socks, shirts and trousers. Blink's big boots are under his bed.

Remembering the overnight bag, I begin filling it with other clothes and things. Max glances across at me, then starts sprinkling powder over Blink.

'I'm going to get these all freshly washed and ironed,' I say. 'Blink likes that. I know you do a good job in the laundry here but it makes him feel special when we do it once a month or so.'

'There you are, Mr Johns,' says Max, 'good as new.'

There is a wheelchair in the hall and I get it as Max finishes dressing Blink, tying his bootlaces in the double knot he prefers, before easing him into the chair and running a brush through his grey, but still plentiful, hair.

'And where are we off to today?'

'Just an afternoon around the gardens,' I tell Max. 'Up to Windmill Hill, maybe Garden Villa. Wherever he wants to go.'

'He likes the gardens here,' says the orderly. 'Gives the grounds staff hell some days. Seems to know what he's talking about, though.'

Max peels off the mattress cover and carefully picks up the rest of the soiled clothes and bedding.

'We'll have the bed all fresh and warm when you get back, Mr Johns,' he says, before adding, 'Have a good afternoon, Mr Johns. It's a good day for it. But stay out of the cold.'

'Thank you,' I say and watch as Max leaves, holding the sheets and blankets as far in front of him as he can.

'Poofter,' says Blink.

I hang the overnight bag over the handle of the wheelchair and check the bedside table for anything else Blink might need. There is a small box of plastic gloves next to Stan, who's still snoring, and I chuck them in the bag.

Removing an envelope from my shirt pocket, I prop it against a small water jug on the bedside table, then wheel Blink quickly out of the room, turning right into the hallway and back towards Lisa, who smiles.

Once through the smooth sliding doors, we take the walkway to the car park. It's cold outside but I'm sweating and feel conspicuous.

As I turn the car into Mount Pleasant Road and Pleasant View Home for the Aged disappears behind us, Blink speaks for the first time since leaving his room.

'You're a good bloke, Angus,' he says. 'Are we going to the gardens? Is there time to see the gardens?'

'Yes, Blink.'

I ease the car into the turn that leads up to Windmill Hill.

chapter 2

We do all the things we usually do, the things that temporarily respark the faltering circuits in Blink's mind.

At Windmill Hill, I park near the radio station and Blink gazes up at the transmission tower and says what he always says: 'Geez, Angus, you get a good view of the town from here.'

It's true. The scenery expands before your eyes. But Launceston is no longer a town, at least not in the way Blink knew it and probably still sees it.

Perhaps if he could climb to the very top of the tower and see further, absorbing all the change and growth that have occurred below, and which continue to spread down and out from each bank of the silty river, he would still see Launceston as it was when he was young.

Just as Launceston is no longer a town, there is no longer a windmill on Windmill Hill.

Instead, there is a small garden where the windmill stood and in its centre is a bronze plaque that marks the day in 1926 when the windmill stopped turning and its role in harnessing the breezes to pump the river water up, over and down Windmill Hill was taken over by what was then flash new technology.

Blink has told me how the windmill, which had operated for more than sixty years, was demolished without a second thought. The bricks were taken away and crushed, the glass was smashed and the timber and fabric of the windmill blades were burnt.

'The new pipes and pumps may have delivered the water as promised, but years later people still said it tasted funny and didn't wash the clothes the same,' Blink has told me. Isobel too.

Windmill or not, the view from here remains spectacular and, as he takes it in, Blink smiles and appears to straighten slightly, as if the cricks in his back and hips have been loosened and oiled.

'Come on, Blink,' I say after a few minutes, applying some pressure to his forearm. He notices the urgency in my voice and tries to pull away.

'Plenty of time, Angus,' he says. 'Enjoy the breeze. Take in the view.'

'No, Blink. There's no time. There's still Garden Villa.'

'Geez, Angus. I'll be in that place soon enough and I won't be going anywhere else once I'm there. Geez.'

But he's moving and grinning and I'm relieved. He faces into the wind and takes a deep breath.

'Real air,' he says.

The draught of a fresh breeze drawn into his lungs energises him, as opposed to the air at Pleasant View, which is artificially heated and cooled, and where the coughing and wheezing never let up. And where, as far as I can recall, I've never seen an open window.

I support Blink's arm as we make our way back to the car and feel him struggling with the pace I'm trying to set. I want to make our day out as routine as possible, so as not to alarm him. I also need to complete that routine in a hurry.

Thinking of Pleasant View makes me wonder whether my envelope and the note inside it have been discovered yet. I feel a nervous twitch in my gut and let out a strained, high-pitched fart.

'Loose in the caboose?' asks Blink. 'Slack in the back? By the sound of that, Angus, you need to eat more meat.'

'I'll be right, Blink. Come on.'

I strap him into the front passenger seat and before driving off check that he hasn't unfastened the belt. He's done it before and I know how he feels about such things, how he hates being confined. I'm like that.

When I was a boy, my brother Stevie and I would stay at Blink and Isobel's place in Raymond Street and it was there that I first saw how I slept like Blink, with the bedclothes all untucked and unruly, and with my legs and feet hanging out, even on winter nights.

Blink likes two pillows, like me, and he hates being too hot, again like me.

All his life he's been a man of the open, thriving on space, and it's the same when he goes to bed.

Not even his eyes enjoy being closed and he sleeps always with one eye and his mouth wide open.

Garden Villa is a home for the dead that Blink once brought to life.

North of the city centre, Garden Villa has entrances from the south and northeast, but it is the western gate that most visitors choose.

To get there, you have to turn off the busy main road that leads all the way to Hobart.

The clamour of the traffic quickly fades as you travel down a half-mile lane flanked by pine trees, which scent the air cool and lemony.

Cobbled walkways curl around the trees and there are polished hardwood benches on the lawns. There is solace and silence to be had sitting there.

Where the pines end, hydrangeas in muted blues and pinks bracket the lane and usher people into Garden Villa.

Once through the western gate, the visitor—or incoming permanent resident—passes through a red stone archway and then enters Hollow House, a shell of a building which is shaped like a chapel and has paintings and scriptures on its walls. The road goes straight through it.

The superstitious, like my mother, refuse to drive through Hollow House and instead use the road that skirts around one side.

'The only time to go through there is when you're in the box in the back of the hearse and you've got no choice about it,' she says.

I've always driven through Hollow House. Blink likes it too. It makes us both smile, like we've taken something on and won.

The cemetery has thousands of graves and markers, ranging from crudely painted wooden crosses to the most elaborately carved and decorated marble headstones.

When I was young, Blink took me with him to work one day and, touching one of the huge and ornate headstones, I remarked how much the person buried there must have been loved.

'Maybe. But come with me,' said Blink. He stabbed his small trowel into the dirt.

Taking my hand, brushing the loose dirt off his knees, he led me down the hill into another part of the cemetery.

I saw a man on his knees, with his hands over his eyes, and a little way from him a woman, who changed old flowers for new and then stood there quietly.

I saw that some of the older gravesites had darkened and mildewed over the years and that some slabs had stained black, a result of the moisture seeping through from underneath and the Tasmanian rain falling from above, settling in pools and then leaching through the weaknesses in the stone.

I saw some graves with chips and widening cracks and others that hadn't seen a visitor or fresh flowers for donkey's years.

When we stopped, it was at the foot of an unbordered, tiny plot. Grass had grown soft over the burial mound and there was a painted steel pinwheel at one end. Blink pointed.

I followed his finger to the four thin petals on the pinwheel, coloured blue, green, red and yellow. The stem was tarnishing with rust but the pinwheel still demanded attention, especially when the wind whistled through and it began to spin.

It was a child's toy and Blink let the whirring petals flick his open hand before grabbing one between his fingers to stop the motion.

On one petal was written a girl's name, "Alison Devine", and her age, four. On another was a browning photograph of a smiling girl with red, curly hair flowing easily to her shoulders. On the third petal was a message "Always loved". On the fourth was written, "Mummy & Daddy".

'You don't measure love by the size of things,' said Blink. 'You measure it by the heart of things.'

Blink worked at Garden Villa for more than forty years, joining the gardening staff not long after he came back from the fighting on the Western Front.

He was more than a tradesman, though that much was known before the war.

He seemed to possess an instinctive understanding of any landscape, its possibilities, the richness and poverty of the soil, the span of the light and the flow of the water, and he would use all this knowledge to transform the ground.

He loved Garden Villa. It offered challenge, space and potential.

When he first arrived he couldn't abide the impersonal practicality of the part-gravel, part-bitumen road that snaked its way through the grounds and which over the years had been crudely extended as Launceston grew and more people required a final resting place.

Once the head gardener's job became Blink's, after poor old Mortie Donald dropped dead of a heart attack and fell into a grave he was digging for someone else, among his first priorities was to minimise the austerity of that road.

He did it with a series of trellissed arches webbed with climbers and blooms. And with carved hedges—Christ, angels, Father Time, Mother Mary, cherubs—with beds of the brightest flowers and expanses of the greenest lawn on either side of the road.

So beautiful were the surrounds and coverings that people visiting Garden Villa soon remarked that they felt as though they had entered an evolving story.

It was another part of a journey, not the end of one.

The colours and fragrances of the plants, the buzz and whir of the insects, created such vitality.

It wasn't irony. It was artistry.

It was Blink.

chapter 3

Blink was cautious and precise when it came to planning a garden. Just because roses or rhododendrons or dahlias might grow well in a particular location didn't mean that Blink automatically planted them there.

Once he knew the ground, he could experiment with it and only then would he begin to make his choices and get his hands dirty.

He retired from Garden Villa years ago, but many of the features he designed have been kept.

For instance, the crematorium at the northern end of the grounds is part of an imposing red-brick chapel and Blink sought to cool the surrounds, providing a contrast to the building and the fire within it.

To do so, he planted shade trees that dapple the light, sending down golden beams through the branches and leaves on sunny days.

Elsewhere, pink and white roses ramble, their appearance and sweet scents a further and necessary softness.

No sound or odour ever escaped from the crematorium, but Blink had seen enough people emerging from the chapel, clutching handkerchiefs to their mouths and noses, to know how the mind could play tricks.

'Grief,' he once told me, 'invades all the senses.'

So, in both long, loose rows and in tight, circular clusters, in shapes of crowns and cameos, he planted the mauve of rhododendrons, the pink of camellias, the white of baby's breath and other ensembles in blue and violet.

It is a cushion of colour, the aim of which is never to distract people from their grief but to empathise with them.

As they arrive and depart, Blink wanted to show them that just as beauty dies, so too is it renewed.

The lawn cemetery is an easy walk from the crematorium and runs along Garden Villa's eastern border. Tiered lawns lead down to a lake filled with waterlilies and surrounded by eucalypts with blanching trunks.

The lawn cemetery is of a decent size and Blink had been discreet in the way he used the space, making the most of the flow of the land to create a garden as calming in its openness as the crematorium garden was with its caresses of colour.

Wherever you stand, the lawn cemetery offers fresh discoveries. Blink didn't want it to be absorbed entirely from one vantage point. He wanted people to delve into the area and mine its gems along the way.

Over a small rise, he had planted a tear-shaped bed of velvety red Chateau de Clos Vougeot roses.

There are four pathways to this location, but Blink shaped the land and embedded the feature so it was hidden until the last moment.

A short distance away, burial plaques placed like stepping stones are separated by squares of close-cut grass and, as you follow them, the sound of trickling water becomes louder.

It emanates from a small waterfall Blink helped design that spills down three levels.

On the top one, water pours from the outstretched hands of a sculpted cherub, curling its way down and down until it gurgles into a small pond edged with irises.

The effect is simple and stunning, yet its most impressive feature is often overlooked.

For there, again almost hidden, is another pair of small sculpted hands dipping into the water, belonging to another cherub—this one kneeling at the pond and about to drink the offering from the one above.

The lawn cemetery is filled with such wonders—three rock pools connected by a wooden walkway forming the shape of a crucifix; a sculpted angel, her wings spread to their limit with water running beneath them to give her flight; a small stone bridge that spans no waterway but shelters a series of plaques honouring members of the one family: the Rivers.

I loved it when Blink brought me to Garden Villa when I was a boy. These days I see it as my duty to return the privilege.

Each week we walk the grounds. I take hold of his arm and help him to sit at one of the benches or bend to touch and smell the grass and soil, the buds and petals.

As he looks at the stone bridge, the flying angel, the cherubs, the roses which ramble freely or cluster to form the shape of a tear, I wonder whether he recognises any of it as the result of his own imagination and labour.

Mostly, he just smiles.

And, rightly or wrongly, even on his worst days, I take that smile as a yes.

chapter 4

The crooked old man hobbling towards us is my old man. In one hand he carries a plastic grocery bag, crumpled as an unironed shirt and, so he tells me, filled with peacharines, a hybrid of the peach and nectarine and a speciality of Tasmania's northern midlands.

The fruit is payment from a pensioner down the road whose house my father, Tommy Johns, has been fixing up.

In his other hand is a carpenter's saw, and hooked into his leather tool belt with the nail pouch at the front is a hammer. From a distance, it looks like a gunslinger's Colt.

Dad may not be so quick on the draw anymore, but he keeps busy doing carpentry repairs for the people of Longford, the village in the centre of a farming district where he's lived for the past six years, ever since the divorce from Mum.

'The Australian Grand Prix used to be driven at Longford,' he tells me regularly, going on to say that, in the 1950s and '60s, some of the great names in world motorsport—

Brabham, McLaren, Hill and others—roared around the place.

'The noise of the cars terrified the cattle so much that it dried up their milk for days,' he says. 'No chance of that now. The old racetrack is overgrown and cars cruise along the new highway, bypassing us completely if they want to.'

When he is not arguing with Longford's publicans or pub patrons—my father is a man of strong opinions, even when they are plainly wrong, and his willingness to back his claims with his fists has seen him barred from two of the town's three hotels—he has so much outside work that his own house is neglected.

He rents a soldier's settlement, semi-detached place with small rooms, high ceilings, an outside laundry and hardly any natural light. Of all the houses in town, I reckon it's his that's most in need of a few nails and a fresh coat of paint.

'I don't strain myself,' he says, pointing to a row of houses which have benefited in some way from his handiwork.

He reaches into the plastic bag and takes out two peacharines. They are on the cusp of rotting and he hands one to me, his son, and the other to Blink, his father.

'Mick never grew these, did he?' asks Blink. 'Down at the orchard?'

My father looks at him quizzically.

'It's been a long time since I've thought of Mick,' he says.

'These old houses out here,' he continues, 'the foundations were never up to much and so, any time there's a bit of extra damp or a hotter spell than normal, things start to crack and shift. That's where I come in, to do the fixing up.'

I nod, taking a bite out of the fruit and it explodes with warm juice.

'And the upshot, when it comes to payment, is that most of these people don't have two spare coins to rub together and the rest have even less than that. That's why I've got more fruit than Golden bloody Circle.'

As I look at him, I cannot help but think that my father also needs some fixing up. He could do with a handy bloke coming round to bolster and straighten him, and all for a bag of peacharines as payment.

Too many years of twisting and turning, hunching over plans, sawing and hammering and holding up thick and heavy Tasmanian timber, balancing on roofs and beams, working outside in the wind and cold, have folded my father almost in half.

He says standing straight causes him such pain that he's stopped bothering.

'I just try to find a position that hurts less,' he says.

'Angus, who's this bloke?' asks Blink, out of the blue.

'You remember,' I say. 'It's Tommy, your youngest. You always called him Whiskers. Remember? Remember Whiskers?'

Blink puts a finger to his temple.

'Whiskers? Yep, I remember Whiskers. Big and strong he was. Tall. Not like this bloke. Whiskers was much taller.'

My father asks me how Blink has been and I tell him fine.

'Bloody strange how he still calls you Angus,' he says. 'You know, I can't get to the home to see him as much these days, not since I sold the car.'

'That's okay,' I say. 'Give me a call and I'll pick you up.'

'Nah, I've had the phone changed too. Cost-cutting. I can take calls but I can't make them. Not that I ever made many.'

'Well, I'll call you then,' I say. 'We'll sort out something. But give us a month or so. I've taken time off from work and I'm going to get away for a while.'

'I thought you and that little architecture firm of yours were joined at the hip,' he says. 'It's a bugger getting you out of the place for a game of golf, let alone time off. What's brought this on?'

'Just some things I have to sort out,' I say. 'The guys can do without me for a while. Anyway, I own the place. I can do what I like. No point being the boss otherwise.'

'Going anywhere special?' asks my father.

'Here and there,' I say, and he doesn't press.

As we walk down the street towards my father's place, I notice the similarities between him and Blink. The same gait, the same bends and bows, the same little movement of the head, the same tug at the right earlobe.

Tommy Johns used to be a fair golfer but now needs a few days' notice before a game, so he can load up on anti-inflammatories and painkillers.

Even then, before teeing off he gulps three quick scotches, and they set him up for fourteen of the eighteen holes. He either stops playing or cheats on the last four.

He looks greyer, but I haven't seen him for a while. Maybe it's a Longford thing anyway. Everything seems older here.

People know him, wave and say, 'G'day, Tommy' as he passes. Some tell him they've got a few stubbies with his name on them, or a packet of fags, a bag of fruit, a "cupla dozen" eggs to pick up the next time he's round.

'My salary is made up of groceries,' he says. 'The pension's all right but it doesn't leave much room for extras. But with all this other stuff I pick up, I get by okay.

'I can have a trifecta, a couple of beers, a ticket in the Friday meat tray at the bowls club. Can't complain.'

Tasmania is the only place my father has ever known. The only time he travelled by plane was on a flight from Launceston to Hobart, an experience he found so alarming that he threw away his return ticket and took the bus back, vowing never to leave the ground again.

'Can you stay for a beer?' he says, fiddling with the gate and its dodgy hinge. 'Must get around to fixing that.'

I tell him we can stay for one and that Blink probably needs a pee. I want to tell Dad what I've done and what I have planned.

But I don't. Once inside, I just sip the beer, which is so cold it hurts my teeth.

'Like I said, I'll be away for the next month or so, maybe longer. But I'll give you a yell when I get back.'

'That's all right, mate,' says my father. 'I'm off to Green's Beach for three weeks to do some work on Andy Barrington's shack. He's picking me up first thing tomorrow.'

I try to disguise my relief, knowing there is no telephone at the shack and also knowing that it is built a tough haul away from the general store, where messages are left or collected.

Further to that is the comforting knowledge that Andy Barrington looks after Dad as if he was royalty, always making sure the fridge is stocked with beer and food and that the firewood is cut and stacked outside. There's no reason for him to leave.

The toilet flushes and Blink emerges, fumbling with his belt and fly. He looks up and his face fills with sudden recognition.

'Hello, Whiskers. How long have you been here? Angus, where have you been hiding him?'

'G'day, Blink,' says my father. 'Good to see you.'

We drink one beer and, though I would like to stay longer, I feel time closing in.

Dad cadges a lift to the one pub in Longford that'll still have him.

'Just drop me here,' he says.

Pulling into the kerb, I keep the engine running and Dad opens his door, pats my shoulder and then does the same to Blink. Three generations touching.

'You two take care,' he says, 'whatever you're up to.'

'I'll ring you,' I tell him, not looking at him.

'Righto.'

Shuffling across the footpath, he leans into the heavy wooden door to the bar and turns for a second and waves, the act out of character. Then he closes the door and is gone.

The car still idling, I turn the ignition key and the engine screeches in protest. It brings me back.

I check the petrol and oil gauges, the temperature and mirrors and finally steer back onto the narrow road.

There is a green metal sign by the sliplane which takes cars onto the highway. An arrow points right—right to Launceston, right to Pleasant View.

I idle there, thinking, not noticing the cars stacking up behind me until one gives a *bip-bip* on the horn.

'You strapped in?' I ask Blink, grabbing at his seatbelt.

I put my foot on the accelerator.

Flick the indicator.

Turn left.

chapter 5

My father grew up in the most detached of families. It was as if there was not one Johns' family tree but several, each one growing of its own accord, like seeds dropped and blown away to strike wherever they might land.

I know they love each other, as deeply as any family. It's just that they've never felt the need to say it, never felt the need for each other's proximity or to reinforce who they are, how they feel or where they have sprung from.

My mother never quite came to grips with what she calls the Johns' aloofness towards each other and how comfortable they have always seemed to find it.

She grew up in an inclusive family, all hugs and kisses and closeness. She says it made them stronger and better able to deal with the knocks they had taken and would have to take.

Her family's laughter and lightness put a brave face on the daily difficulties of life in the place nicknamed by Launceston's toffs, in their big warm houses across the river, as the Bog.

The name became so entrenched that the suburb's proper title was all but forgotten and people not from the Bog would whisper when they spoke about it, as though saying the name too loudly invited bad luck.

'It had dark and narrow streets,' recalls my mother, 'and they were lined with scrappy timber and tin houses built on land between the river and the railway yards.

'In all, that land wouldn't have taken up more than twenty floodprone acres, I suppose, but hundreds of families packed in there and we all called it home.'

I grew up with my mother's stories about the Bog, about how, when the Great Depression really hit in the 1930s, people living in the Bog didn't notice much difference.

'We were used to going without. Nothing too great about that. Certainly not great enough to need a capital G.'

She has told me of the hard, low-paid work on the wharves, where the Bog men loaded and unloaded merchant ships.

'It was never a surprise to see the men come home with tins of jam, spiced meat or pineapple chunks. And after tea, with all the kids out playing until last light, we could hear the adults laughing as they spoke about the crate that just happened to fall, break open and send tins every which way.'

I've seen pictures of the Bog men of my mother's childhood and adolescence. They are mostly short, nuggety blokes, reputed to be fearless footballers on a Saturday afternoon when they were adored by the supporters and shouted a few beers after a win.

'Everyone, kids and all, crowded into the Railroad Hotel, and the other pubs, the Ship or the Harbour,' says Mum, who reminisces when she's had a couple of wines. 'Dark as caves those places were and run by men whose noses were all out of shape.

'And the women! You should have seen some of them. Huge busts, dyed hair and make-up slapped on so thick we used to say they'd given away the trowel and slapped it on with a spade.

'Those girls knew how to swear, drink and handle themselves. They called everyone "Duck". "Another beer, Duck?" "One for the road, Duck?" "Bugger off, Duck." "Not tonight, Duck."'

The men who didn't work on the wharves—apart from those who didn't work at all—were either doing long shifts at the railway yards or the textile factory.

Mum says you could always tell a Bog person later in life because they were hard of hearing after all the years amid the roar, clang and rattle of heavy industry.

'Their first response to any conversation was "Eh?" and they'd lean in towards you, searching for your words.'

The railway yards offered a worker hardness and danger. Men's feet and legs were broken after lengths of rail slipped off benches or out of their hands. Fingers were chopped off and crushed, eyes were blinded and skin was burned and cut by sparks and flying bits of iron.

Mum talks of men caught between and under carriages who had the life squeezed out of them, and others permanently stooped from years of bending over sleepers and anvils. Unable to straighten themselves, they talked into their chests.

'Tough as it was, the railway yards did at least offer some sense of community and camaraderie. There was a men's and women's bowls team and two bowling greens. There was a brass band, a footy team in winter and two cricket teams in summer. And a funeral every other week.'

The yards were always working and at night, when all else in the city was closed and quiet, the sound of metal and labour from the nightshift echoed from the yards, across the Bog and over the river.

'It was almost comforting,' she says. 'It was like something you could depend on.'

The textile factory employed as many women as men and when they came home after work they'd still be shaking their heads and banging their ears to try and belt out the racket of the looms.

The factory churned out products renowned throughout the world. Making the thick tartan blankets, jumpers, cardigans and travel rugs, however, was as close as the workers got to them. They created what they could never spare the money to buy.

'We made do,' says Mum. 'Had to.'

She has told me of tea leaves being used over and over until the hot water didn't change colour at all, of milk on the turn but drunk anyway, of small cuts of meat divided into smaller portions and grilled, the fat from the meat drained into a tray and left to harden to fill the next day's school sandwiches.

The houses in the Bog were built so close together that a couple having a blue two doors down could be heard plain as day four doors up.

'And you could hear them making up.'

Women shared cigarettes and cuppas as they chatted over the corrugated iron fences and imposed their own strict moral and social code on Bog matters.

'The street names lacked any imagination. Main Street. Small Street. Crooked Street. Dry Street. New Street. Old Street. I mean, I ask you.

'But we stuck together. Neighbours became friends, friends became in-laws and the streets became family centres.'

My mother's mother raised her family alone and the absent father was rarely mentioned, no matter how powerful his absence or how much more difficult it made life.

They owed much to the generosity and understanding of others, who often gave what they could not do without. Food. Clothing. A few coins.

My mother was fourteen before she wore shoes that had not been run-in by someone else's feet.

'But I never felt poor. I never felt as if I lacked for anything. We were all in the same boat in the Bog.'

The Bog had been nicknamed by people with no subtlety to their motivation. It was meant to be hurtful and degrading. Instead, it had the opposite effect. The people of the Bog became stronger for their refusal to be discarded.

Today, years after the Bog was refurbished and renamed Tamarheart, the old houses torn down and replaced by smart villa units, and the railway yards closed and transformed into a shopping and entertainment centre, people who left the Bog long ago speak with fondness about growing up there.

Like they miss it.

'Despite what some people believed—and those who didn't know the Bog were ready to believe anything anyone said about it—crime was never really a problem. Not for us, was it, Barb?' said my Auntie Joycey one day, back from Sydney for a holiday.

One by one, my mother Barbara had waved and cried her brother and sisters away from Launceston. William went to Queensland, Joycey to Sydney, Jane to Hobart and Brenda to New Zealand, while Mum stayed behind with Dad and me and Stevie.

She was well aware of the irony that the Johns had all stayed in Launceston yet barely saw each other, while her own family, so close and so loving, had spread to all corners, out of reach.

The phone could be tied up for hours when she talked to them and sometimes, after hanging up, she would sit still in the chair beside the phone table and we knew to leave her be.

'Sure, there was some stealing from the boats, the railway toolshed and the textile factory fabric boxes, and there were occasions when pub brawls and drunkenness spilled over into the streets and homes,' said Joycey.

'But there was a...oh, what's the word, Barb?...a morality. Yes, a morality that existed in the Bog and it was rarely breached.'

'That's right, love. We shared everything,' said my mother, 'so there was no need to take anything.'

'And what's more, we had fuck-all to take,' said Joycey, and the pair of them got the giggles.

My mother likes to get out the old photo album and the black and whites reveal her and the others as peas in a pod.

William's hair was shorter, but under their winter hats with the flaps over the ears they look like those Russian dolls, one pulled out of the other, each one identical in all but height.

Even now, each seems to know what the others are feeling.

My mother is happy that Stevie and I have a rapport and are at ease with each other. I suspect she is less comfortable with the same ease with which Stevie and I can move apart and stay that way for long stretches.

'No doubt where you got that from,' she says. 'You got that from your father and he got it from his, Blink.'

My mother knows a thing or two about what Blink went through during the Great War—that's what she calls World War I—and what befell him and Isobel afterwards.

She knows the shaping of their characters has something to do with Blink's father, Stocky, and something to do with the war and something to do with this Angus, who Blink talks about constantly and seems so consumed by that he attaches the name and the identity to me.

She knows it has something to do with Noel, Blink and Isobel's first child, whom they welcomed with open hearts in 1922 only to have them break when, fourteen months later, the little boy reached up to the stove in search of his bottle, took down a pot of fat just coming to the boil and tried to drink it. The burns, inside and out, killed him within the hour.

She knows it has something to do with Mick down at the orchard, although that was so much later.

After poor Noel, other children came for Blink and Isobel—Rex, Phil and Dorothy, or Dot, who married Mick. My father Tommy, who Blink called Whiskers from the start, was the last of them.

All the children were loved but not with any display, as if Blink and Isobel were shielding themselves from the type of wrenching pain they had suffered when Noel died.

Only Dot, perhaps because she was the one girl among the boys, showed any signs of mischief and real liveliness. In this way, she was out of kilter with her brothers who were as straight as the York Park goalposts and protected her like royal guards.

There were times when my mother would say quietly to Stevie and me, holding us close to affirm the point, 'Your father is proud of you both. He talks to me at night and tells me things. You don't have to worry. He doesn't say much, but he does feel things.'

We never really worried. Our father may not have shown his affection through hugs and heart-to-heart talks with his sons but he was always there, maybe in the background, but still there at every important occasion in our young lives.

Like the time in my teens I'd joined a knockabout rock band. We rehearsed at my place and Mum would sit at the kitchen table, tapping her feet and nodding her head.

My father would leave the house. He hated the noise of our electric guitars and drums and was out of step with the style of music. He liked country and western, as traditional and with as much twang as it could muster. He also liked Dame Nellie Melba.

We rehearsed more than we performed in public but we did once earn a spot supporting an American singer-songwriter, whose main claim to fame was having had Elvis Presley record one of his tunes. We'd never heard of it.

Our set was to last thirty minutes and we played well. At one stage, as I grinned across to the bass player, I saw that behind him, standing in the half-dark of the wings of the Duchess Theatre, was my father.

He was smoking in the No Smoking area. How he got in there was anybody's guess.

All I know is that when he nodded to me, it felt like an ovation.

My father was not from the Bog but was raised across the river, up and over Windmill Hill and down Raymond Street.

He was the youngest of the Johns and I know he always felt as if he was born at the wrong time. He yearned to be a fighting soldier but was too young for World War II and Korea, and too old for Vietnam.

'I would have been a bloody hero,' he said. 'Too bloody stupid to stay out of trouble.'

He grew tall and strong, with jet black, Brylcreemed hair swept back from his forehead. He had a gold tooth.

Like Stocky Johns, the grandfather he never knew, he had a way with timber and a reputation for quality work.

He wasn't a loner as much as he was impatient with company and readily showed his disdain by being impolite.

After a while, you'd notice he wasn't there. He'd have drifted downstairs into the garage or his workshop, where he tinkered and swore until the house was his again.

Of course, the Johns family did come together sometimes. Twice a year, in fact.

Every Christmas and every Easter, the various strands of the family assembled down at Dot and Mick's orchard.

As Dot unfolded a cloth over the wooden table outside the main house, not for reasons of daintiness but to protect us all from splinters ('if it's the last thing I do I'll get Mick to plane off this table,' she'd say) the arrival of the family would be signalled by the sound of car tyres crackling along the bumpy dirt driveway.

The men unloaded bags, bottles and spare blankets while the women—my mother, Dot, Rex's wife Myrtle, and Isobel—would peck each other's cheeks and start preparing lunch, which was always roast lamb followed by fruit pie.

My father, Rex, Phil, Blink and Mick would stow the gear in the big house for the women to sort out later and open the first of what would be several beers.

Mick fitted in superbly, speaking only when he had something to say. But it was Uncle Phil who said least of all, content to get as full as a boot and have a kip under a tree, from where he would punctuate the afternoon with his long farts.

We kids wolfed down our food at a separate table and excused ourselves, desperate to get into the orchard to run and climb.

Mick and Dot's two kids were countrified. They had feet with hard soles accustomed to the orchard ground. They played without shoes and dared us to do the same, never seeming to notice the sharp stones and nettles that had the rest of us hopping.

Karen could kick a football further than any of us and sometimes, if we gave her money or lollies, she'd pull up her dress or lift her top.

Her brother Terry was quieter. He was good with his hands and helped Mick build the treehouse which sat rock solid among the thick branches of an old oak in the middle of the orchard.

Rex and Myrtle's son, Simon, was the oldest among us but he never pulled rank. He too leapt into the fun of the orchard.

For kids like me and Stevie, used to small suburban backyards, swing sets and cricket on the road, the orchard was like Sherwood Forest, the African jungle, the Wild West, Disneyland and the MCG all rolled into one.

We played Robin Hood, Lone Ranger, Tarzan, Three Musketeers, King Arthur, cowboys and indians, war games and footy finals, hurling ourselves headlong into piles of leaves and batches of fallen and rotting fruit.

We scampered from the cover of bushes, clambered up trees and tested our weight on the thinnest of the limbs. Then we swung down, landing lightly on the balls of our feet and checked to see if the coast was clear.

'Enemy at twelve o'clock high,' Stevie liked to say.

'We'll rendezvous back here at 0-Four Hundred,' I'd say, even though none of us wore a watch.

As the adults drank afternoon tea from an enormous pot and passed around scones, they could hear our games.

When Dot rang the brass bell to summon us for dinner, we would emerge from the orchard black and bruised, nicked and stained.

Without that brass bell, we would have played into the night, our eyes adapting to the fading light and our bodies to the chill, our stomachs not registering the slightest pang of hunger.

Uncle Rex was born a year to the day after little Noel's death. I like him but he is not an easy man to know.

Rex served during World War II. He joined the army on his eighteenth birthday and saw action against the Japanese in New Guinea.

There were times after the war, when he was back at Raymond Street and safe, that Rex would scream out in the middle of the night and dive under his bed, yelling, 'Here they come!'.

Isobel still shudders at the memory of it.

Blink would go into Rex's room and talk softly to him, as a comrade more than a father, and what they shared fired something in my own father which he has carried ever since.

It's not animosity or envy, but a sense that something indescribable is missing from his own life.

Uncle Phil, on the other hand, only had a sense of something missing if a beer wasn't in front of him or on the way.

His room at Raymond Street was off-limits but Stevie and I snuck in and counted how many bottles of beer he had stashed under his bed and which new girlie magazines he'd hidden in the top drawer of his dresser, underneath his singlets.

His room ponged of stale smoke and beer and so did he.

Nevertheless, he was as lovely a bloke as you could meet, a happy drunk who fell down the steps of the Trade Union Hotel twenty-eight times one year.

He never married and the only romance in his life was with one of the ugliest women in Launceston, who tried to stab him.

It's one of my favourite stories from a family that tends not to tell too many.

The woman was Betty Dixon. She had long whiskers sprouting from her chin and teeth the colour of the beer she poured past them. And she was known to carry a knife.

For some reason, Uncle Phil moved in with her, but the arrangement was doomed from the start. One night, Betty lunged at him with her knife after he'd had the cheek to go to the fridge and open the last beer for himself.

With fourteen stitches in his drinking arm, Uncle Phil was sober enough to recognise it was time to leave.

And he knew he was on a good thing when Jack Oliver, the licensee at the Trade Union, offered him a permanent room.

'After all,' slurred Uncle Phil, 'why bother with bottles under your bed when you can have the whole pub under it?'

When Uncle Phil died, Jack paid a thousand dollars for the funeral and a real crowd, mostly drinking mates, turned up at Garden Villa for the service.

When they returned to the pub, parched, they toasted Uncle Phil until after closing time and Jack Oliver soon made his money back.

Dot, the only daughter, was pretty like her mother when Isobel was young.

Whereas her brothers followed their father's looks and colouring, Dot had her mother's blonde curls, all loose and bouncing, and eyes that gleamed.

As she matured, Blink could see in Dot the Isobel he had known as a boy and as a young man. He drew silent strength from his daughter's energy.

Dot was tall and lithe and her body took its shape with a nonchalance. Her curves were subtle and alluring and her mind was as sharp as Blink's secateurs.

She had a laugh that roared its joy to the world and a wit that could make others laugh as quickly as it could put them in their places.

Dot was an imposing character, one who knew her own mind and liked to speak it. She also knew when to do otherwise.

She was balance personified, able to shin up trees with her brothers, kick a football and roll in the March mud, before fixing her hair and applying some make-up to look stunning in her best dress.

Dot had faith in God and in herself.

When she met Mick, they fell for each other there and then.

chapter 6

I wonder what he's thinking. Since leaving Longford, the speedo has been clicking away the distance and Blink has been silent.

'Back in the '20s,' he says, immediately startling me with the suddenness of it, 'it was easier to bump your bum on the moon than get to Green's Beach by road.'

I'm pleased he's talking. My father's impending trip to Green's Beach must have awakened something in him.

Then, as quickly as he had broken his silence, Blink shuts up again.

'It's a nice place, Green's Beach,' I say, trying to engage him. 'I might take you there one day. Be good for you to have a paddle, feel the sand between your toes.'

Blink shakes his head and I begin to think that's all I'm going to get out of him, until he turns to me, fixes me with his eyes, and says, 'No, don't take me there, Angus. There's nothing good about sand.'

A few minutes later he's asleep, his head rolling to the bumps and bends in the road.

Blink and the beach were never the best of mates, yet no matter how many times he told Isobel how much he disliked it, she marched him there anyway.

More accurately, she sailed him there.

In those days, the best way to get to Green's Beach was by boat and, unfortunately for Blink, Dan Stephens had one.

Dan was a butcher by trade and said you could always tell a good one by how many fingers he had left. Then he'd hold up his hands and count off nine.

Each summer, Dan, his wife Marjorie, Blink and Isobel boarded Dan's ketch, *The Breeze*, and sailed down the Tamar River, chasing gusts that seemed to Blink to run out of breath just as they reached them, thereby prolonging his ordeal.

The Tamar was beautiful then, blue and wide and full, but Blink couldn't wait to be back on land, even if it was Green's Beach.

'Lesser of two evils,' he'd say.

'I like Dan but once he gets in that boat of his he thinks he's Captain bloody Cook,' Blink said to Isobel.

Isobel still talks about how Dan loved the river, how he'd tack *The Breeze* from one bank to the other, steering into inlets to wave to the picnickers on the grass and cheer the kids as they swung on a tyre roped to a strong branch before they dropped, squealing and with their legs kicking, into the water.

Out in the middle, Dan would applaud the rowing crews in their white singlets as they puffed and pulled by.

He'd circle the boat around Tamar Island, just for the lark of it, then take a zigzag course to where the river widened past the little village of Rosevears, the old Windemere church and Gravelly Beach.

From the deck, a miserable Blink held on for dear life and sought diversions for his stomach, away from the plain truth that his was a body meant for the land.

Isobel, on the other hand, was at ease with the water. She could stroll the deck of *The Breeze* and never lose her balance. Her insides were immune to the pitch and roll that turned Blink green.

She would hold her head high and laugh as the wind threw her hair behind her and pushed her clothes firm against her body.

Neither a sailor, or a swimmer, when Blink swam he did so without a skerrick of expertise. He punched and wrestled his way through the water, swallowing big, salty mouthfuls of Bass Strait as he went.

His skinny legs looked like white sticks and, together with his arms, flailed as he fought to keep his head above the water. His slender waist always seemed at the longest odds to be able to keep up his shorts which, once wet, would fan around him like a flower opening.

Blink's only pleasure in swimming came from watching Isobel.

'It's like the water understands her, like it moves out of her way to let her through,' he once told me, going on to say how long it had been since the day Isobel fell into old Smithy's fish pond.

That was the only mistake he had ever seen her make in the water and he would smile at the memory of it.

'We were just kids at the time.'

Isobel could swim for hours, tireless, her stroke never failing as she glided through the water.

There were days Blink would not have been surprised had she swum right past Green's Beach and kept going, around the headland and all the way to the northwest coast and further, right around the island state, reappearing a few weeks later from the other direction, still stroking calmly and freely.

It was different for Blink. Too much time in the water brought up his phlegm and though he swam to be with, and please, Isobel, he never swam for long.

Blink is awake again. 'You didn't know Dan, did you, Angus?'

'No, he was your mate,' I say, keeping my eyes on the road.

'Dan was a rough nut but a good bloke and he did his bit in France, though we never talked about it much. Anyway, with that wife of his, we were lucky to get a word in. I couldn't do anything right with her. Many's the time I pondered chucking her overboard.'

Blink tells me that Marj Stephens was pencil-thin and pernickety, always organising, talking, assuming she knew best.

She made sandwiches that were too small for a man's hands and she served tea in cups which Blink had to hold by the rim, not the handle. Marj would roll her eyes at his manners.

'That Marj Stephens has more airs and graces than His Majesty,' Blink would say and Isobel would shoosh him out loud or hold her index finger to her lips.

At the shack, the two men would sit outside in canvas chairs and talk about work and their wives and whose turn it was to get the next beer.

'You boys and your war stories,' Marj would say, presumptuous as ever, walking up the track from the beach. 'Anyone would think you want to be back there, the way you go on about it. Well, we girls had to put up with a lot as well and we don't go blabbing on about it all day. Come on, there's work to do. Wood for the fire. Chop, chop.'

No, Blink didn't like Marj Stephens at all.

'It's all very well to say what you think, but surely you've got to think about what you're going to say,' he said to Isobel.

'Shoosh,' she said, 'they're just in the next room.'

'You know, between Marj and that bloody boat, I think I'd choose the boat.'

'Shoosh!' said Isobel again, this time more firmly.

Blink didn't like the way the beach sand got in everywhere, from between his toes and then right up, until it was in his mouth, where it crunched between his teeth. He didn't like the coastal wind that flicked sharp grains of the stuff into his eyes and up his nose and he didn't like the freezing ocean and the way it constricted his lungs and made his shoulder ache.

Most of all, Blink didn't like the barrenness of the beach and how the only things that grew there were ugly, sharp grasses and his own discomfort.

He loved the way Isobel reacted to this place and came alive in the water. But all he ever wanted to do was leave.

'I was never the best of sailors, Angus. I threw up all the way from Hobart to the front,' says Blink. I glance across at him and in that split-second the car veers into the oncoming lane.

A woman blasts her car horn and gives me the finger.

'There's nothing good about sand,' says Blink.

'What are you on about?'

'We're not going to Green's Beach are we, Angus? I don't want to go there.'

He is gazing past me, across to the water of Bass Strait, which becomes visible as we emerge from the inland and begin to head along the coast highway.

'No, Blink, we're not going there.'

chapter 7

Cassidy North has always known what he wanted out of life. He is a good friend and I know he can be trusted.

'Whatever you might hear, I promise you there's nothing sinister going on,' I tell him. 'I just need to do this for Blink. And for me.'

Cassidy puts down the big mug of tea he drinks in rude slurps and takes with fresh cow's milk and four sugars.

He picks up a homemade biscuit from the plate between us and it crumbles in his hands.

Glancing across to a dozing Blink, Cassidy shoves the biscuit into his mouth and says, spitting crumbs, 'Let's take a stroll.'

Blink and I arrived mid-afternoon. The drive had taken longer than it should have, thanks to my paranoia about the likelihood of being seen on the main road.

Not so long after turning onto the coast highway, I turned back off it and took the old roads that wind between little places like Mole Creek, Sheffield, Railton and Latrobe.

By the time I finally turned into Cassidy's driveway I was busting for a pee and a cuppa and the car needed petrol.

I met Cassidy at high school. We played footy together but he was always a notch or two above me or anyone else in the team.

Cassidy was strong, fearless and fair. He wasn't huge in size but protected his team-mates as if he were a giant.

Many was the time I felt ashamed after a match to see Cassidy bloodied and bruised from his efforts, while I wore barely a smudge of dirt or the slightest scratch.

I still think he's the best Aussie Rules footballer I've ever seen and though the offers and inducements were many from the big league in Melbourne, he turned them all down.

He loved the game but he loved the land more and knew the city would choke the life out of him.

'It's just a game,' he says. 'A great game, but there are more important things to worry about.'

Because he had always preferred a farmer's boots to footy boots, it seemed out of character when Cassidy went to teacher's college and I recall talking to him over a couple of beers the night after his college acceptance arrived in the mail.

'Why don't you work on a farm? That's what you really want.'

'It is. But I don't have a farm yet,' he said.

He graduated high among his fellow student teachers and never complained about where he was posted.

He spent terms in big schools with hundreds of kids and other terms in country classes where all the grades sat in one small, draughty room.

Eventually, he was posted to the northwest farming town of Latrobe and he says it felt like a homecoming. He dug in.

It was there he met his wife Alex, who was teaching at the same school, and they married within a year. The ceremony was held in the school gym and, as we were waiting for the fashionably late bride, the groom and groomsmen, me included, found a basketball and shot free throws.

Pooling their pays, Cassidy and Alex found the deposit for a farmhouse and rolling green spread overlooking the Mersey River. It's an easy fifteen-minute bike ride along the back track to school.

They've been here ever since and they're here to stay.

Pulling on his gumboots and pointing to a pair for me, Cassidy takes me to the top of a hill and onto an impressive plot of land where he and Alex are growing the proteas they hope will one day fund their retirement.

He also shows me the laden fruit trees in one corner and the thriving vegetable garden beside the house.

The soil is rich in this part of the world, billionaire rich, richer than anywhere else in Tasmania. It's thick and chocolaty and fertile.

'You can lose a shoe in this soil, come back a week later and a new pair will have broken through the surface,' says Cassidy.

A low siren blares and I peer across to where a white passenger ferry is pulling out of the Mersey dock and has begun the slow, wide arc to start another Bass Strait crossing.

We walk through a wooden gate—'Don't touch the electric fence,' says Cassidy—and wend our way up towards a dilapidated shed that appears to remain upright out of sheer stubbornness.

Behind the shed is what can best be described as an alcove. It has an entrance and a window—although the glass has long gone—which frames a view down the hill, over the road, all the way to the river and out to the open sea.

I can see Cassidy's neighbour's place and its apple trees.

'Years ago,' he says, 'the government paid the farmers to dig out their apple trees and plant other crops. Now they're paying the farmers to put the apple trees back in. Silly buggers.'

I hear a shuffling behind me and I turn to see Cassidy's oldest boy, Keith, wedged in the middle branches of a nearby mulberry tree. He is gleefully stuffing his face. His lips and chin are purple from the runny juice.

The alcove is Cassidy's milking shed.

'Fresh milk every day, fresh from Frolic the cow,' he says. 'I get up here at first light, sit on my stool and milk Frolic, look out that window and I never want to leave. If I have an element, then I believe this is it.'

'What's more,' he continues, 'with Frolic, I get to play with her tits and she doesn't kick up a stink.'

We talk a little about the local footy, about how things are going at school. Cassidy is patient, letting me take my time, knowing the conversation must turn.

'It really is good soil here, isn't it?' I say.

'There's none better,' he says, chewing on a fingernail.

'What about down the west coast? What's the soil like down there? What would it take for something to grow there?'

Cassidy leans against the alcove's wooden wall and it bends with his weight. I half-expect it, and the entire shed, to come crashing down on the pair of us.

'I taught there for a term, down at Queenstown, not long after I got out of teacher's college. All I can tell you is what most people already know,' says Cassidy.

'Yeah, I know,' I say, 'the moonscape. The pink, purple and yellow bald hills, the gravel footy field, no trees. Rain and more rain.'

'I can tell you plenty about that bloody footy field,' he says. 'I was picking rocks out of my knees for weeks. They play it hard down there.'

'But what about elsewhere?' I ask. 'Surely there's some goodness in the ground somewhere.'

'Why?'

'For Blink.'

Alex is at the back door of the main house and when she sees us coming out of the milking shed she waves us in.

'Look, all I can tell you is what I learned down there,' says Cassidy, as we stroll back to the house. 'And that was that the land around Queenstown was felled and stripped bare over decades, either for the loggers or to keep the smelters going at the mine.

'Then pollution from the mine and good ol' reliable Tassie bushfires sucked any nutrients out of the soil and, after that, anything that could be grown was washed away by the rains.

'You'd have to be a hell of a gardener to get anything to come up out of that ground. The soil was rooted long ago.'

We slip off our boots.

'I read that since the mine stopped full production, some of the land is coming back,' I tell him. 'There's greenness. And anyway, Blink is a hell of a gardener.'

'Was,' says Cassidy, not unkindly. 'He's an old man now.'

Inside, Blink has woken from his nap and is thrown by his surroundings. He doesn't know Alex or the kids and his confusion is leading to panic.

'Blink, it's all right. It's me, Angus,' I say, trying to calm him.

'Angus?' says Cassidy. 'Oh yes, I'd forgotten about that.'

The old man is staring at me, through me, searching for recognition.

I take his hands and, bit by bit, he stops pulling against me and the anxiety leaves his eyes.

'Angus,' he says. 'Angus. I thought you'd bought it.'

Alex has boiled the kettle for another cup of tea and I sit Blink at the table, pushing the plate of crumbly biscuits in front of him.

'Cassidy,' I start, my eyes not leaving Blink's, 'I might need some soil. Good soil. The "none better" type of soil. Probably a lot of it.'

The late afternoon sun has become a fierce yellow, signalling the verge of evening. I remark that it's going to be a long drive in the dark down to the west coast.

'Don't be silly,' says Alex. 'You'll stay here for the night, for dinner, and we can all talk more later.'

chapter 8

'They're such hardy bastards and they love this soil,' says Cassidy, flicking a finger towards the proteas.

'And there's a market for them. Or at least there's interest. We buy the seeds for bugger-all and sell the plants for a couple of dollars, sometimes more, depending on the size and strength.'

There are scores of the spiky shrubs in the garden and Cassidy says each is protected within its own rubber tyre and is watered by an automatic system.

'They'll get me and Alex out of the classroom for good one day,' he says.

I can see the proteas from here on the balcony, which trains and warps its way around three sides of the house. The fourth side is taken up by the carport, where a tarp has been draped over my car.

There is no balcony rail. A boundary of sorts is formed by a line of plants which serve as evidence of the other great botanical love of Cassidy North's life—cactus.

'Is it cacti or cactuses?' he asks.

'I don't know. You're the school teacher.'

There must be sixty or seventy, all in plastic pots, and Cassidy, this tough-as-teak former footballer, begins to wax lyrical about the cactus flowers.

'Something about them,' he says, holding up a plant and poking his hard thumb into the quills. 'I like their irony.'

'That's very deep,' I say. I take a swallow of red wine. 'I think this rural caper has brought out the bard in you.'

Still, I know what he means, and so would Blink, about the rough exterior shielding the softness within and protecting the frail flowers.

The light has not quite faded and the sky is that lovely half-life of day and night. A few stars are out, the sinking sun and rising moon are both visible and Cassidy and I stay outside while Alex prepares the kids' bath.

He opens a fresh bottle, the cork makes a satisfying pop, and he places the wine on the small table between our low-slung wicker chairs, chairs so close to the ground that when I first go to sit in one it feels like falling.

'Shall we let it breathe?' I say to him.

'Nah,' he says, 'let's strangle the hell out of it.'

The taste bites the back of my tongue but it's not long before the wine relaxes me. I need it after what has been an unusual and unnerving day. I think about Pleasant View. The note.

Again Cassidy waits. When I speak, he's ready.

'It seemed like such a good idea at the time,' I say. 'The trouble is, now I look at Blink and listen to him babbling or going off at tangents or calling me Angus and I can't help thinking I've made one almighty mistake.'

Cassidy drains his glass and pours another.

'Queenstown,' he says. 'You've chosen a doozey there.'

'I know. But it's not my choosing. It's Blink. It's what he's talked about for as long as I can remember. It's what he's said from the moment he started to call me Angus, or see me as Angus, or whatever it is that happens to him when I'm around him.'

'What does he say?'

'He says that all it will take is to make a garden. In Queenstown, of all places. Make a garden and he will have made things right. That's what he says, like it's a matter of honour or duty. Couldn't throw some light on it, could you?'

Cassidy takes a long pour of the wine. He holds it in his mouth for a few seconds, swirling it, then swallows.

'Do you have any idea what he means by it?' he asks.

'Who knows?' I say. 'He's always talked to me about the war and I know it has something to do with that. I know that Angus, whoever he was, died over there.

'But dead or not, Blink sees Angus in me. The trouble is that when I ask him what happened, he acts as if I already know. I wish I did, but I don't.

'I've even tried going through the old war archives, the Queenstown records, family histories, but I can't find anything. Just bits and pieces, nothing major.'

Cassidy tells me about a football match played on the gravel oval at Queenstown.

'This big bloke rode his bike like a bloody maniac down from the copper mine to the ground. The players were already making their way on to the field when he pedalled in. He jumped off his bike while it was still rolling, threw off his workclothes and had his footy gear on underneath.

'You should have seen him. He ran and leapt, dived at the feet of the other players, took a real battering on the gravel. He played like a man possessed.'

Cassidy pauses, eyeing the wine.

'And the point of this story is what?' I ask.

'Shut up, I haven't finished. After the game, when the match was won and the beer was flowing in the old tin shed that was used as a changeroom, storeroom, bar and meeting hall all in one, someone noticed that Jack Hodgetts—that was his name, Hodgetts, or Hodgkins maybe—anyway, he wasn't looking too good.

'When he collapsed, everyone could see why. Blood and muck had soaked through his guernsey and when some bloke peeled it off him we could see this ugly great ring charred into his back and inside that was this bloodied, blackish mess. Angriest thing I've ever seen. Must have been agony.'

According to Cassidy, the burn occurred that morning when a coal shot from the furnace Jack Hodgetts, or

Hodgkins, had been stoking. It was down the back of his singlet and into his skin in a flash and he'd spent the rest of his shift laid up in sick bay, biting down on his knotted-up handkerchief as the doctor tried to swab and disinfect the wound.

'Nice story,' I say.

'Yep. I couldn't understand why he played. I mean, why would you? It was just a game of footy,' says Cassidy. 'But maybe this bloke, like Blink, thought he owed something. To his team-mates. To the club. Simple as that.'

I'm sceptical.

'That just sounds like footy coach talk,' I say. 'All for one, one for all, ultimate sacrifice, that kind of crap.'

'Maybe,' says Cassidy, 'but there it is.'

'And that's completely different from what I'm doing,' I continue. 'If it was me acting alone, then fine. But I've dragged in someone else and I've done it pretty much under false pretences because I am not who Blink believes me to be.

'And that football player, Jack Whatsisname, wasn't making amends for anything. He just wanted to play footy and would do anything for a game. We both knew blokes like that.'

Cassidy empties the bottle into my glass. I hold it to the moonlight. The sun has set.

'Then again,' he says, 'what if, while he was in that sick bay, he thought about not playing and saw it as a weakness? Perhaps he'd let the side down before. Or perhaps, and this is what I reckon, or how I hope it went, perhaps his weekly game of football was the one escape he had from the front of a furnace. I knew a few of those mine blokes and they worked like slaves. Maybe Jack reckoned he owed it to himself.'

'I know what I reckon,' I say. 'I reckon we should open another red.'

Before either of us can rise, Alex is there with a bottle.

'You two are deep in conversation, I see,' she says. She looks pretty and peaceful.

'Maybe Blink feels he owes something to himself as well as to this Angus,' says Cassidy. 'Maybe. Buggered if I know.'

Alex, frowning at Cassidy's language, swigs straight from the bottle and a dribble of red runs off her lips.

'Speaking of Blink,' she says, 'he's asleep, snoring like the foghorn on the Bass Strait ferry. He's a dear.'

She seats herself on Cassidy's armrest.

'Quite a dear,' she says again. 'He was talking to me.'

Later, as I'm curled up on a foldout bed, my lazy limbs can feel the effect of the last bottle, but my mind is clear as I consider our situation.

There were a lot of ifs, buts and maybes as Cassidy and I talked but I believe it is right to keep going, at least for now.

Blink may not be sure of much anymore, but he is sure about his debt to Angus.

And there's another reason to go on, namely my own debt to Blink and the hope that by helping him make amends, I too can atone.

Cassidy is shaking me.

'Jesus, what time is it?' I rub my eyes and burp. The taste is of stale claret.

'It's time to meet Frolic,' he says.

The sun is just beginning to rise and as it does the signs are of a fine morning, good for driving down to the west coast.

'Blink should be here to see this,' I say, putting on the jacket Cassidy passes me.

'I woke him too,' says Cassidy. 'He shouldn't be far away.'

I tiptoe to the spare room, knock lightly and go in. Blink is dressed but is having trouble with his boots. I tie his thick laces and I can see he's put his trousers on over his pyjamas.

I hold his wrist and elbow as we step out onto the balcony. He is painfully slow and his bones creak their disapproval.

Cassidy tells us to be careful not to slip on the frost, which makes an ice rink of the balcony boards and then has the grass squelching under our feet.

Up in the milking shed, inside the little alcove I'd seen the previous day, Cassidy gives a whistle and within seconds the sound of hooves and snorting can be heard. Frolic the cow strolls in with the easy confidence of a favourite customer.

I do what Cassidy says he does each morning and study the view through the alcove's glassless window. Dawn is framed and lovely.

Blink strokes Frolic's strong back and she flicks him playfully with her tail, swish-swoosh, bringing a cheeky smile to his face.

It is an old face and yet this morning it looks so much younger in this new light.

'Good girl, good girl,' he soothes.

Cassidy squeezes the teats and warm milk squirts out.

'Why not go electric?' I say, not looking down at Cassidy but instead watching a fishing boat chug into the mouth of the river. I think I can make out the breath of the fishermen.

'Because there's only one cow for a start,' he says, 'and, to tell you the truth, Frolic and I enjoy ourselves up here of a morning. It's a hands-on experience. Anyway, where would I fit technology in this little area?'

I raise my eyebrows.

'Yes, yes, all right,' he says, 'I know it would fit in terms of space. But I'm talking about the mood of the place. All that noise, all that machinery. It wouldn't fit, would it?'

The point is well made. There is a peace to this place and I can understand why Cassidy loves it, why he bounds into every day.

Blink is still grinning and says something I don't catch.

'Sorry, Blink, what was that?'

He makes his way out of the shed, giving Frolic a good pat as he goes, and walks to the side and then to the front so that he is momentarily framed in the window.

'It's like morning down at Mick's place,' he says, 'like mornings in the orchard.'

I feel as if I've been punched. I fight for breath.

'I'd better go to him,' I say as Cassidy yanks away, his head hard against Frolic's flank. Frolic is patient, her big mouth chewing on nothing.

In the short time it takes me to reach the front of the shed, Blink has made his way down and through a gate into the next paddock. It is lush and green and when he kicks his boots into the ground it surrenders easily, rolling back to reveal a divot of thick soil.

Blink, on his knees now, runs his hands through it, holding a clump and breaking small pieces between his thumb and forefinger. He smells it, then brushes it away.

Hearing me, he turns and almost loses his balance as he tries to get up. His knees are wet. I hurry forward to steady him.

'A bloke could do good work with earth like this,' he says. 'Angus, am I here for work?'

'No, Blink. Work will start soon enough, if you're ready.'

'Can I have a cuppa first?'

I haul Blink fully to his feet and his knees crack as we go back to Cassidy and a freshly milked and frisky Frolic.

The milk slops up the sides of the bucket as we walk to the house where Alex is in the kitchen in her dressing-gown. I can smell toast cooking and the kettle is on.

Cassidy scoops a plastic jug into the bucket and fills it with milk. Alex pours a dribble of milk into her tea cup and takes a long swallow.

'That's the stuff,' she says. 'Another day.'

Cassidy shakes my hand and Alex gives Blink and me a warm hug as well as a plastic lunchbox each, filled with sandwiches.

I am unsure of what lies ahead and tell Cassidy not to be surprised if we turn up again in the next day or two.

He shakes his head and does what he has never done before, grabbing both of my shoulders as if he is about to hug me.

'You find the land,' he says. 'If you can find a spot where a garden can be made down there—and I wish you luck with that little challenge, mate—then I will bring the soil.'

I back the car down the driveway and out onto the road.

Before moving off, I see that Blink has something in his hand.

'What's that?' I ask him.

He opens his palm and I see a square chunk of earth. Topped with grass, thin roots reach in and cling to the brown soil.

'That woman gave it to me,' he says. 'That one back there at the house. You could do good work with earth like this.'

I am driving Cassidy's car. Mine has stayed under the tarp. Cassidy says he'll keep it out of sight while we're away and they can use Alex's old bomb for a while, or ride the bikes.

I keep to the speed limit as we travel towards the city of Burnie, before taking a hard left onto another highway, which will take us deep inland and then veer west towards Queenstown.

The landscape changes. It starts with fertile farmland planted with crops—potatoes, corn, rhubarb—then gives way to pastures trodden down and picked by horses, sheep and cattle.

Next is thickly wooded land, giving the first clue that the going is becoming more demanding, a truth confirmed by the road which begins to wind and roll and turn back on itself.

There are times when the narrow strip of road is all that separates us from wilderness, dense and unyielding, on either side.

Eventually, though, the forest thins and the real and notorious ravages of the west can be seen.

'Tough country,' says Blink, scanning the bare land which has paid so dearly for the things it held inside—copper, gold, silver, tin—as well as for the trees.

Trees were here in tens of thousands but they were hacked down to fuel the smelters, be shaped into railway sleepers, shipped away for mansions on the mainland or put to use building the mining and forestry towns of the west.

'Tough country,' says Blink again.

And for better or worse, we are here.

chapter 9

I'm uncertain about what lies ahead, but it's good to be out of the car. I stretch and yawn.

The woman who greets us is round and robust and she wears a long dress, the colours of which match the Queenstown hills. The house is enormous and I ask her about it.

'I was a happy housewife, doing my cooking, cleaning, sewing and raising my family,' she explains, making easy conversation in such a way that I learn how her husband died years ago and that, one day, bored with having little to do, she wandered through the big house and realised that its potential and her talents were going to waste.

'I think I was born to look after people and when I walked around the empty place that day I saw that what it needed, and what I needed, was company,' she says.

'Then Bob's your uncle, or in my case Bob's my little grandson'—she laughs at a joke she's clearly told many times and of which she just as clearly never tires—'I'd opened the place up as a Bed & Breakfast.

'Well, it's more a bed and all meals, really,' she continues, leading Blink and me into the office.

She opens the register, finds the date, grabs an impressive silver fountain pen and says, 'Name? By the way, mine's Gemma. Gemma Woodley. Just call me Gemma. Welcome to Queenstown.'

We go through the formalities. She requires only a driver's licence for identification, although she is taken aback slightly when Blink calls me Angus, which is not the Christian name registered on my licence.

'It's a nickname,' I tell her and it's not really a lie.

She takes a set of keys off a hook behind her.

'This one is for the room,' she says, 'you're in Room 4, overlooking the town. And this key is for the toilet and bathroom just down the hall. How will you be paying, may I ask?'

She is chuffed at the news of a cash transaction.

'I'm not much for cheques or credit cards,' she says.

I pay her for a week and hint that we might be staying longer, then follow as she ushers Blink, who looks worn out, and me through the house and to the bottom of a grand staircase.

'Up there, last on the left down the hall,' she says. 'I can do you some sandwiches and a pot of tea. There's a kettle, tea and cups in the room but I'll make this one. I was going to have a cuppa anyway, so it's no bother. I'll leave it outside the door and give a little tap. Dinner's at six. A roast.'

It's just after five o'clock and the night is closing in.

'Angus, I think I'll have a lie down,' says Blink. He moves up the stairs so slowly, holding the rail. I'm right behind him.

In the room, I help him undress, leaving his underpants and socks on, and get him under the covers. I don't worry about pyjamas. Blink ruffles the bedding, making it loose and light. I hope he stays warm.

'The gear's in the car,' I say and when I return with the bags Blink is asleep. Not long after, so am I.

Outside, the tea and sandwiches go untouched and we sleep through until morning, missing Gemma's dinner.

Queenstown nights are darker and more silent than I could ever have imagined. Nevertheless, it's the mornings that are especially hard on Blink.

At night, the small fireplace in the room sends out a pleasant heat once the wood has been burning a while. If I wedge a towel under the bottom of the door it keeps out the draught.

By morning, only the smell and the sight of the ash gathered at the bottom of the grate prove there's been a fire at all.

Mornings here offer the kind of cold that makes you frightened to move. Even under a flannelette sheet, two thick blankets and a garish pink bedspread, the slightest shift of position opens vents and pockets in the bedding and the chilly air blasts its way into your bones. There's no preventing your teeth from chattering.

The thin mattresses have seen better days and the bedsprings have loosened with age. The beds sag like hammocks when any significant weight is placed upon them.

Blink doesn't complain and I wonder whether that's because he's not the complaining type, or because he's slept in worse beds and worse places, or because he simply can't remember the support and comfort of his bed back at Pleasant View.

Our room boasts few mod-cons. There is a kettle, a teapot, two cups, a small jug of milk which Gemma fills each evening after dinner, a bowl of sugar and a tin filled with proper leaf tea.

'There are some things that should never change,' she says, 'and tea is one of them.'

Blink usually wakes just before the alarm goes off each morning. He needs my help to dress so he stays in bed.

I've established a daily routine which begins with boiling the kettle and rebuilding the fire and, while the room is thawing, I find Blink's clothes for the day and hang them over a chair in front of the fireplace to warm.

I throw back the curtains to witness another dawn breaking with little enthusiasm.

Then, supporting Blink's head with my hand, I use my other hand to lift his pillow and rest it against the bedhead.

Reaching across him, I take him under the arms and hoist him into a sitting position. The slack bed and his stiff body fight me all the way.

I spoon him the first four or five mouthfuls of his sweet tea until there's no danger of a scalding spill once I hand him his cup and saucer and he can take over for himself.

'Just what a bloke needs, Angus,' he says, as the tea courses through him.

I take his clothes from the chair and lay them on the bed. Blink hands me his cup and saucer when he's finished.

I dress him from the top down, making sure his bottom half stays loosely covered by the blankets as we progress.

Firstly, it's off with his flannelette pyjama shirt—never buttoned—and on with a singlet. I see his purple scar and every morning he fingers it uncertainly, tracing its passage down from his left shoulder.

Over the singlet goes a thick workshirt and over that a woollen jumper. Then I grab his knees and say, 'Ready?'

I swing him around and adjust him so that he is sitting up on the side of the bed.

'Watch out for the big fella,' he says always, cheeky as a kid, as I pull down his pyjama pants and his old dick flops against him.

I am never thrilled by this part of our daily routine and Blink's chuckling doesn't help. It seems that no matter how quickly I try to get him into his clean underpants, and his so-called "big fella" away from my face, the act is always prolonged by the underwear snagging on his toes, his ankles or his knees.

The old bastard just laughs and it's deep and rheumy and full of stories.

I stretch his socks over his feet and manoeuvre him most of the way into his trousers before reaching for his boots. I rub his legs for a minute or so and he closes his eyes.

Then I take him under the arms, feeling his ribs as I lift him to his feet. He rests his hands on me for balance as I pull up his trousers. He leaves them unzipped, holding the tops.

He does a jig of sorts, bouncing from foot to foot until his boots are comfortable. He stretches his neck and starts to totter across to the fireplace. Once there, he lets go of the trouser tops and they fall to his ankles.

Resting one hand on the mantelpiece and using the other to steer, he pisses into the fire. When he's finished, shaken and tucked away, I reach around from behind him, pull up his pants, turn him, zip him and tie his belt.

Downstairs, Gemma Woodley is cooking up a storm in the kitchen as she fries sausages, eggs and bacon in a black skillet.

Slabs of toast cool in a rack in the middle of a large table covered by a coronation commemorative tablecloth. The strawberry jam conceals the young Queen Elizabeth's right eye, and her slender neck is hosting a plate of mostly bruised fruit. She has the butter dish sticking out of her mouth.

A transistor radio crackles the news in the background. I listen for mention of Blink and me but there is none. The weather forecast is for showers.

'Surprise, surprise, not telling us anything there,' says Gemma, tonging bacon rashers onto our plates, where they settle in their own grease.

I know not to bother asking for cereal. The look Gemma gave me on our first morning told me in no uncertain terms that, at her place, breakfast is always fried.

More's the pity because my insides, attuned to a healthy regularity encouraged by oats, bran and the like, are usually still groaning under the weight of Gemma's cooked breakfasts several hours later.

It must be said, however, that her evening meals are just the ticket and Blink never leaves much on his plate.

We've been here over a week now and Blink is on the improve or maybe I'm just hoping.

He's still a slow starter in the morning but once he's down in the kitchen, he leaps into Gemma's breakfast and after that has an energy I've not seen in him for a long time.

'Eat up, Angus,' he says, enthusiastically. 'Every meal might be your last. We know that, don't we? The war taught us that.'

'No bullet could get through the layer of fat you're building up, Blink,' I reply, giving him cheek.

'If only, Angus,' he says, his mouth full. 'All the more reason to tuck in. Eat up.'

The B & B hasn't been overrun with guests. Apart from Blink and me, the only others have been a young couple passing through on their honeymoon, a tour around the state.

They spent most of their time locked together, staring full moons at each other, oblivious of us or anything else.

I was relieved by their lack of interest, but know that Blink and I can't be completely hidden or anonymous.

If alarms are raised and events are set in motion—if they are not already—then we will be found.

'You wouldn't believe the characters we used to get in this house and in this town in the old days,' says Gemma. I have asked her to call me Angus. I said it would be easier for Blink.

'You just had to walk down the street and look at the folk.

'Everyone was here because of the mining but everyone had a different story to tell. It's a hard way to make a living, is mining. You don't make that choice lightly. But being in a mining town is a good way to hide or start again.'

'Is it?' I ask.

'Oh, yes. Especially down here. The edge or the end of the world it is down here. Artie, that's my husband, he used to say that people came here and swapped their old lives for new ones.'

'What did he mean by that?'

'He meant that often they came to the west as a way of avoiding or escaping some bad situation somewhere else, whether they came on their own or with their husbands, wives or whole families. That situation might be poverty or shame or just plain bad luck, but Artie used to say that if it brought them here, then what they left behind must have been something awful.'

I decline a runny jam sponge.

'But you came here and stayed,' I say. 'And you told me your husband mined here for years. Was he escaping? Were you swapping a life? Old for new?'

'Indeed not,' she says.

'We were born here, grew up here and went to school for as long as we needed to. Then Artie went mining, like most of the boys in town, we went courting and the rest is the rest.'

'But what about this house?' I say, digging for the sake of it and reaching for the runny sponge I previously turned down. 'Surely, not many ordinary miners ever earned enough on their own or with the mining company to have a place like this. I've seen the cottages in town and around and about. This is something out of the ordinary.'

'It was left to us, Mr Johns,' she says, calling an end to the conversation by swishing out of the room.

Gemma Woodley does not trouble herself too much with the workings of the outside world.

I am comforted by her refusal to have the newspapers delivered—'You can't believe a dashed word in them,' she says—and her use of the radio is minimal. Meanwhile, the television, when it is on, picks up one Hobart station and poorly at that.

None of this should imply ignorance. Rather, I sense elements in Gemma's conversations that convey worldliness and wisdom. She is an intriguing, insightful woman, one at ease with and in charge of her own territory.

The hallmark of that territory is this four-chimney house turned B & B at the end of Quartz Street and Gemma spends little time away from here.

Her groceries and other supplies, like firewood, are delivered and paid for on the spot, in cash, with the receipt always ticked off with the silver fountain pen. It's no nonsense and there's not much small talk.

Gemma saves her ebullience for her guests because, I think, she likes their transience.

It's as if she is resigned to never leaving Queenstown herself and so gains some form of escape through the stories she tells and the impact she has on her guests.

I am sure it will be the same for Blink and me and, even though I seem to have upset her a little tonight, I know she won't be upset for long and soon we'll be talking again.

I feel quite safe and concealed under Gemma's strong roof and she's taken a real shine to Blink.

As for me, I am sure that all she requires is to know I am being honest and good in what I am trying to do.

A trust, or a loyalty, is building between us.

Gemma has begun to talk about her past and I am doing the same and, as we reveal more, we are finding common ground.

chapter 10

When Angus Bain was born, the hills outside Queenstown were still green and forested. Timber-cutting and chemicals had yet to leave the landscape, like sores on old skin.

Angus's grandfather, Fraser Bain, had come all the way from Yorkshire back in the 1880s to dig for his own gold and silver.

He never found enough and so in 1895 signed on at Mount Lyell to mine for copper. He was surrounded by others who had done the same thing.

As soon as he was old enough, Angus's father Harold joined him and, as he grew, Angus, being the son and grandson of miners, had little reason to doubt what the future held for him.

His mother Maggie had lost her zest and her looks to the relentless worry that was the life of a miner's wife and mother.

The emotion she knew best was fear. The skill she applied best was concealing it. She hummed constantly and most nights she prayed herself to sleep.

Harold Bain was an honest and hard-working man and Angus knew that his parents were not alone in bearing the hardness of mining life in their faces.

He could see it everywhere in town and knew that it would only be a matter of time before he too was aged by the same expression and carried himself in the same way, beaten down by the work.

He never felt quite clean, no matter how much he scrubbed before dinner or church, and he felt sorry for the wives and mothers, like his own mother, who had thin lips and ground their teeth.

Angus wanted to know if there was a more exhausting place in Tasmania, perhaps the world, than the west, where nothing came easily.

There was bounty there, of course. That was why people came. But it had to be wrenched from the earth and doing so was back-breaking and perilous.

'Look at these names, Ma,' he said, reading a map of the west outside church one Sunday. 'Hell's Gates, Trial Harbour. Why do people keep coming? With names like that, why would you?'

The ore and the minerals extracted from it helped build towns and services, but retrieving them cost the land and took a terrible toll on those doing the digging and the pulling, the lifting and the drilling, and the waiting at home.

The work, the conditions, the weather, all combined to lock people in.

Yet still they came to the west.

'Look at me, Ma,' said Angus, 'I'm built for mining.'

Maggie Bain sized up her son and said she agreed. Angus was short and stocky, with thick red hair and freckles.

Powerfully put together, he had thick arms, strong shoulders, round calves and meaty thighs, a package ideal for gouging and drilling through rock.

Each morning, Maggie Bain would hand Harold and Angus their metal lunchboxes into which she had crammed two slabs of bread and dripping and whatever cold meat might be left over.

Fruit was scarce but they might have a small pear each if they were lucky. Both took a bottle of milk and there was plenty of water at the mine.

Angus ate on the job, working on while others knocked off to eat their lunches around wooden tables and hung their filthy, sodden singlets over the backs of the benches to dry.

Angus wasn't trying to impress anyone and there were others like him who remained working.

'If I stop, even if it's just for half an hour,' he told his father, 'it's like torture to go back and start again. I can't bear that.'

So Angus ate as he dug, waiting for the signal at the end of the day which meant he was at that point farthest away from when his work began again.

The miners left home in the dark, trudged to the mine and came home in the dark.

The Bains lived in a small, unpainted timber house, the same sort of shanty that could be found everywhere in town.

The house sat at the end of a narrow dirt lane and black smoke choofed from the chimney from morning until night.

Maggie Bain always kept a pot over the coals for the stew or porridge. There was a smaller pot for the water.

It was cramped inside, with only a thin wall separating Angus's room from that of his parents. He had trained himself not to listen to anything that went on in there.

The house was lit by lanterns and candles and Angus would always need one or the other after dinner, when he headed to the outhouse for what he called his nightly constitutional.

The toilet was a planed board with a hole cut out of the middle and it was balanced between two shelves and above a large bucket. Angus put the light on one shelf and read whatever book was on the other.

When he was done, he tore a page from the book and wiped himself clean.

The only respite from the mine came on Sundays and after morning church Angus would run home, get himself out of the confines of his "Sunday worst" clothes, grab a crust of loaf he smeared with dripping, and head for the hills.

'I'll be home for tea, Ma,' he'd say, rushing past his parents on the way out.

He could wander for hours, circling the town, and on good days the sun glinted off the tin roofs of the houses and sparkled off the quartzite streets. Chimneys smoke-signalled to each other and Angus could see men outside making their way to the pubs or to Broom Sherman's big four-chimney house on Quartz Street.

Turning his back on the town, Angus would walk further into the trees and among the great stands he would find a comfortable spot, lean his back against a smooth trunk and eat.

Sometimes he brought his fishing rod along with the thought of catching something different for Sunday dinner. But he lacked the stillness and patience for fishing. Angus wanted to move; to think on his feet.

In summer he would walk the streams, following the fat trout, feeling the cool running water and the river stones on his bare feet. Later, he would luxuriate in the warmth of putting his thick socks on.

On those Sunday walks he had seen black snakes lazing on rocks and spiders that had spun webs the size of fishing nets between the trees. He had heard the growl of Tasmanian tigers and followed their tracks.

Once, as the sun dipped below the treeline and reminded him to start making his way home, Angus heard the slop and chop of Tasmanian devils and he found a group feeding on the carcase of a horse. How it got there he could only imagine.

Sunday was the day Angus most anticipated and most dreaded because it offered him both the longest break from the rigours of the mine but also the reality that, when the day was done, another six long days of digging stretched ahead of him.

Although powerfully built, Angus knew he was powerless to enact change. Like others his age, he would have his life shaped for him by the west—and that meant a life of mining.

To escape was rare, because escape required either the desire and motivation to try something else, when all you had ever known was mining, or an external force of such magnitude that it was difficult to even ponder the possibility of its existence.

'I work hard, I don't shirk,' he said to his father one evening, 'but what I find isn't mine. It's not ours.'

'I don't know what you mean,' said Harold. 'What we find puts food on this table and clothing on our backs. Good enough.'

'But what if you want more than that, Pa?'

'I don't know what you mean,' repeated Harold. 'What do you want? What else is there?'

When the call-to-arms came in mid-1915, more than a quarter of the Mount Lyell workforce joined up.

Angus Bain was one of the first. He didn't know if this was the kind of escape he wanted. All he knew was that he had to grasp it, to prove it was really there.

Angus was taken aback by the scene at the station.

'Crikey, Pa. Looks like it's double shifts for you from now on. There'll be no one left up at the mine to do the work.'

Some were laden with cases, but Angus was travelling light, with just a canvas bag slung over his shoulder. The mood on the platform was solemn. Card games were under way and cheers, groans and the odd curse could be heard.

Groups of two and three milled as near to the track as possible, as if there might be a danger the train wouldn't stop and they'd have to leap aboard while it was moving, or worse, walk all the way to Strahan, then Zeehan and on to Burnie. Others kept to themselves or chatted quietly with family.

Angus stood with his mother and father on a gravel path that led to the platform.

'Don't worry, Ma, the war can't be worse than that mine. And the pay's better—I'll send plenty back for you. You can buy something nice for yourself.'

The Bains exchanged pleasantries but avoided any kind of overt closeness that could be construed as weakness or making a scene.

It was a quiet leaving, with those going and those staying feeling awkward about the sentimentality of it all and yearning for the whistle of the train. When it came and smoke and steam billowed into the air, a sense of relief rippled all along the platform.

Harold Bain had worn his church suit and his boots had been shined. His red beard, just beginning to fleck with grey, had been neatly trimmed.

When he took off his hat, it was plain the scissors had gone to work on his hair.

'Your boy heading off as well?' said Eric Smith, another miner. Harold opened his mouth to say something but nothing came.

He fidgeted with his collar and bow-tie but did not undo the top button. Nor did he take his eyes off his son for a second.

Meanwhile, Maggie Bain was wearing lipstick which was fighting to stay on her lips. There was colour in her cheeks and a blue ribbon in her hair. She looked, for the first time in Angus's memory, pretty.

They talked about writing home, doing what the officers said, staying out of trouble. It was guff, there to fill in the time.

When it was time to board, Angus kissed his mother on the cheek and she put her arms around his broad back, though not for too long. She told him to look after himself, to keep that red hair of his out of sight and to, 'Go on, away with you, son.'

'I'll be right, Ma.' Angus allowed his gaze to linger on her sad face.

Then Angus went to shake his father's hand but Harold beat him to the punch and gripped his son's hand in both of his.

Harold's eyes never dropped as he memorised Angus's face. 'Good luck, son.'

Three words, the last one cracking into two sad syllables.

Angus boarded and noticed how quiet it had become. He felt the ache of a lump building in his throat and tried to swallow it down, all the time glancing about the carriage, hoping to find someone who could engage him in conversation and take his mind away.

He tried to write in the journal he had vowed to keep—*My Thoughts*, read the title on the leather cover—but no thoughts came to him.

As the train pulled out, steam hissing, Angus watched families leaving the platform and tried to find the backs of his own parents making their way home.

They were still there, standing on the same spot on the gravel path. They didn't wave but Angus could tell they were following the slow passage of the train.

Then Maggie Bain dropped her head onto her husband's shoulder and Harold Bain put his arm around her and pulled her in close.

Watching from his seat, Angus thought it the most intimate and natural thing he'd ever seen his parents do.

chapter 11

Broom Sherman was a rich man, almost up there with mine manager Robert Sticht, an American metallurgist running the mine at Mount Lyell.

At 5000 pounds a year, Sticht earned more than the prime minister and he showed it. Broom would see him in the flash Daimler car in which he was driven around Queenstown.

'Show pony,' he muttered.

Broom Sherman was self-made and self-aware.

He'd made his start in Zeehan, another mining town just northeast of Queenstown and when Broom arrived there in Queenstown at the dawn of the twentieth century, Zeehan was booming. Some called it Silver City.

'How'd you get that nickname?' blokes would ask him, gently mocking Broom's thick brown moustache which swept across his upper lip and which he twitched constantly.

He was not conventionally handsome, but then he was not a conventional man.

What he did have was an air of calm authority and the courage of his convictions. Both qualities had brought him to the west.

Coming up from Hobart with money borrowed from his father, Broom secured a mining lease and began to seek buried treasure.

'I'm glad to have spent the majority of my time in Zeehan looking down at the ground because there was little of any worth or pleasure to be found by looking up,' he said, after his mining days were behind him and he could be proud of the life he had made.

He found Zeehan to be practical and graceless. Typical of boom towns, it had a proliferation of hotels and a constant stream of poor hopefuls wandering in on legs still wobbly from the long and arduous journeys they'd had to make to get there.

Some seemed never to find their feet again, but Broom Sherman was not among them. Within six months he had dug up enough silver to pay back his father and within a year he had struck a vein of such purity that he was able to buy fine clothes and pay two men to do his digging for him.

Never greedy, never arrogant, over the next few years Broom became one of the west's wealthiest men.

He chose not to speculate on other leases, nor to seek partnerships or expansions, though many were offered. Above all, he wanted to remain his own man.

'What I did—and I think I did it quite well—was save and wait, save and wait,' he'd say.

And what he was waiting for, more than anything, was the first sign of the silver petering out.

By 1907, after seven years of success, Zeehan's yields began to decline.

Broom shook his head as he witnessed men, lulled by the good years, refuse to believe the leases were drying up, convincing themselves that new veins would be opened.

He watched as they poured their money into digging deeper and further until, too late, they knew that all they had dug was their ruin.

Broom was the acquaintance of many a once rich and independent silver man in Zeehan, who ended up broke and digging for copper for the company at Mount Lyell.

He sold his lease for a pittance, and took himself and his money to Queenstown.

Copper may not be as valuable or possess the same mythology as silver or gold, but Queenstown was sitting on a fortune of the stuff and more than a decade of mining at Mount Lyell had hardly dented the reserves.

Not that Broom had any plan to go mining himself.

Far from it.

He built a house.

Broom Sherman's Queenstown Gentlemen's Club was one of the biggest and most plushly appointed houses in the west and probably all of Tasmania, maybe even the entire country at the time.

The stone and bricks were shipped from Hobart and the timber was cut from the Huon pine forest that curtained Queenstown to the east and south. Broom hired labourers and tradesmen who answered advertisements he had printed up and placed in Queenstown's thirteen pubs.

The house took six months to build and another month to furnish and, when it was finished, Broom Sherman promptly locked it up, left Queenstown and boarded a boat for Melbourne.

Four weeks later he was back and with him were four attractive women who knew nothing about mining but who were about to learn plenty about miners.

Broom's moustache twitched a fit as he carriaged his girls through town and out to the four-chimney house. On the street, people pointed and their tongues wagged.

The Queenstown Gentlemen's Club opened for business at the beginning of winter 1908 and immediately warmed the hearts and minds of the single men and those married ones who could get away with it.

'My girls,' as Broom lovingly called them, plied their tantalising trade from the four upstairs bedrooms six days a week, an hour off for a meal and a bath, and every Sunday off for God.

Appointments were for half an hour, with five minutes of that granted for undressing and dressing.

'That last chap I had in here was so eager he jumped into the bed with his boots and socks still on,' one of Broom's girls told him one night. Again, his moustache twitched.

He paid the girls a fair salary and they were allowed to keep whatever the customers might offer in gratitude. Some were exceedingly grateful.

'Not bad for a hand-to-mouth existence,' the girls would laugh and say on Sundays, the day they emptied their jars and purses on to their beds and tallied up.

Regular medical check-ups were given by Dr Ivan Sturmie—"Spermy" Sturmie, the girls whispered to each other—who was only too happy to offer his services and revelled in the time away from his regular surgery at the mine.

The sight and feel of a woman's full breasts or her long legs made it worth enduring the sight and feel of men's hairy, saggy testicles at check-up time, or the sight and feel of men cut, burned and broken in some accident at the mine.

Dr Sturmie never left Broom's place without a big smile and a wave to the upstairs rooms.

Broom had his own large room which doubled as an office. Each night he would place the day's takings in a calico bag and lock it in the floor safe.

Every Monday morning he would walk with the bag to the bank. He was never robbed, never even threatened.

Patrons soon came to grips with Broom's house rules.

In the room where Gemma Woodley now serves meals to her B & B guests, there was a lounge and bar and there was a strict dress code—collar and tie, clean hands and polished boots.

Broom would serve drinks and make small talk with the men.

No one who arrived smelling of drink was allowed inside. No one who drank too much stayed inside for long. Anyone who caused trouble in the lounge was banished for a month. Anyone who caused trouble with the girls was barred for three months.

Broom employed a doorman, who was taller and wider than most doors and kept the peace by virtue of his sheer size and the fear of what might be unleashed if he was ever riled.

Girls left and new girls joined Broom's operation and he looked after them all with a paternal goodness.

There were hiccups. The forces of temperance and piety in Queenstown often protested the "moral disgrace" of the Queenstown Gentlemen's Club and, while such opinions didn't faze Broom or affect the operation of the club, he never felt fully accepted in the town.

He remained a model citizen, scrupulous in his accounts and unfailingly polite when out in public. In church every Sunday, his donation always made the loudest and longest clatter in the collection bowl.

The local constabulary, such as it was, couldn't fault him because incidents of violence in the town actually declined after the club opened for business.

And so far as anyone could remember, no one had ever seen Broom Sherman drunk, utter a curse, speak ill of another, mistreat his employees or swindle his customers. He was a good man and he knew it irked a good many to admit it.

In November, 1914, World War I was showing no sign of a quick end. That was when Josephine O'Rourke arrived to begin work at the Queenstown Gentlemen's Club.

From Melbourne, Jo was pretty and petite and had no idea she was pregnant until a month or so later when nature and instinct left her cetain.

Too weak for the long and rough trip back to the mainland, too afraid to face her parents, who thought she had left for the west to take up work as a nurse, and too far gone for Dr Sturmie to perform an abortion, Jo fell upon the mercy of her new employer.

Broom Sherman responded typically.

A storeroom was quickly converted into a bedroom for Jo and there was a basin, a mirror and a small window which looked out to an untidy garden and then up into the hills.

There was also a small fireplace and, once the room was done up, with Broom providing the finishing touch of a varnished cradle, it was cosy and charming.

'You'll be right here, love,' he told Jo. 'We'll look after you and the young one.'

With his moustache bristling and the girls cooing, Broom Sherman proved beyond doubt that he was the finest gentleman in the Queenstown Gentlemen's Club.

Initially, Broom was concerned at the exodus of young men from the mine and into the military. He worried for their safety and what their absence meant for his business.

He soon realised that there were always men coming to

Queenstown for work. The big four-chimney house was always alive.

Then, on a July day in 1915, Jo O'Rourke gave birth to a healthy baby girl in that cosy little room.

She named her Gemma.

'That's quite a story, Gemma,' I say, feeling the words stumble out of my mouth. A quick check confirms a whisky bottle with considerably less in it than when she began talking.

'Have we drunk all that?'

'Not so much we,' says Gemma, who is standing by the fire and prodding at the coals.

Replacing the poker in its stand, Gemma resumes her seat and says, 'When I was old enough, Broom would walk with me and tell me his story. How he came to be here, how he met my mother.

'He hid nothing from me. He was not a man to gild the lily about anything in life. And what would be the point of doing so down here in a place like this?'

'How do you mean, Gemma?'

'This is a mining town,' she says. 'There's no value in pretending. Pretending is tiring and people are tired enough in places like this.'

'It's a good story,' I tell her.

'I think so too,' she says. 'I think I'll have another drop. All this talking has left me parched.'

She takes a drink, waits for the warmth and, when it comes, lets out a sigh as sweet as a happy memory.

chapter 12

'My father,' says Gemma, 'was a businessman first and foremost. Making money was his talent and he planned and worked to ensure his talent was not wasted.

'But the one thing he always said was that a man needed a quieter side, some time and space to think about other things. I suppose that was the spiritual part of him. I liked that about him.'

Usually, I like listening to Gemma. Even more, I like the way Blink is so comfortable in her presence.

On this particular evening, however, I am fed up, disillusioned and resigned to driving Blink and myself back to Launceston to face whatever comeuppance awaits me. I become churlish.

'Why do you call him your father?' I ask her. 'You've told me your story. You didn't know your real father. I thought you were against gilding the lily.'

There is a steely defiance in Gemma's gaze.

'Broom Sherman was a father to me,' she says, ever so quietly, ever so mightily.

I see my thoughtlessness and it's not just in goading this kind woman or in bringing an old and fading man from care and comfort to a place like Queenstown. It's there in the fact that I have made no further plans. Me, an architect, with no plans.

Instead, I have been foolishly hoping that things will simply fall into place and that good intentions will be rewarded by good outcomes.

As Gemma returns to the many merits of Broom Sherman, my mind searches for options it cannot find. I chomp angrily into a piece of chocolate cake.

'The one thing Broom Sherman always did was plan ahead. He always said there was more value in foresight than hindsight,' she says, eyeing me. 'There's chocolate on your chin.'

For one dismal moment, I consider whether Gemma might grant us use of the small garden area at the back of the B & B. Maybe Blink and I could do something with it.

The more I think about it, the more defeated I feel.

Worse, I know I have let Blink down, putting him through so much for an act of futility, something I should have known from the start.

I should have seen it on the drive down the coast, should have realised as the temperature grew colder and the landscape bleaker that things just do not grow here. In the west, they are only dug up, chopped down, poisoned and removed.

Blink has nodded off and there is a blob of cake on his chin as well. I lean across and wipe it away.

'The one thing Broom Sherman always said was that self-pity was self-destructive,' says Gemma. 'You reap what you sow, he always said. You reap what you sow.'

'For Christ's sake, Gemma! For a man who only said one thing, it sounds like he never shut up and, anyway, none of it is any good to me now,' I snap at her.

I have made up my mind to settle our bill in the morning, drive back to Cassidy's, pick up my car and head home.

And I am about to say as much when Gemma leaves her chair and the room. I sulk, thinking I've finally gone too far, but then she returns, carrying a bottle of port and two glasses.

'Here,' she says. The sweet brown liquid nestles in my belly.

Gemma sits down and leans towards me. 'Tell me what you want.'

I do. As naturally as water, it pours out of me and when I've finished Gemma leans forward again and says, almost to herself, 'I have some land. It might be gardened.'

Gemma calls on Sarah Trotter, a young mother who lives in the street and helps in the office now and again, to mind the reception desk for the morning.

After giving Sarah details of any expected visitors, Gemma says she's happy to be out of the house.

The land is on the road between Queenstown and Zeehan and when I ask how far I am told it is almost precisely halfway.

'In answer to your question from last night,' she says as we drive out, 'and I have forgiven you for your rudeness, I call him my father because in every respect Broom Sherman behaved as my father and treated me as his daughter.

'He held no ill-feeling or disrespect for my mother and he never allowed anyone to put either of us down about how we had come to be here.

'I just want to clear that up, all right?'

'I suppose it must have been a little easier here in Queenstown,' I say, moving close to the road verge to avoid a lane-hopping truck coming the other way.

'Why would that be?'

'I don't know, I just suppose it would not have had the same social stigma in a place like this, as opposed to somewhere like Launceston or Hobart—any city, for that matter.'

'Angus,' says Gemma, 'people create their own stigmas, no matter where they are. Queenstown has never been an exception.

'Broom Sherman tried to protect us but he couldn't do it all the time and we didn't expect it. Other children and other parents certainly scored plenty of points off my mother and me.'

'What was your mother like?'

'Grateful,' says Gemma. 'We were both very lucky and she made it clear that I was never to forget it.

'Broom Sherman may not have married my mother but he came to love her and he loved me and he was—turn off here, to the right, head up that dirt road.'

The car sprays mud behind us as the road becomes a lane and then a track.

'Stop here.'

Gemma leads us through a gate and we make our way up a small incline. The ground has a chemical odour but not as much as land closer to Queenstown and the mine. I hold Blink's arm and he huffs and puffs.

'Broom Sherman bought this land in the '20s,' says Gemma. 'I can remember coming here for picnics, travelling up from Queenstown in a horse and buggy.

'There were trees on this land then and the grass was still green and the dirt was still brown.'

As the ground flattens out, I help Blink sit to catch his breath. As soon as he's comfortable, he lights a smoke and surveys the scene.

'Empty,' he says. 'This land's done it hard.'

'Not quite empty,' says Gemma, breathing heavily. 'I won't sit down just yet, otherwise I may never get up.'

Strange, Gemma had seemed so much younger than Blink and it is only now it occurs to me that there can't be so much distance between them, maybe only fifteen or twenty years.

I pull Blink to his feet and he groans with the effort.

Gemma walks a little further and then stands quite still, her arms loose at her sides and her head bowed. The land expands around her.

It has a slope, because it would be asking too much for land in this part of the world not to have a slope. Also, the land has suffered its share of poisoning on, and beneath, the surface.

But the land has assets too, and the best of them is its setting, concealed between the scalped hills and the eastern forest. In that regard, the location is perfect.

Also, the land does not drop away as suddenly as I've seen elsewhere. The slope is gentle and easy, as close to a plateau as the west can offer.

I gather from the untouched forest to the east that the trees that grew here were among the last to be taken before the mine slowed production.

The cutting and clearing that did occur still left the ground vulnerable to the pollution, which drifted on the air before dropping and seeping into the soil.

Then again, the distance from the mine and the end of the furnaces also means it was spared the worst of the ravaging.

In outlying areas such as this, I can see that what I have heard is true—in places green is beginning to poke gamely through the garish colours.

The soft fall of the land and its proximity to the other hills and the forest provide some shelter from the biting winds.

Nothing in the west can hide from the rain but being able to keep the wind at reasonable bay is invaluable.

Most comfortingly, the land is hidden from the highway—to reach it requires a turn-off from the main road, and few ever do that. People either want to reach or leave Queenstown. Detours only complicate matters.

When we reach her, Gemma is kneeling between two headstones in the centre of the land. Each one is carved from granite and each one is tablet-shaped and adorned with a cross.

One is inscribed to the memory of Sebastian "Broom" Sherman, born 1880, died 1955. The other signifies the final resting place of Josephine Elizabeth O'Rourke, born 1893, died 1937. The graves face east, towards the trees.

'My father liked that this place was halfway between Zeehan and Queenstown, the two places that had given him so much,' says Gemma. 'When my mother died, he thought it was perfect for her.'

'She was still young,' I say. 'What happened?'

'TB. It took a few down this way,' says Gemma.

'And she's been here all these years,' I say.

'No, not all that time,' says Gemma, and she explains how the outbreak of World War II prompted Broom Sherman to sell the land to the mining company.

'We were told the war effort was more important than sentiment and that the land, any land with trees on it, was crucial to helping support the effort.

'The mine had to be kept going. They even tried growing vegetables on this land. Not that it worked. Anything that did come up tasted like sulphur.

'The war meant that giving up the land was something that couldn't be refused and my father wouldn't have refused anyway. He sold up for a song and my mother's grave was moved to town.'

I tell Gemma that Blink had been a gardener in a cemetery.

'I know,' she says, 'he's told me. Tells me quite a bit.'

'Are we going to Garden Villa?' asks Blink, his hand brushing back and forth along the top of Broom Sherman's headstone.

'No,' I say, 'another day.'

'There's never been much of a garden here,' says Gemma.

She goes on to say that when Broom Sherman died, she inherited the four-chimney house and some money.

By then the Queenstown Gentlemen's Club no longer existed and Gemma's husband Artie had developed health problems from his mining years.

'In his blood mainly,' she says. 'He was a decent man and we raised our children and had a good life, but then his blood gave up on him.

'When he went, there was some money. Not a fortune, but a bit. I used some of it to buy back this land. It wasn't up to much and it still isn't. But it was cheap. I bought it back. For my parents.'

Gemma sits quietly.

'Mind you,' she begins again, 'it still took a fair whack out of my kitty and even more when I wanted to relocate my father and mother's graves from the town to here. Worth it, though, worth every penny, don't you think?'

I agree and understand. As I know would Blink, on better days.

'That's when I decided to try to make a living out of the house again,' she says. 'I could see its value as a place to stay for the tourists who'd started coming down to the west to have a look at our ruined hills.'

'Foresight, not hindsight,' I say.

As Gemma slowly rises, I realise that bringing Broom Sherman and Jo O'Rourke back to this piece of earth is one way she has repaid what she felt, and knew, was her debt.

With luck, on this piece of land, two more debts will be repaid.

chapter 13

Blink's having a kip before tea. I feel like talking. I begin by telling Gemma that if her debt is linked to Broom Sherman's goodness, part of my debt to Blink has its origins in selfishness.

We were young, Stevie and I, but old enough to know better and, in any case, it didn't matter how old we were. One look at the Raymond Street garden was all anyone of any age ever needed to know it commanded respect.

It was grand final day, late September, 1970, and Stevie's and my beloved Collingwood, the most popular and most hated Aussie Rules club in the land, were taking on Carlton at the MCG.

Stevie and I were to spend most of the day with Blink and Isobel. We'd watch the game there.

That morning we dressed from head to toe in the black and white club colours. Our beanies were turned up at the bottom to sit better on our heads and the black pompoms bobbled on top.

Our Collingwood jumpers had been knitted by someone, I forget who, but Mum had arranged it. We had arrived home from school one afternoon and there they were on our beds.

Both had No. 6 sewn on the back, a declaration of allegiance to our favourite player, full-forward Peter McKenna.

Stevie and I couldn't bolt down our breakfast quickly enough and we were soon sliding across the dew and kicking the footy in the backyard, playing our own grand final.

Our parents were not gardeners of any great skill, but in the backyard they had gone to some effort by planting a rose bush, which crept along the fence and prevented next door's kids from climbing over.

'They're bad eggs,' my mother said.

The back lawn was always reasonably trim, kept so with a stubborn push mower, but it suffered from being our play area.

At the front of the house was another lawn and this one was close-cut, always watered and rimmed by hydrangeas. Stevie and I were warned time and again never to play there.

'This is what people see,' my mother often told us, hammering home the point. 'This is where we make our first impression.'

On grand final day, the street began filling with cars about mid-morning and couples carrying beer and containers full of food filed into our place. Stevie and I were called in to say hello.

The gathering was Mum's idea and Dad eased his discomfort among company by tapping the keg early, just as the under-19s were getting under way on the black and white telly he had to thump into life with the flat of his hand.

Tired of having our cheeks pinched and hair ruffled, Stevie and I couldn't wait to get back outside and, when Mum gave us the nod, we took off.

I don't know why, perhaps we were too excited to think properly, but we headed out the front. I do know that bad things happen in slow motion.

Stevie scooped up the ball and was running at close to full tilt when he executed a stunning blind turn out of imagined trouble, dodged a couple of invisible opponents and dropped the ball onto his right foot.

Two, maybe three hydrangeas burst like bombs as the ball spun its way through them before it found clear air. Their petals fluttered to the ground.

I kept my eyes on the ball, moving in from the side and dropping to my knees to begin a long slide on the wet grass, my actions timed to meet the ball at just the right moment.

It worked a treat. To the cheers of the crowd I could hear in my head, I caught the ball in front of my face, not noticing a second burst of blooms as I ploughed through them.

Stevie realised before me what we had done. There was no disguising the look of horror on my brother's face, nor the sinking feeling which then punched into the pit of my stomach.

'You two having fun?' Dad called out from the front veranda. 'That was a good kick, Stevie, and you picked it up well too. Not a bad grab. Chuck the ball here, mate, I'll show you how your old man does it.'

I handpassed the ball to Dad, amazed at how relaxed he was, given how many times he'd said the front lawn was off-limits.

I saw what we'd done. The hydrangeas were a shambles and there were long, muddy skidmarks across the lawn.

Holding the ball between his arm and his side, Dad took a pocket knife from his trousers, flicked open the silver blade and plunged it deep into the leather and bladder of the ball. It *fssshhhed* and died.

When the time came to leave for Raymond Street, Stevie and I had only a red plastic footy with the dog's teethmarks in it. It was a bastard to kick.

And, even then, we didn't learn.

Collingwood were seven goals in front at half-time and looked unbeatable. Stevie and I downed one of Isobel's bitter lemonades, pips and all, and went out to relive the glories of the first half in Blink's garden.

When Blink came out to the top of the back stairs to call us inside for the second half, I remember seeing him sort of lose his balance and reach for the rail. He sat down on the top step, struck dumb.

Then I saw why. In a few short minutes, Stevie and I had torn through the garden.

We had churned damp ground to mud. Our swerves and high marks and slides had ripped tomatoes from vines and stakes, lemons from branches, strawberries from their beds.

There were holes in the hedge and flower petals strewn across the ground.

Blink's beloved roses remained unscathed. We boys had become familiar enough with the sting of their thorns to keep our distance from them.

Almost everything else, however, was in ruins and for the second time that day I felt my stomach plummet.

I tried to say sorry but the words wouldn't come. Blink stared at his boots as we passed. 'The second half's starting,' he said.

He clomped down into the garden and I watched as he began his repairs, picking up petals, tamping down grass divots, breaking off half-hanging stems, shaking his head, at times holding a hand to his eyes.

Collingwood lost the 1970 grand final. Carlton came from nowhere. I felt it was something of a repayment.

Nowhere near enough. But something.

Gemma spoons another chunk of cauliflower onto her plate and holds the bowl out to me.

'No thanks,' I say, patting my belly and pushing my plate away as Blink scrapes a last mouthful of bread through his gravy.

'Cup of tea, Blink? Angus?'

I help Gemma clear the table and use a napkin to wipe gravy and potato smears from Blink's face. He leans back in his chair and burps unashamedly.

'Tribute to an enjoyed meal,' says Gemma, laughing as we head into the kitchen and set the plates and cutlery by the sink.

She looks at the pile of dishes. 'Later,' she says.

After filling the kettle, she places it on the stove and lights the gas, which makes a pleasing *whomp* on ignition and glows blue–red. Gemma then tips four spoonfuls of tea into the pot and says, 'One for each person, one for the pot.'

'I know it's not my business,' she says, reaching into a cupboard for cups and saucers, 'but all that about the football and the ruined gardens doesn't sound, not to me at least, to be something so terrible that you had to come all the way down here to make amends.

'I mean, you were just children, and excited children at that, although I've never understood what people see in that game. They play on gravel down here, for heaven's sake!'

I pour milk into the cups and tap a crusty sugar lump back into granules. The cups have red roses painted on them.

'It wasn't just that,' I say. 'I owe him for more than that.'

Gemma is about to say something else when the kettle whistles.

Blink coughs an oily one in the next room.

chapter 14

Sometimes, up at Gemma's land, Blink digs his hands into the earth and watches it sift between his fingers until all that's left in his palms are a few tiny pebbles and some brown muck.

In his more lucid moments, he wonders aloud how much time and effort, how much blood and bone and digging and turning it will take to make this ground work for itself and be good again.

He is an old man and he has a right to wonder about time and whether there can possibly be enough of it to transform a patch of terrain like this one.

'Nothing wants to be here. It's almost given up,' he says to me, or so I believe, but now that I look at him I can't be sure. There's a distance to him and he seems to have left me again.

I've seen it happen enough that I know there is nothing to do but wait.

It usually doesn't take long. I suppose that's the way of his old mind. It jumps between the real and the unreal, never staying long enough in one world or the other.

It happened in the car on that first day, driving down from Longford. It's happened a few times since we've been in Queenstown.

Blink comes and goes. I keep a watch on him, ready for both.

This time he says he can hear his mother's voice.

'She's cooking a roast. She cooks a good roast,' he says.

Elizabeth Johns cooked to eat and to take her mind off things.

I know this from what I've read, from the things Isobel has told me and from the disjointed snippets of information I get from Blink, just as I know that Elizabeth Johns was miserable beyond words the day Blink told her he had decided to enlist.

She sat on the garden bench under the sun, the brightness and warmth painting the Raymond Street garden in colours she'd never thought could be so brilliant.

The roses were lustrous red, blinding white and yellow, and the hollyhocks seemed taller than ever as they stretched skyward.

Greens and pinks and golds were set off against the profound black of shadows.

The hedge was a gorgeous green and when a sparrow flitted in to drink at the birdbath, water flicked off its beak and sparkled like little diamonds.

Despite all this beauty, Elizabeth was in a gloom.

She could hear the trudge of her son's boots heading up Raymond Street and gradually fading.

At the top of the street, she knew he'd turn left and probably wave to old Daisy Davies who was always out on her balcony at this time if the weather was fine. Then he'd cross Mary Street to High Street, walk over to Windmill Hill and down into the town.

She couldn't imagine her son's stringy body filling a soldier's uniform. Nor could she imagine how he would fare when confined by regulations and orders. She tried not to think about the army which would depend on his courage or the enemy baying for blood and not caring if it was his. She tried not to think of any of these things. Failing, she took a small handkerchief from her sleeve and dabbed her eyes.

Gazing about the garden, she recognised anew the beautiful work Blink had performed there. Then, with all her strength, she sought to will away any thought of the terrible work that lay ahead of him.

Elizabeth feared for her son's life, as she knew all mothers did for theirs. She knew some who had already lost their sons.

But her son had magic in his hands and she couldn't bear to imagine that soldiering might take that gift away, blinding him to beauty and his ability to conjure it from the ground.

Composing herself, Elizabeth left the garden and went inside, going into her room and taking out her diary.

It was no use. She wasn't yet ready to write about this. She returned to the kitchen where vegetables waited to be peeled.

Something extra special for dinner tonight, she'd promised Blink: a roast with all the trimmings, gravy and white sauce, a crusty loaf in the middle of the table and a jug of iced tea.

The pantry door couldn't take the weight of Elizabeth's grief and she slid down, a long splinter spearing into her palm.

She slumped to the floor, a tin of flour spilling from her hand. Potatoes rolled around as her body jolted in a seizure of sadness. The tin clattered. Flour sprayed.

Elizabeth's tears poured from her eyes, down her cheeks, falling, falling, until they too hit the floor and turned the spilled flour to a lumpy paste.

As he walked, Blink felt so light as to be tipsy.

Raymond Street was a street of gardens, with colour and fragrance abounding on both sides.

At home, on dry days and in the afternoons when the shadows were lengthening and the grass was cool and soft, Blink would take off his workboots and workshirt, roll off his socks and lie on his back on the ground. He'd rub his hands and feet into the lawn as if drawing his own nourishment up through the soil.

Reaching into his trouser pocket, he'd take out the leather pouch which had belonged to his father, Stocky, and which he kept filled with tobacco and papers, a few matches and a scratch. Still on his back, he'd roll the tobacco in his palms, take the paper from the edge of his lip and fashion a rollie, thin and straight, never too tight. Lighting up, he'd take a couple of strong draws and hold the smoke deep inside him before slowly releasing it through his mouth and nose.

This was the best part of the day and he could have stayed there for hours.

But something always caught his eye: a brown spot out of place on a petal, a caterpillar munching its way through a green leaf, a discoloration or sign of disturbance in the roses.

He'd take a last good drag of the smoke, grind it into the turf and place the butt in his pocket. Elizabeth would find it and others on washing day and be both miffed at his habit and taken with his sensitivity.

'You worry more about that garden being spoiled by one small cigarette end than you do about a good pair of work trousers that need to last the summer,' she'd tell him.

With his secateurs and trowel, Blink would cut away the problems he'd seen or nudge around the plant bases, easing the flow of air and water. He used an old cloth hung on a nail hammered into the back fence to wipe away any scale and he never forgot to change the water in the birdbath.

When he was finished, as the last of the sun lit the garden, he would gaze at every corner and work his way inward, taking in every detail from every angle, all the way back to where he was in the middle of the lawn. Only then, content that nothing else needed to be done that day, would he pick up his boots, socks and shirt and think about what his mother was cooking for dinner.

Blink stopped at Windmill Hill and admired the full circle of the view and the slow spinning of the windmill blades.

Straight ahead, as he looked north, the Tamar River was wide and boats were coming and going, loading and unloading everything from fish, timber, fabric, fruit and vegetables to mining equipment, paper, steel and railway sleepers.

He could see ships' crews swapping places, either ready for a few days sailing to the mainland or a few days holed up and gloriously drunk in one of the Bog pubs.

There was contrast in the boats. Some were hoisted out of the water for scraping and cleaning, their dignity gone. Others were bobbing in the water, freshly painted and with dignity intact.

Turning west, Blink saw a landscape that dipped into a valley and was filling with homes, schools, stores and other services that further evidenced Launceston growing.

From the floor of the valley rose a series of cuttings taken up by roads and new subdivisions. Beyond them, out of Blink's sight, the town stretched even further.

Blink knew the kinds of houses that had been built out that way and he had worked in the gardens of quite a few.

Even though he was still a young man, his talent had been obvious from the start and his reputation had grown quickly.

He knew the fruit trees, the walled garden and hawthorn hedge at Entally House; the cherry orchard at Franklin

House; the mulberry tree and roses at Fullers; the beautiful displays of camellias, peonies and magnolias at Mount Pleasant; the orchard at Newnham Hall.

'Are you all right, Blink?' I ask. The look in his eyes is still one of distance and he is turning, as if seeking something lost in every direction.

'I was thinking about an orchard,' he says. 'Not Mick's, though. Mick had an orchard.'

'I don't think Mick would look at this place too fondly for his apples and pears,' I say. 'Not too much fruit growing on the west coast.'

I try to be easygoing, but I am uncomfortable talking about Mick.

'I can't see the houses,' says Blink, still turning, slowly, hoping to latch on to something familiar.

'No, there they are,' he says. 'There they are. I've got 'em.'

He is away from me once more.

Facing south, Blink could see the thin brown–blue line that was the main road out of Launceston. A train pulled eight carriages along the adjacent railway line.

Turning east, back towards Raymond Street and home, he took in the view from Windmill Hill. Blink could see his house and imagined his mother sitting on the garden bench, as he knew was her habit at this time of the day, not knowing how different the scene really was, as she cleaned up spilled flour and tried desperately to steer her mind back to the details of the evening meal.

Beyond the house, his gaze was drawn towards the farms at Waverley, St Leonards and White Hills. Blink could make out clusters of sheep and herds of slow cows.

The green of the fields lightened the further he cast his gaze and the land was patterned by fences and rows of trees. Every second or third field broke the run of green by being fresh-ploughed and brown. Winding tracks led to huge estate homes and off them could be seen smaller buildings, for staff, animals and equipment.

The farms looked tiny from Windmill Hill and that perception was enhanced by the backdrop of the mountains. Blink thought they had sinister faces and when the snow melted and streams ran down their slopes, that their expressions were grave.

Somewhere just beyond the mountains, were tin mining communities with rugged men and their wives and sniffling children who were always cold, always dirty and always caused a ruckus when they came to Launceston for supplies.

The mountains held nothing for Blink. The stories that filtered down from them were unpleasant and sad as they told of mine collapses, in-breeding and fights between the locals and the migrant Chinks.

Blink returned to his starting point, facing north and the river, and he was glad to put the misery of the mountains behind him.

He sat to retie his bootlaces, then stood and caught a gentle breeze from the spinning windmill.

He tucked in his shirt and strode down into the town.

chapter 15

Just as Elizabeth Johns admired her son's garden, so did Isobel, who came to live at Raymond Street when she and Blink married after the war. Occasionally, she would need lemons, tomatoes, carrots for a meal or a clutch of flowers to brighten up the dinner table.

In the Raymond Street garden there was, thought Isobel, a place for everything and everything in its place. There were flowers and shrubs, fruits and vegetables, hedges, paths, lawns and small trees. No part overwhelmed any other.

The garden was quite a size, though hardly compared with the sprawling estate layouts on which Blink had worked, like Entally House, Mount Pleasant and Rosemount. It grew on a shade more than half an acre and was fenced on two sides. At the bottom of the block, a barrier was formed by the back wall of Tuckey's Tool Repairs.

Blink used the windowless wall for climbers. Old man Tuckey, who lost a son on the Western Front, didn't mind.

At the bottom of the back stairs, a green and yellow-leaved box hedge was cut at such a tempting height that it almost defied you not to run your hands along its prickly top.

To the right, a tiny patch of lawn was the dampest spot in the garden because it was shaded by the house and the Trevors' place next door. Blink had planted hydrangeas there and his boots squelched and dented the earth.

A small cement path led left of the stairs and around the little hedge to a larger lawn, this one more open to the sun and clipped as close as a schoolboy's crewcut.

A wooden garden bench was backed by a row of petunias, themselves backed by chrysanthemums, and a lemon tree stood a few yards away, its greens and yellows off-setting the purples, pinks and whites of the other blooms.

This part of the garden was squared off at the front by a row of shrubs, mainly daphne, which in bloom brought forth clutches of sweet flowers. The daphne grew either side of an arch through and over which jasmine sprawled. Dahlias lined the left side fence.

As you walked under the arch, Blink's birdbath came into view and centred a new section, although it was never long before the eye was caught by the roses.

Dupont roses rambled along the fence, taking up where the dahlias left off, forming a cloud of white and yellow.

A path of stepping stones curved in such a way that Blink had been able to plant different species of roses at regular intervals. The contrast was glorious. Deep reds and blinding whites. Soft pinks.

The pattern and placement of heritage roses and hybrids had been grafted first in Blink's mind, then by his hands, then by the earth. There were gallicas and damasks, which bloomed just once a year, albas ideal for the borders, centifolias with their thick flowers and tough thorns, bourbons prone to black spot but monitored like a hawk and kept clean by Blink.

Of all flowers, Blink believed roses had true character. He saw in them an incomparable beauty and femininity and yet they were also stubborn, fickle and aggressive.

He had also been careful to include variety, complementing the roses through partnerships with daffodils, petunias and impatiens.

Whereas the climbing roses spread out and up of their own accord, the bedded roses had been shaped and trained.

Like Blink, Isobel would touch the rose petals and press her thumb and forefinger against the thorns. Like Blink, she recognised their fragility and strength.

She loved this part of the garden because she believed this was where Blink revealed his true self. She couldn't imagine that something like this could come from aloofness or so plain an explanation as tradesmanship.

Hollyhocks separated the roses from the practicalities of the vegetable garden, which was entered via a grassed walkway. Staked tomatoes climbed, carrots and parsnips sprouted.

A tree presented small apples, beans grew on runners alongside radishes, fat pumpkins, zucchini and sweetcorn.

Slap-bang in the middle was an old stump on which Blink sat and smoked. We'd talk there.

Stevie's fondest memory is of the lemon tree.

'It was the scent more than anything,' he says, 'and, even today, the scent of lemons makes me think of Isobel's lemonade.'

We've always called her Isobel. She said Nan or Grandma made her sound old.

We didn't just stay with Blink and Isobel on grand final days. We were regulars at Raymond Street and knew the lemon tree was the sturdiest one in the garden and the easiest to climb. It had low, thick branches, ideal for footholds, but you had to be careful if you looked up or climbed higher because the short twigs could take out an eye.

We were light enough to sit high in the branches and pretend to be scanning the horizon for pirate ships or searching the garden for baddies. We'd be up there, our holsters tied to our legs with Blink's spare bootlaces, holding on to a branch with one hand and a cap pistol cocked and ready in the other.

Blink was never overjoyed to see too many lemons lying at the base of the tree, dislodged by our ups and downs, but he let us play on.

Isobel made her lemonade from the fallen fruit and I can still taste its tartness on my tongue and feel the discomfort of stray pips swallowed or lodged at the back of my throat.

She would halve the lemons then press them hard down onto the top of the glass juicer. The liquid would dribble out. When enough juice had been extracted to fill about a quarter of a jug, she would spoon in sugar and water, stirring all the time with a wooden spatula. Stevie and I were the tastemasters and the lemonade was only finished when we said so, after which Isobel would place it in the fridge to chill.

It was sweet and tart at the same time, the most perfect drink I have ever tasted.

Not so long ago, Stevie drove me back to Raymond Street and we saw that the house had been painted a nasty custard yellow over the chocolate brown we had known. But just seeing the old place again filled me with nostalgia.

We walked up the steep concrete drive with the strip of lawn down its centre and laughed at the way it was always a bugger to mow, because you could lose your footing going up and coming down.

We went past the wooden garage which had never held a car, not for the few years that Elizabeth and Stocky Johns had lived there, and all the years Blink and Isobel lived there after them.

Isobel used the garage as a laundry. A double sink was made of cement and there was an archaic washing machine and a mangle through which she fed shirts, sheets, towels, undies and the occasional pound note and grocery list, turning a handle and pressing out the excess water before laying the clothes flat across her wooden basket and lugging them out to the line.

Stevie grabbed my arm as we walked under the back stairs and I saw he was pointing to the lemon tree.

'Are we too old to climb it?' he asked.

The people who owned the house were pleasant enough but were not keen on letting us inside. Stevie and I apologised for being a nuisance on a Sunday morning.

Stevie thinks of the lemon tree. I think of the secret cupboard.

All right, so it wasn't really secret, seeing as it was in Blink and Isobel's bedroom, which was large and had a view of Mount Barrow and the pastures below it.

The secret cupboard was also large, a walk-in with floor space and shelving on three sides. A stepstool sat in a corner.

On the left was the conventional stuff—underwear, towels and bedding—which filled two shelves. On the top were boxes containing cookbooks, placemats, doilies and old postcards.

It was the right and rear shelves of the secret cupboard that hid the real delights and surprises.

Along the top were jars of preserved plums, nectarines and peaches, while the rest of the shelving was devoted to gadgets and tools, boxes of letters, biscuit tins containing medals, buttons and old notes.

An old typewriter had keys so stiff you needed two fingers to push them down. There was a small cracked mirror, there were women's hats, and there was a wicker basket full of brooches and pins.

When we were small enough and Blink could still lift us off the ground, one boy on each arm, the shelves in the secret cupboard were strong enough to take our weight and we would climb and wriggle and giggle from level to level.

We'd throw the towels and blankets onto the floor and, pretending to be shot down by bad guys, fall from the shelving to soft, joyful deaths.

We contrived uses for all the gadgets. They became mines, grenades, all kinds of exotic weapons, magic keys.

Stevie and I could spend hours in the secret cupboard. Just close the door. Flick on our torches.

New discoveries were made every time, like the day I found a locked box, surprised I hadn't seen it before.

Isobel said she'd only recently put it there. She had the key and it stuck a little before the box opened.

'Some are mine, some were Elizabeth's,' said Isobel of the batch of diaries and letters inside. She sorted through them, putting some aside and keeping them with her. 'You can read the rest if you like. Just put them back when you're done.'

At first, I was too young to grasp what I was reading and Isobel seemed to find it difficult to read them at all, especially the letters from Blink, which were brief and bare of real detail.

But from then on I was drawn to them and often, after Stevie and I had finished playing, I would ask Isobel for the key and she would leave me to read.

Gradually, the items she set aside that first day were returned. Then she gave me the key for good.

I still have it, at home, with the box.

It was Stevie who found the money but I worked out what we could do with it.

Playing in the secret cupboard one day, up on the second level behind a stack of tins, Stevie found a bundle of plastic tubes, each one with a green lid, each one bearing the symbol of the City Baptist Church, each one filled with silver coins.

There were ten tubes all told and, to small boys, that added up to a fortune.

I figured there was no way Isobel, who was the only one who attended church, would miss two or three.

I pocketed two tubes and Stevie two more and we emerged from the secret cupboard and walked out to the kitchen to beg Blink to take us to the shop, a small milkbar five minutes away which did a thriving trade, thanks to its being so close to a school.

As it happened, Blink needed a packet of fags.

Unloading the jangling money on the counter, almost wetting ourselves at the prospect of what we could buy, we reloaded our pockets with Big Boss bubble gum, sherbies, milk bottles, gobstoppers and musk sticks. We left the milkbar still rattling with the money we hadn't spent.

I had a mouth full of delicious chocolate buddies as I jumped up the back stairs, then almost choked at what I saw on the kitchen table—six plastic tubes, each with a green lid and a church symbol and filled with coins.

'I have to go to church tomorrow.' Isobel looked up from stirring something pink and gluggy in a bowl. 'I thought I had more money than this for the poor people. Perhaps I lost count. I suppose the poor people won't know.

'They're grateful for any help they can get. I suppose someone will make up the difference so the poor people won't go without.'

Three times in the one little speech Isobel had mentioned the "poor people".

She didn't scold us, accuse us, smack us or punish us in any way. Rather, she used a grandmother's guile to encourage guilt and contrition.

I had chocolate all over my gob and my pockets bulged with stuff. I wondered if the poor people could eat sherbies or were allowed to chew Big Boss bubble gum.

Stevie, two years younger, chomped away behind me, led astray but too young to be culpable.

Blink sat at the table and lit a smoke, sucking in his cheeks as he inhaled.

'I better go and lock that cupboard,' he said, 'just in case.'

There were other delights for small boys at the Raymond Street house. Like the beds.

Maybe it was because we were small, but the beds seemed huge and there was space underneath for games.

Elsewhere, the smells from the kitchen and Blink's tobacco permeated and were intoxicating.

The house had plump chairs a boy could get lost in and hide behind. There were floor to ceiling cupboards, little nooks and large expanses of hall and floor for races and playing with toy cars or toy soldiers.

In the living room, Blink sat next to the heater and butted his smokes in a standing ashtray. He'd press a button and the tray would spin, whirring the butt out of sight and into the bowl below.

'Centrifugal force, boys,' he'd say as we watched.

Then he'd light up another one.

A Prudential Insurance calendar, updated each year and with a map of the world always as its illustration, hung above the heater, while a bookshelf behind Blink's chair held Readers Digest condensed novels which he read in the toilet.

'Bugger it,' you'd hear him curse from the loo and you'd know he'd picked up the index again.

When Isobel sat down for the evening she did so in a recliner. She would knit and sew and only glance up at the telly every now and again.

To Stevie and me the telly seemed miles away, so we sat close, plonking ourselves down on velvety cushions.

On one of the walls in the living room, there was a painting of a snow-capped peak and next to it was a framed photograph of another snow-capped peak. There were no family portraits, no wedding or baby photos, nothing remotely sentimental.

Windmill Hill

The Raymond Street house was probably austere in its decoration and forced in its warmth. But no boys anywhere loved a place as much as Stevie and I loved that one.

chapter 16

Most Tasmanians knew the story of Charlie Forster and either felt sorry for him or dismissed him as weak, or worse, a coward.

Blink knew the story better than most because he and Charlie had worked together on a couple of gardens.

'I can't figure it out,' said Blink to his mother. 'It's just the strangest thing. I was only talking to him not long ago. It doesn't sit right. This whole thing doesn't sit right. Poor bugger. I hope his Mum's all right. I don't know.'

What he did know was that Charlie Forster had been among the first to enlist and was keen to go but had come down with a fever that kept him out of uniform for more than two months.

In that time, news of the ongoing and increasing carnage in Turkey had made it back home and people around the traps said that Charlie's mother Beth, whose ears for gossip were as big as the mouth she used to spread it, became hysterical.

In the end, for his mother's sake, Charlie stayed home.

'The police and the military came for him,' said George Collis, a neighbour, over a beer with Blink. 'And when they did, Beth Forster went for them with a broom, screaming, "Don't take my little boy! Don't take my little boy!"

'Little boy?' George continued, pouring another. 'Charlie was twenty-two and built like a brick shithouse, for Christ's sake.'

Beth Forster had to be restrained as Police Sergeant Will Redding went looking for Charlie. He found him in the back shed.

Blink imagined the scene—as Will had told everyone it had panned out—of poor Charlie, dressed only in his singlet and underpants, carrying a short-handled axe and something in his other hand that Will said he couldn't make out at first.

'The lad was wild-eyed and white as a bloody sheet but then his eyes just rolled back in his head,' said Will afterwards, to anyone who'd listen and buy him a beer to keep talking.

'He just dead-fainted, clunk. That was when I saw the clean cut, straight through Charlie's foot.

'Never seen anything like it. The exposed bone and all the blood turned a man's stomach, I can tell you, and I've seen some things over the years.'

Blink had heard the rest, of how Beth Forster, held at the wrists by two young soldiers, slumped between them at the sight of her son. Of how Charlie was lifted to his feet and out of his left hand dropped the other half of his severed foot.

'Hairy toes and all,' said Will, who would shudder at the memory and, at the same time, look around for anyone who hadn't yet heard the story.

'I tried to staunch the bleeding with a wad of material that was slung over a post in the shed. I had to do something,' said Will, and people would pat his back and murmur their agreement and support.

Six weeks later, Charlie Forster died from septicaemia, the stench of his wound becoming so bad that the hospital authorities gave him a room of his own, near the furnaces, into which every day a nurse tossed his stinking, green–yellow bandages.

'It doesn't sit right, this Charlie Forster thing,' said Blink at the time. 'It sits badly.'

'How do you mean?' asked Elizabeth.

'Well, I sort of see it like this. Is one man changing his mind about going off to the war worth all the effort and all the sadness that came about as people tried to keep him to it? It's just one bloke. Maybe he should have stayed home.

'I mean, what if he went to pieces at the front and more men died because of it?

'Everyone's saying there's a lesson in what happened to Charlie. But I'm buggered if I can work out what it is.

'By the way, Davie Tomkins copped a white feather the other day. Poor bugger, he's not much use to anyone even on the best of days. How's he going to go at the front?'

'So he's going then?' asked Elizabeth.

'No choice now,' said Blink. 'Wouldn't be able to live it down otherwise. That's what it's come to.'

Heading towards the army barracks, Blink passed other lads and heard snatches of their conversation as they sauntered, throwing light punches into the air and draping their arms across each other's shoulders.

'Fancy us going to Egypt?' said one.

'Yeah,' replied his mate, 'pretty strange, considerin' I've never even been to Hobart.'

The two men separated to let Blink through, making a jig of it, then rejoined as one, wheeled right and danced up the stairs of the Courthouse Hotel.

Blink stood outside the recruiting office. Out in front, a stone walkway was lined on either side with a rose hedge.

They were Dupont roses, clustering on their canes. Blink had read that the Dupont had been named for the founder of the Luxembourg Gardens in Paris and he wondered if he'd see those same gardens when he got to France. He used his pocket knife to take a small cutting.

Two men stood nervous and shuffling on the balcony and as they smoked they stole furtive glances inside.

'Signed up?' asked Blink, and one of the men jumped.

'Not yet, mate,' said the other, 'just waitin' for a mate.'

'Righto,' said Blink.

Inside, three flags hung from the ceiling—a Union Jack, an Australian flag and the Australian Imperial Forces standard. They fell just behind the recruiting officer and fluttered ever so slightly when the breeze blew through.

Ahead of Blink was a tall man with a long neck and an Adam's apple that stuck out like an extra chin. Blink turned and saw that the men outside were still there but were no more resolved to coming in.

Further up the line was a fellow dressed in farmer's overalls and gumboots. In front of him was a man in a flash suit and ahead of him a boy in bare feet, trying hard to look older than he was.

There were others and most looked of age or thereabouts, except for one boy who was so obviously not eighteen and who appeared so childlike that Blink half-expected to see the lad's mother there, holding his hand or licking a handkerchief and wiping grime from his face.

'David Burkett!' barked the recruiting officer. 'You were not of age last week, you were not of age yesterday, you will not be of age next week or next year for that matter. Go home. We admire you for your courage and commitment, son, but the army does not need fourteen-year-olds just yet.'

Blink watched as the boy dropped his head for a second, then jerked back to attention and saluted. Dropping his head again, he about-turned and forlornly left the line.

'This bloody war better not end too soon,' he mumbled.

Blink saw him leave and noted that the two men on the balcony had also gone.

At home that afternoon, Blink stooped in the garden and tended to the rose cutting he'd snipped at the barracks. There was space along the side fence, where he thought it might do well in good sun. He wanted the Dupont to stand out, imagining its pink buds turning to white blooms and the golden stamens shining like individual suns.

He knew it was probably the wrong time of the year to be planting but he'd succeeded in the past and he knew the sun, soil and drainage at Raymond Street were in his favour.

Blink tamped down the earth and left nature to its own devices.

'We'll see,' he said to himself.

Reaching for the leather tobacco pouch in his pocket, his fingers brushed the enlistment papers.

They registered that his presence would be required the following Monday at Paterson Barracks, that he was to be ranked as private and paid the princely sum of five shillings a day, with an extra shilling a day put aside by the army for when he came home.

Blink read and re-read the papers before folding them and shoving them back whence they came. He decided against the cigarette.

The smell of roast lamb, gravy and other delights wafted down from the kitchen. He saw his mother staring out of the window at him.

'Smells good, Mum,' he said. 'How long?'

'Not long, love. Best you get cleaned up and take your seat.'

There was half a cake of soap in a bowl beside an outside tap and Blink scrubbed his hands and face, using fast movements for behind his ears, around the back of his neck and through his hair. He dried himself with a small towel.

Upstairs, Elizabeth stirred the gravy until her arm ached and it was only the sound of her son tramping up the back stairs that broke her sad reverie.

The wooden spoon plopped into the gravy and she burned her fingers fishing it out. The carrots started to boil over.

Blink didn't notice a thing. He ate with more vigour than ever, while his mother picked, pushing the food around her plate.

'Patience is supposed to be a virtue, especially for a gardener,' said Blink to his mother. 'But I'm having a hard time now.'

The few days remaining before he had to leave seemed five times their duration and, although Blink got plenty of good work done in the garden, his mind raced with impatience.

Elizabeth, on the other hand, felt the days fly by as seconds.

On that last Sunday, she and Blink sat to a farewell lunch. Another roast, chicken this time, followed by apple pie and thick custard. A pot of tea. Fresh lemonade.

Later, Blink led his mother into the garden and they sat on the bench.

'You'll know what's ready and what's not, won't you?' he asked. 'The strawberries are coming on nicely and the apples are due, but the tomatoes are a bit late. Just keep an eye out, Mum, that's all. Don't put yourself out.'

'I won't, love,' she said.

'I don't know about that new rose,' said Blink. 'I've put a bit of work into that one these past few days. Have to wait and see, I expect. Just watch out for blight.'

Elizabeth nodded. Inside, she was imploding.

Blink promised to run the mower over the lawn before dark and then sharpen the blades.

When he'd finished talking, mother and son quietly looked at everything in the garden except each other.

'I'll be right,' he said, after a while.

Next morning at breakfast, Blink emptied a tea urn full of notes and coins onto the kitchen table.

'That's for you, Mum,' he said. 'They'll be paying me and feeding me and clothing me and there won't be anything I'll need to spend this on.'

Elizabeth had cut him sandwiches because she felt it was the thing to do and it had occupied her attention.

'Righto, love,' she said. 'Off you go.'

They stared at each other, expressionless, and then moved together. Elizabeth fitted neatly beneath Blink's chin and he felt as if he could wrap his arms twice around her.

She held him and rocked him, just as she had when he was a baby and the colic was hurting him. She held him and closed her eyes tight. There were no tears, not yet.

No, first she had to take him in, absorb the kiss curl of his fringe, the shape of his face, the smell of his cigarettes, his youth and trade, the strength and gentleness of his hands, his height and width, his gait and his idiosyncrasies, like biting his nails and sleeping with one eye open and the bedding thrown every which way.

She took it all in.

'Come on, Mum.'

She let him go. And as she stepped back and saw the baby, the boy, the youth and the man in him, still she didn't cry.

She felt pride and frustration, a blend of loss and discovery.

Blink leaned forward and kissed his mother on the cheek and Elizabeth heard herself say, 'Take care of yourself, my son' and 'Don't forget to write' and other things she couldn't remember later on, no matter how she tried.

She heard him clomp down the back stairs, open the iron gate and once more head up Raymond Street.

She strained to hear until there was nothing left to hear, until there was only herself in a suddenly strange house with furniture and paintings and ornaments and dirty dishes she didn't seem to recognise.

She wandered from room to room, trying to find her place in it, trying to find her bearings.

In Blink's room, she sat on the edge of his bed and studied the shape of his body in its centre, the indentation of his head in the pillow, his trousers and braces on the floor.

A white shirt hung over the bedpost and she held it to her face and breathed in deeply.

'Yes,' she said, 'that's him.'

She paced around the room and wondered whether he was all right, whether he'd be up at Windmill Hill yet, whether he'd eat those tomato sandwiches before the bread got too soggy, because she knew how much he disliked it when that happened.

Then, for the second time that week, she dissolved into tears that fell so many and so large that Elizabeth Johns thought she might be washed away and that Blink would come home to find a salt lake where this house, this garden and this woman used to be.

chapter 17

Saying goodbye to his mother had tested Blink's resolve. The previous day, with Isobel, had been no easier.

He knew it was wrong to think it but he couldn't wait to be on his way.

They were the two most important people in his life. He simply wanted the weight of departure taken from him.

Blink looked forward to the emotionless certainty of army life, knowing that the next few weeks and months would be an ordered existence of training, discipline, obedience and then travel, all to a strict timetable and purpose.

He was grateful for his mother's stoicism because he feared the mess he may otherwise have become and, if so, the decision he may have made.

He thought of Charlie Forster, holding the remains of his severed foot, and then thought of his own shed, which contained many axes.

Blink had drawn strength from his mother's courage and he loved her all the more for it, knowing he would need something similar in the army.

What he had grown to love about Isobel McQuade was her lightness. She lifted him, and the times they spent alone together passed without self-consciousness.

Isobel had grace, a kind that Blink observed was not learned or affected. It came naturally and Blink found her beautiful.

Unfortunately, when Isobel looked at herself in a mirror, she did not see anything like beauty. She saw nothing like the women in the posters outside the Duchess Theatre in town, with their confident, seductive smiles, scarlet lips and figures which curved and rolled and jutted with such allure. Neither were there the wide, beckoning eyes able to summon such alluring expressions as she had seen on the back of a pack of dirty playing cards one day at a friend's place.

'Look at these, Isobel,' Ruth Free's brother Rick had said, his eyes bulging and a salacious grin on his face as he awaited Isobel's response to the lurid pictures spread before her.

'Gosh, they're so lovely,' she'd said. 'May I keep one?'

Rick Free had been suitably unimpressed.

Isobel's blonde hair never took to curlers, always breaking away, and there was little daintiness to her walk. Her laugh was too loud for some.

By the age of fourteen, she was already as tall as her dad Ted and a good head higher than her mother, Daph. At that age, Isobel preferred her father's company, though she was no tomboy. His life, she thought, was just more interesting. She could do what her mother called "women's work"—needlepoint, knitting, sewing and cooking—and she liked the quiet concentration they required. But she preferred it down at the workshop with her father, playing there with Blink after school in the timber shavings and the sawdust piles as they waited for Ted and Stocky to walk them home.

Isobel's fingernails were forever broken, her mother said she'd love a threepence for the number of times Isobel had needed a splinter dug from her skin.

'Honestly, Isobel, I sometimes wonder whether the little girl I send off to school looking so neat and clean, and the little grub who returns home with her hair everywhere and her knees filthy, are one and the same,' remarked Daph McQuade, regularly.

'Sorry, Mum,' said Isobel, just as regularly.

Isobel was long and straight-backed and when her body began to mature she took on a shape that was athletic but still feminine.

Looking in the mirror, she may not have seen what she took to be beauty, but as long as Blink saw it, she was happy.

Even as a child, Blink revelled in Isobel's vivaciousness and she became all the more attractive to him as they grew. They had met as children when their fathers worked together at Smith's Carpenters & Joiners.

The boss, Smithy, was generally held to be an old bastard who wore a permanent scowl and had few kind words for anyone. He worked his employees hard and made them earn every penny they took away at the end of the week, plenty of which was put over the bar to buy beers raised to Smithy's ill-health.

He was a canny old codger, though. He knew the men couldn't spend all their pay at the pub on a Friday because he only paid them part of it. He left the bulk to be distributed on Monday, the start of the working week, when men were less inclined to drown their sorrows or hail their happiness and more inclined to go home with their earnings.

It meant more book-keeping to pay the men twice, but Smithy's wife didn't mind the work and the wives of the employees were always grateful.

Shirkers or lesser tradesmen didn't last long at Smith's. Smithy would soon see they weren't up to it, pay them a week's wages and they'd be looking for a new job the next day.

In fact, one joke that did the rounds when the war broke out was that Smithy had to find a whole new workforce because his had joined up to a man, preferring the demands of the army and the bullets of the Turk and Hun to Smithy.

Albert—named for Queen Victoria's prince—Smith had built a flourishing business and men like Stocky Johns and Ted McQuade, if they wanted, could wander the town and point out any number of buildings either built or improved by their skill.

Stocky and Ted had also helped build Smithy's big house west of town. He'd named it Prospect because that's exactly what it offered all around: a panorama equal to that of Windmill Hill.

Smithy's house was built on one level and sprawled in all directions. Every entrance led to lawns and gardens.

There was even a waterfall, a generous splash and flow of water that was pumped from a pond, spilled down steps into another pond and then recirculated to repeat the process.

Smithy's cat would sit at the side of the lower pond, looking longingly at the goldfish and mournfully at the water.

During construction of the house, Ted and Stocky would sometimes bring the kids and let them loose on the grounds, first warning them not to get into any mischief or do anything to give Smithy cause for anger.

Blink followed the gardener.

'Here you go, young fella,' the gardener said one day, after Blink had spent the best part of an hour no more than two small steps behind the man.

'If you're going to follow me around all day and leave that lovely young lady on her own'—he pointed to Isobel—'then you might as well make yourself useful.'

Blink saw Isobel dangling her bare feet in the water, rippling it to attract the big goldfish to swim across and nibble at her toes. She giggled as she dipped a hand in and then playfully flicked droplets at the cat.

The gardener held out a handful of seeds and when Blink took them they felt smooth and alive in his small hands. Next, the gardener handed him a trowel.

'Just over there,' he said, 'dig a row about two or three inches deep, sprinkle those seeds, cover them lightly with dirt, give them a gentle watering, then leave them alone. And then go and play with that young lass.'

Blink lingered over the small patch of ground he'd been assigned and he furrowed and planted with care, wishing the seeds would break through, bud and flower right then and there.

He knew he should be with Isobel but he waited a little longer, on his knees, feeling the dirt in his hands.

He leaned down, stuck his nose as close to the ground as he could without sneezing, and breathed in where he had been working. He was lost in this until a sound brought him back—a splash and a shrieking.

He couldn't see Isobel as he ran towards the pond and he was worried for her until he heard her raucous laughter.

And there she was, on her back in the pond, a giggling gertie all red-faced, holding her sides and soaked to the skin.

'I slipped,' she said, 'I saw that fat orange one go under the lilypad and when I leaned over I slipped.'

'Your dad's going to kill you,' said Blink, as Isobel began to chortle all over again.

Thinking about that now, just a day or so before he was to leave for the army, Blink knew he should be grateful to old Smithy for two things—through him, Blink had fallen for the scent of the earth as well as for the sound of Isobel's laughter.

Isobel was there for Blink when his father died.

Blink was sixteen, she had just turned the same age and their friendship had begun to become something more. When the news came through about Stocky, Isobel was the first one at Blink's side and the one who held him tightest.

Ted McQuade and Stocky Johns had been working on the town clock, which rose above the post office, making it the tallest building in Launceston.

Some of the interior timber had weakened over the years and it was a simple but important job for it to be reinforced or replaced. Smithy won the contract and Ted and Stocky went to work.

Ted's back was turned when Stocky fell.

He heard wood breaking and Stocky yell, 'Shit!' He heard the thump.

It wasn't far, twenty feet or so down the clock shaft, but as Ted lowered himself to see if Stocky was all right, laughing and calling him a "bloody goose" on the way down, he saw the wracked expression on Stocky's face and the weird angle of his head and neck.

Within a month, Stocky Johns had become a ghost story drummed up by kids who talked in low voices about the haunted clock tower, about how the movement of the pulleys and ropes and wheels, and the clock's mechanism, was the sound of a man trying to claw his way out.

In the evening it was Isobel who held Blink close to her as aunts, uncles and friends made tea, drank beer and shook their heads in disbelief as they passed around biscuits and scones.

Elizabeth Johns stayed quiet, her lips set together and her chin firm. She seemed not to hear anything anyone was saying.

Isobel held Blink close again a few days later, when Stocky's coffin was lowered into the ground at Garden Villa. The only time she let go was when he scooped a handful of earth from the side of the grave and held it to his face, breathing it in, before tossing it onto his father's coffin.

Isobel was like a balm for Blink. He knew he needed her then, just as he knew he needed her now that he was leaving.

Reaching her house, Blink politely made his greetings to Isobel's mother and father and she emerged from behind them, like a party trick, and he was dazzled by her. And yet, even though she was dressed as brightly as ever, this time he couldn't help but notice how the laughter he loved was catching in her throat.

After tea, when the McQuades adjourned to their sitting room and left their daughter with Blink, the young couple said nothing but realised, instinctively and finally, that they had always been meant to be. They recognised the love between them, that it was good and profound and had been there, just waiting to be discovered, all the time.

They kissed.

When it was time for him to go, Isobel stood at the front gate and waited until Blink was out of sight before she reached for the handkerchief in her sleeve.

Blink walked away with awkward strides.

And then, perhaps at the same moment, the pair of them cursed the time they had wasted and pondered whether that was all the time they would ever have.

chapter 18

Two months went by.
To Blink, it seemed no time at all since he'd hopped off the troop train that had carried him from Launceston south to the training barracks constructed on good dairy land about half an hour out of Hobart.

On that first day, as Blink and his fellow recruits took in all they could of what was to be their home for the next several weeks, he couldn't prevent his mind drifting to Isobel, then his mother and the garden at Raymond Street.

Next day, with the sun not yet up, he had begun his training proper and, from then on, there was little time or opportunity to think of anyone or anything else.

Running his eyes up and down Blink's naked body, pushing here, pinching there, poking this and that, the medical officer made notes on a sheet of paper clipped to a board.

Blink was embarrassed and shivering but the doctor either didn't notice or simply wasn't concerned.

It was the latter, because this was not a job Captain Monroe Harris enjoyed. He'd made it clear he would much prefer to be at the front saving the lives of the wounded, rather than performing the doubtlessly necessary but dreary duty of declaring new soldiers fit for service.

Cradling testicles, monitoring lung capacity and poking his finger up backsides to check for piles was not the way he had envisioned serving his country.

'Like me, Private, you'll learn quickly that a soldier's duty is to obey, whether at the front or worlds away from it,' he said.

'Pardon, Sir?' said Blink.

'Never mind, Private.'

Captain Harris yearned to bring soldiers back from the brink of death, not send them to it, which is why he cursed the phlegm that was forever in his own lungs, as well as the weakness of his own heart, both of which had conspired to keep him at home.

He put on a brave face but it was not easy, particularly given that as deeply as he probed about past medical histories and ongoing complaints, he knew these young men were so eager to fight they would tell him anything he needed to hear.

'How did you get that scar?' he asked, touching the raised skin to the left of Blink's nose and just above his lip.

'In the garden,' said Blink.

'You have an unusually violent garden, Private.'

'Not really, Sir. It was an accident sharpening the blades on the lawn mower.'

'You'll have to be a good deal more careful at the front.'

'Will we be doing much mowing at the front, Sir?' asked Blink.

'Private—young man—I am about to take your balls in my hand. Not the ideal moment for flippancy towards an officer.'

As Blink dressed, Captain Harris made some final entries on his paper.

'Here,' he said, 'you'll need this. And good luck to you.'

Blink read his medical certificate as he left Captain Harris's office and was struck by the ordinariness of the man it described. Nothing about him stood out. He was young, of medium height and build, with a fair complexion, blue eyes, black hair, sound physical health and no sign of madness. Even his name was plain. Johns. 'Common as muck,' he said to himself, 'must be thousands of us.'

Yet, as dull as his certificate painted him to be, Blink took relief at the various conditions which Captain Harris had noted he didn't suffer.

Dutifully checked off with a pencilled tick were ailments of which Blink had never heard and others he hoped he would never hear of again: scrofula; ptithisis; syphilis; impaired constitution; defective intelligence; defects of vision, voice or hearing; hernia; haemorrhoids; varicose veins; marked varicocele with unusally pendant testicle; inveterate cutaneous disease; chronic ulcers; traces of corporal punishment; contracted or deformed chest; abnormal curvature of the spine.

Blink had good eyes, good lungs, good freedom of the joints and limbs and was not prone to fits. In every way he was everything the army required.

The medical examination was one of the final steps before embarkation on a ship bound for the mainland and then another bound for Egypt, then France and what would become the Western Front.

Blink took his medical certificate to the Attesting Officer, who read it, eyed Blink from top to toe and casually completed his transformation from civilian to recruit to fully-fledged soldier about to leave for the pointy end of the war, as the AO called it.

'Good luck at the pointy end,' said the AO. 'Kill one for me.' He said that to all the boys: his way of wishing them well.

Outside, Blink saw that a bed of petunias needed a little work.

Strangely, he felt as if his step was heavier than normal, as if the ground was grabbing at his boots in some kind of game, refusing to let go, like on the day he'd said goodbye to Isobel.

He hoped his mother was looking after the roses, then for some reason he started to run, all the time looking around for a place away from militariness, this new world in which the bark of orders and the tramp of marching feet and the firing of guns at precise intervals had become his life.

It had hit him as suddenly and profoundly as any bullet—in the next few days he would be leaving. And as that bullet tore through him, so came another, armed with visions of all the people and things he loved.

After some time he found a place that felt right to him, or right enough. It was a patch of lawn enclosed by hedges at the far southern end of the barracks grounds.

Blink wrenched off his boots, unfurled his puttees, lay on his back and dug his feet and hands into the soft, damp grass. He turned and breathed in the fragrance and texture of the Tasmanian ground.

Back at his barracks, Blink took out his army greatcoat and flicked open the penknife he always kept handy. He cut into the cloth.

It was pointless trying to explain to the sergeant what he had done or why.

It was pointless trying to explain anything to Sergeant Townshend. He was as sergeants everywhere seem to be—angry, unflinching, sticklers for the book.

Every soldier was aware that a crime against the army, no matter how petty, was a crime against the sergeant and was felt personally.

Sergeant Townshend held the violated greatcoat under Blink's nose and bawled, 'Private Johns, do you think that His Majesty's army is made of money? Do you think that His Majesty's army has an endless supply of uniforms? Do you think at all, Private?'

Blink truly thought the answer to all of Sergeant Townshend's questions was a resounding "Yes". Yes, the army was made of money. Yes, there was an endless supply of uniforms. And yes, he was thinking all the time. He wisely decided to keep those thoughts to himself.

'It was an accident, Sir,' started Blink, 'I tore it while on an exercise. It must have caught on—'

Sergeant Townshend wasn't interested in explanations, true or false. His only purpose was to note that a breach of army regulations had been committed and to ensure the errant soldier was made to pay.

Blink was officially charged with mutilating government property and was fined both the cost of a new greatcoat and the unexpired value of the original coat.

'Unexpired value, that's a charming term. Does the value go up or down if I expire in it?' Blink asked a fellow private.

All up, the twenty-five shillings put a hole in Blink's ready cash but the material he had cut from the greatcoat had been worth it. Anyway, they'd be sailing soon. What was he going to spend twenty-five shillings on?

Blink paid the fine and on the way back from the supply depot, where he took delivery of a new coat, he detoured to the spot he had found earlier. He checked that no one could see him and, when satisfied, he knelt and began scrabbling through a patch of soil beneath one of the hedges.

Shoving his hand down his trousers and into his underwear, Blink pulled out a square of greatcoat cloth. Placing it flat in the hole he had dug, he took a last look before gently covering it with the soil. He patted down the surface so the spot would not stand out.

Three days later, Blink was in Melbourne. He thought it might be the biggest place in the world. Five days after that, the troopship docked in Adelaide.

A few weeks further on, the other side of the world appeared in the distance.

chapter 19

Before people came, the west evolved its shape and purpose as determined by the wind, the rain, the sun and the earth.

As Blink says, it's tough country.

Still, it was not tough enough to thwart those who teemed west when the ground betrayed what it held inside and when profit could be seen in a place once thought to be of use only for the transportation of convicts.

This landscape has been changed so much and here are Blink and I, in our own small way, trying to change it again.

The change is not restricted to the ground. It is within the pair of us. I can feel it and see it.

Each morning at Gemma's, I dress Blink as usual and make him his first cuppa, despite it being an effort to drag myself out of bed. The temptation is always there to steal an extra hour of sleep and wait until there's at least some light in the day. While at night I flop into bed and fall asleep quickly, mornings find me stiff and sore and reluctant.

My first movements are jerky, as if my bones don't fit, and my tender muscles tug hard at me. The land is the cause of it. Turning hard soil like that is arduous at the best of times, but especially so for someone like me, who is unused to such activity. I have to put my back into it, and my feet and knees and hips, pushing hard down on the blade of the shovel for better purchase and depth. My wrists hurt from tossing the soil left and right. My fingers ache from gripping the shovel or wheelbarrow and my palms are blistered, Band-aids have now been cast aside for bandages wrapped around my hands. Each evening, I rub ointment into them and the effect is soothing but temporary, because I know that in the morning, when the work begins, it's never too long before the blisters start to rub.

As for Blink, at first I tried to convince myself that this is nothing new to him, that aching bones and tender muscles have been his companions throughout life, not just now that he is old and here with me. His life has been full of digging and turning and bending and pushing and pulling and surely his mind, as fickle as it is, must remember the feel of a working body.

I try to lighten his load, to restrict him to the fork work, chopping through and breaking down the hard clumps I dig up, but it's as if his past keeps catching up with him and he can't help but reach for a shovel or a mattock.

'You'll wear yourself out,' I tell him. 'You can hardly lift that bloody mattock, let alone swing it. Just tell me what to do, Blink. I'll follow your orders.'

'Hard work never hurt anybody,' he says, and he tries again.

I watch him. All the time I watch him.

That first day of real work was the hardest, although I was pleased with our efforts and the way Blink had held up.

'Kettle's on,' Gemma called out, after we'd arrived home and cleaned ourselves up.

Blink reached for his cup, gripped his hand around it and I saw his eyes widen when the pain struck him. There was a crash and hot tea spilled across Gemma's floor.

'Angus?' he said.

Blink had both hands in front of his face and was staring.

'Angus?'

I could see that the skin had torn away from his palms, the blisters were angry and red.

'It's all right, Blink,' I said. 'Just blisters. Like mine. Our hands aren't used to the work yet.'

'I'm a gardener,' he said, still looking at his hands.

'Not for a long time, Blink,' I said. 'But it'll be right. Just give it a little time.'

'Always,' he said. 'Always.'

Gemma turned her head away.

Later, with his hands wrapped, I looked at Blink as he dozed.

'Not much comes easy down here,' said Gemma. 'Do you mind if I come with you tomorrow?'

It dawned fine and the three of us were soon up at the land.

'You've achieved quite a lot for just one day,' said Gemma. 'Come on, Blink, show me what you've done.'

She put her arm through his and left me to my digging, blisters and other aches and pains.

Gemma stayed with him for hours that day.

Gemma says we have achieved so much, but I'm unsure.

The days are passing and if I look at the ground still to be worked, or look from our land and across to the other hills, I can start to feel dejected.

The colours are so hideous and the ruin is entrenched. So I try not to look beyond our land and I try not to think about what there is to do. I just dig and when I'm finished I see whether there is any change and whether it might be for the better.

The good news is that Blink, despite his sore hands, is changing for the better. With every day, he seems stronger and more assured.

'The smell's going,' he says.

'What?'

'The smell. The chemicals. That's a good sign. In places it's starting to smell like the earth again.'

I check his bandages before digging with renewed energy.

That night, after the meal, I ask Gemma if she thinks Blink is any different.

'It's the way of things down here,' she says. She corrects a tress of hair that has broken loose and speaks with a bobby pin clamped in the corner of her mouth. 'In a mining town, and don't forget that I was born and raised in one, nothing stays the same,' she says.

'Mining takes from underneath the ground, and from on top of it, and changes everything. Even the air. We breathed sulphur fumes when I was a girl.

'Then people change. My father told me about people sent frantic by what they've found or what they haven't found or what someone else has found.

'That's probably why this place was such a hit,' she says, referring to the Queenstown Gentlemen's Club. 'It wasn't just a matter of running a clean house with nice girls, although that must have helped. And I don't think it was just a release of tensions.'

'What was it then?' I ask. 'Because I know what I think.'

'Well, in my humble opinion,' says Gemma, 'it was that people could be sure of things here. Probably one of the only places in town that you could be.

'I think Blink is changing because he's more sure of himself.'

She nods, pleased with her observation.

'You see, a miner may know what he's looking for and may slave to find it but he can never really know if it's actually there.

'That's something else my father told me: a miner never knows if he's digging a few inches away from a big strike or if the seam he has found fades to nothing just a few inches away.

'But here, in this house, there was no guesswork. What you saw was what you got and, as long as you behaved and paid, you knew you were on a certainty.'

It's a persuasive argument but I cannot help cheekily applying a touch of devil's advocacy to keep the conversation vibrant. Plus, I fancy a port.

'But Gemma,' I say, 'wouldn't plain old lust be the driving force behind a man coming here? I mean, all that time digging, sweating and working from before dawn to after dusk—you'd crave relief. You'd have to. And this place offered it.'

Gemma sizes me up.

'Angus,' she says, 'this is a mining town and once it was a very wealthy one. People came here by the thousands. Any lust was for the ore. Always for the ore.'

Blink's hands are hardening. His body is finding something of its former self and he is warming to his task.

'No birds, Angus,' he says, wiping his hands down the back of his pants and flicking a bead of sweat off the point of his nose.

I think about it and it occurs to me that for as long as we have been out here—and there's no sign yet of us being discovered—I have not seen or heard any birdlife.

Of course, there's nothing here for them. While there are gulls near the coast and birdlife aplenty further inland, there is no presence here.

In town, where people have planted rough, weak gardens and put in birdbaths that cascade over their rims every time it rains, the occasional sparrow or blackbird might peck about.

'You never know,' says Blink, 'with a bit of luck we might bring the birds back. That'd be something.'

I am becoming used to the work, but I am still muscle-sore and my hands, though also hardening, still have some blisters. My fingernails are split and dirty. This is not me at all.

But that's the point. To Blink, I am not who I am. I am someone he knew and maybe loved, someone he felt he owed or owes.

So I put up with things and follow his instructions.

I dig where I'm told and as deeply as I'm told. I water where he says and drain where he says and turn clods and pat clumps and barrow stuff away.

With ingredients collected by Gemma from the local nursery, I mix in blood and bone by the bagful and sprinkle the powdery gypsum, which Blink tells me will break down the soil further and allow roots to spread when the time comes to fertilise and plant.

We mulch and toss and spray and dig, always digging, trying to find where the poisoned ground stops and the good earth begins, if anywhere.

Sometimes I dig so deep it's like we're starting a new mine.

'Angus,' says Blink, pointing with the fork, 'you're not digging a grave or a trench, you're not digging to China.

'Just remove that top layer and hack hell out of what's underneath, keep working it over. Make it as soft and lumpy as you can. Like a good turd.

'You're not digging for the sake of digging. You're digging for the sake of the ground. So be good to it.'

Blink relapses from time to time but mostly he looks younger and alive with the possibilities of the challenge at hand.

I can see the age draining from his limbs, his neck and jowls and I can sense his expertise and his instincts being rehoned.

Each day, I have no trouble finding a second and third wind.

chapter 20

The council tells Gemma the exact dimensions of her land.

'I've got it here somewhere among all my papers,' she says. 'I could rifle through them but it's easier for someone to tap into a computer. It's at their fingertips and it's just an inquiry, nothing suspicious for them to worry about.'

There are no computers at Gemma's, not even a manual typewriter, let alone an electric one. All the reservations, arrivals and departures, costings and supply logs are handwritten on paper backed by a carbon and then kept in a concertina file. She uses the silver fountain pen which I have since learned Broom Sherman had crafted in Hobart from a nugget or two dug from his own claim.

Once we have the exact measurements, Gemma begins making calls to landscaping firms and nurseries, mostly from the northwest.

We have given him plenty of business, much more than he is used to, but there is no way Bill Drummond's little gardening store can handle a job like ours in its entirety. To try would only invite unwanted scrutiny. Bill's supplies have been enough to get us under way.

Playing one firm against another, Gemma negotiates the best deal on materials with which I am starting to become familiar: gypsum, bark mulch, loam, blood and bone, seeds, various tools. Blink is our guide and he is lucid and expert.

With every call, the row of figures Gemma writes down grows longer and larger, despite the bargains she wheedles out of the people on the other end of the line.

I have money but, typically, have not devoted consideration to how much will be required. All I've thought about is the intended result and it is becoming obvious that getting there is going to require a chunk of my savings.

At least Cassidy is happy to supply the topsoil. I phone and ask whether he can collect our other orders.

'No probs,' he says. 'So, we're going ahead with this?'

'It's probably the stupidest thing I've ever done, but yes. You should see Blink down here. He looks like a young man at times. Great to see.'

While ours is a pitiful piece of ground compared with the soil he worked all over Launceston and in his own Raymond Street garden, Blink is inspired.

'It's coming back brown and green,' he says, 'you can see it trying, feel it coming on. It wants its old colour, Angus. That's a good thing.'

We take our breaks by the gravestones and I constantly have to tell Blink not to wolf down Gemma's huge sandwiches.

'Geez, Blink, an extra five minutes chewing your food and allowing it to digest properly is better than being laid up with indigestion.'

But he is excited and it is exciting to see him so.

It always takes such an effort to convince him to rest, and just as much effort to convince myself that he needs to.

First thing in the morning, and later in the evenings, he can drift back to something approaching the old, brittle Blink. On the land, however, he is revived. Prodding his fork through the tough soil, he is never disheartened by its poor quality. He breaks it up and turns it again, doing all he can to summon any substance there.

With some of the money I've given her, Gemma has bought a large stock of seeds and cuttings from Bill Drummond's. We'll need plenty more.

'I didn't know you had a glasshouse,' said Bill, who only runs the nursery as an aside to his machinery shop, which has a sign above the entry reading, "You Break It, We'll Remake It".

'I don't,' Gemma replied.

'Well, the only way you'll get roses and dahlias and carnations to grow is to plant them away from here. Like Hobart maybe, or up north. I dunno why I bother to keep 'em.'

'We'll see,' Gemma said, 'I'm ready for a new challenge.'

'I feel bad taking your money, Gemma,' said Bill, 'I really do. Just the same, that'll be $175.60.'

When it rains, Blink and I stay out in it for as long as I think wise.

When the fat drops begin dribbling under our clothes and down our backs, we are soon soaked and it is best to shelter in the car until it passes, or call it a day and head for home.

The good news is that the rain, which can be so heavy in the west it can wash away almost anything, has not been so devastating to our land.

Our newly dug ground has begun to use the rain, and the water can sink in and enrich it.

Nevertheless, there is always the threat of a drenching—a couple of days of solid downpour would put paid to all the work we've done.

The power of change, however, does not lie solely with the weather. This is confirmed a few days later when Blink and I arrive back at the house to find Gemma waiting for us at the door. She has a newspaper in her hand and, even before she holds the page up to my face, I can guess what I am about to see.

There I am, pictured with Blink, his photo an old one taken years before. The article says relatives—Isobel is the only one quoted—are deeply concerned for our safety and that police have begun enquiries.

Blink and I have been gone for more than a fortnight and it surprises me that it has taken so long for us to be reported missing.

Then I notice that the paper is an old edition and, in fact, that the alarm was raised the very afternoon Blink and I left Pleasant View. Max, the orderly, is quoted as having found my note and the newspaper has repeated its message, calling it "mysterious".

"To my family, Blink is in no danger. I wish him only good. We will return when we are done. My apologies for those concerned by these actions but I can only repeat the good of my intentions. All will be explained in time."

I ask myself how long it will be before we are found.

The land is nowhere near ready.

I sit in the big velour chair in the lounge and try to gather my thoughts. Blink is dozing as Gemma brings in a tray with glasses and a bottle of whisky.

'I'm not a big drinker but I'll have one with you now. We have some serious thinking to do,' she says.

'Not we, Gemma, just me,' I counter. 'I've really gotten myself into something here and it's about to blow up in my face.'

I take a slug of the alcohol and it burns. The calming warmth I crave does not come, only harshness.

'I just didn't think. Same as always. I get carried away with a notion and give no thought to planning or consequences. I gave no real thought to Blink.'

Gemma pours a measure into a small glass and rolls it back and forth with the tips of her fingers.

'Blink talks to me, you know,' she says. 'He tells me things. We've had some lovely chats.'

She still hasn't tasted her whisky.

'What type of things?' I ask.

'Mostly he talks to me about you. About Angus, I should say. He waits until you're in the shower or asleep in the chair and sometimes he comes down the stairs at night. You didn't know that, did you?'

I didn't. I tell her I figured that once I helped Blink into bed he was gone for all money, until morning when we repeated our daily ritual.

'Old people don't sleep so much,' says Gemma. 'You're the one who's gone for all money when your head hits the pillow.

'I get tired and run down and worn out but I don't sleep eight hours a night anymore. Not in one go. Nothing like it.

'I fall asleep in an armchair in front of the fire, or while I'm reading or knitting. I wake up sometimes and a ball of wool has dropped from my hands and almost rolled out the door.

'It's just the way it is when you get older, and Blink is older than both of us.'

Finally, Gemma downs her whisky and glances at the bottle.

'No, better not,' she says.

'Go on,' I tease her. 'It can't hurt.' And she fills her glass once more.

'I heard him come down the stairs about the second night you were here,' she continues.

'It was about 3 a.m. and I was awake. I usually am at that time.

'Anyway, I heard him head into the kitchen and so I got up to see if he was all right. I made him a cup of tea and we sat down and talked.

'I don't think he was sure who I was, or where he was, but he was comfortable enough. He said he couldn't find his dressing-gown and couldn't find the wardrobe where he kept it. He said a man might have stolen it, that things were always being stolen. I gathered he was talking about somewhere else. He swore a bit.'

'Pleasant View Home for the Aged,' I say, 'where he would be a lot better off right now.'

'Nonsense,' she cuts in. 'You only have to look at him and listen to him when he talks about what's going on at the site to see the improvement in him.

'I saw what he was like that day you arrived and I've heard him and seen him since.

'He has a purpose and he is thriving on it. What's more, so is that sorry patch of ground.'

'It's coming along,' I say. 'I can see that. And my shoulders, hands, back and knees can feel it. It's probably all for nothing. My time on the run, as it were, seems to be coming to an end. For all the digging we've done lately, I might have succeeded only in digging a bloody great hole for myself.'

Gemma puts down her glass.

'You might be surprised at what happens next. People can be quick to judge, but that judgment might be good. People will see you've done a good thing here.'

I don't want to be morose. I want to be buoyed by Gemma's soothing words.

As she packs up, I phone Cassidy and explain Blink's and my new celebrity status.

'Yeah, I saw it when it came out. Shocking picture of you,' he says. 'Where was that taken, prison?'

'I think it's an old passport photo,' I say.

'Oooh, nothing like one of them to make you look like a serial killer. You're not a serial killer, are you?'

'Not as yet,' I say, 'although these past few weeks have seen several unexpected new developments in my life. You never know what could be around the next corner.'

'Anyway,' says Cassidy, 'on to more important things. Where do I meet you?'

'What do you mean?'

'I've got the trucks and the soil, all the shit you wanted from the nurseries and landscapers. I can smell the blood and bone from here. Where do you want it?'

As overwhelmed as I am by Cassidy's unflappable nature, I cannot help but be saddened that such a virtue, at least in this case, will come to nothing.

'I'm sorry, mate,' I say, 'I think I'll be spending most of tomorrow with the local cops. The weekend's not a goer. This grand scheme of mine is about to reach a rather poor end.'

'Crap,' says Cassidy. 'Just tell me where to meet you, bright and early. We'll get the stuff down and we'll plan your next move from there. Give it a chance. I've got people organised.'

There is no point arguing. Hanging up, I walk back to the lounge where Gemma is stoking the fire and Blink, awake again, is smoking and chatting easily to her. She smiles.

'What are you two conspiring?' I ask, trying to stay light and breezy for Blink's sake, and mine.

'We are talking about another time,' says Gemma.

Blink draws on his fag and tosses the butt into the fire. Lighting another almost immediately, he sucks hard on the filter.

'I've never had my picture in the paper before,' says Blink, grinning. 'I come up all right for an old digger. I could hardly recognise myself.'

'I don't doubt it,' I say, flopping back into a chair, 'that picture of you was taken a few years ago.'

'I remember,' he says, 'we were all there, down at Mick and Dot's place, with all the family at the orchard.'

'How do you remember?' I ask, unnerved.

'I just do, Angus. One of those things. Clear as day. We were sitting out the back of the house and Mick took a photo of all of us together, and then he took another one of me by myself.

'And you were there too, Angus. Wait a minute, no, that can't be right. How could you have been there?'

Blink is confused, trying to figure it out.

'Good bloke, Mick was,' he says. 'A real good bloke.'

A real good bloke. With those words, the world collapses on my head.

I know the colour is draining from my face and my heart is beating a tattoo. I tremble as if I am freezing, even though the room is toasting.

Gemma eyes me with concern and moves towards me.

'Angus,' she says, 'are you all right? What's the matter? You look as if you've had the wind knocked out of you.'

'My name is not fucking Angus,' I snarl.

I feel weighted down but manage to drag myself out of the chair. I stand, unsteady, my head spinning.

'I'm sorry. Sorry,' I say quietly. 'I didn't mean to swear.'

I try to steer a straight path out of the room but knock the whisky bottle off the table. Brown liquid pours across it and down onto the floor, where it pools before branching away in small streams.

I apologise again, desperate for the door and the stairs. All I want is to lie down and sleep and forget.

There is no forgetting. In my mind, images of trees, apples, pears and members of my family dance around. I know it is them, although they are blurred at the edges and their faces aren't quite clear.

I can also taste blood. The ground is unstable as I walk and the branches and roots of the trees are slippery.

Something is trapped in a fence and the only sound I hear is a whimpering, like a hurt dog. Then it stops and I am relieved, until the sound is replaced by a longer, fuller, more harrowing sound that I cannot will from my mind.

Only when the dream has run its course do I wake. Even then, that last dreadful sound stays with me.

chapter 21

'Angus? Is that you, Angus?'

I was three years old when I found Blink, could run to him and know him as my grandfather.

I was five when he first started to lose me and I began to form as someone else in his eyes and mind.

For a few years after that, I drifted from one to the other. One day I was me, the next I was Angus. But Angus was taking over more and more, and I was disappearing.

At first I called him Uncle Blink, even though he was my grandfather. That was the way of things in Tasmania when I was growing up. Every adult, apart from your parents, was either Uncle or Auntie, whether you were related to them or not.

It was easy and friendly, and probably did nothing to dissuade mocking mainlanders that we Tasmanians were inbred.

Blink was Blink because that is what he did—does—as if there's grit in his eyes. Isobel would go crook at him and tell him to get his eyes checked, though he never wore glasses.

'They're fine, Isobel,' he'd say. 'Just overactive, that's all. Doctor says they're fine.'

Once I became Angus to him, when he talked to me Blink could remember events that occurred at a precise moment on an exact day in a particular setting during World War I. He'd describe towns and times, the meals he ate, the weather and ground conditions, and how this chap and that bloke got knocked either side of him.

He said little about himself, or this Angus I was supposed to be, but he could recall others, how they went and the expressions on their faces.

It wasn't easy to reconcile that Blink with the one who didn't know what he'd eaten for breakfast less than an hour ago, or couldn't recognise that the man talking to Isobel in the kitchen was his youngest son and my father Tommy or Whiskers.

Or that the boy sitting beside him was not a soldier.

Sitting in his chair, a fag resting on the ashtray, Blink would take down the calendar and fold the dates underneath so that only the map of the world on the top sheet was showing.

He'd spread it flat across his knees and point his knotty finger with the dirt under the nail to the red of England and the green of France.

'That's where we were,' he'd tell me. 'Eh, Angus?'

My only experience of war is as Angus. He has been my conduit to another time and I learned to become a willing traveller.

Sometimes the stories Blink told were vivid portraits from which little was omitted. I could see the blood, hear the bombardments, feel the suck of the mud on the boots and the misery of the rain, the cold and rats, as if I really had been there.

At other times, his stories faded away to assumption and I wouldn't know what place or battle or bloke he was talking about.

And there were still other times when his stories would end abruptly and Blink's face would pale.

In those stories, there was always wire.

Long after he retired from Garden Villa and had left the intricate pattern of planting, tending, cutting and culling to younger men whose knees didn't lock and whose backs and shoulders didn't ache, Blink continued to work in the Raymond Street garden.

Occasionally, he would succumb to the wanders.

It was not unusual for Isobel to receive a telephone call late in the afternoon with a council worker on the line saying, 'It's all right, Mrs Johns, he's with us. We'll drop him home.'

Blink would have found his way to the cemetery or to one of the municipal parks where he would bend to smell and touch the beds of rhododendrons and roses and other plants which may once have begun as seeds or cuttings in his hands.

I loved watching him run seeds and soil and water through his fingers. He cupped a new flower with an unlikely tenderness.

I have often wondered whether beautiful moments like that enabled him to mostly keep at bay the nightmarish memories of what he had once seen, and perhaps done, in the green of France under his dirty fingernail.

When Blink did speak of the war he did so only to Angus and, in the beginning, I was clumsy with the privilege, asking stupid questions such as, 'What's war like?' and 'Did you kill anyone?'.

He would consider me with a furrowed brow.

'War has no middle, does it, Angus? You miss the middle of things,' he said.

I would ask him what he meant by that and he'd just wink, as if I was already in the know and the answer was obvious between us.

But I wasn't in the know and there were umpteen times when I wanted to tell him so, to say that I was his grandson, not this other person.

What stopped me was the fear of what that knowledge might do to him and to us, whether our link would be severed and I would become just another stranger in the Raymond Street house.

From then on, I tried not to ask stupid questions. I tried to listen and search later for those meanings I found elusive.

It was in this way I forged an explanation for his assertion that war has no middle. It was years after Blink had first said it.

'War has no middle,' I told him one rainy afternoon, 'because it's either too hot or too cold, too loud or too quiet, too near or too far, too terrifying or too dull. There is no balance, just extremes.'

The old man smiled. The rain stopped, the Raymond Street garden glistened and we walked down the stairs into it.

When I was a kid, Blink took me to an Anzac Day dawn service in Launceston.

The cenotaph was in Regent Park, near the museum and up from the regatta grounds, and it was dark and bitterly cold when we arrived. As dawn edged, more people shuffled in and we occupied our time by hopping from foot to foot and clapping and rubbing our gloved hands together.

Old men with spidery veins in their noses and cheeks, and with jangling medals on their chests, moved in and out of the crowd offering tots of rum, even to youngsters like me. I swigged, almost gagged, but kept it down and soon felt it warm me from inside.

Breath plumed from every mouth and I pretended I was smoking cigarettes with the men.

In my memory of that day, Blink is as clear to me as the perfectly formed smoke rings he would blow while taking a break on his tree stump in the Raymond Street garden. He would send out circles and I would thrill to poke my fingers through them.

Flicking insects away, he would talk to me.

'Angus, how've you been, old boy? Come to help an old bloke in the garden?'

He'd hand me a trowel or a little fork and show me the best way to turn the soil or cut and scrape away some simple problem.

If he was stooped, or had dug and raked for too long, the ache in his shoulder would force him to stop and he would spend a few minutes massaging away the irritation as flies and mozzies buzzed around him.

He'd pull down his braces, fold back his shirt collar and roll away his singlet. The long purple scar would come into view, vivid against the white of his skin.

'War is all about inches,' he said one day, rubbing that shoulder of his.

'A couple of inches to one side and they would have missed me completely. A couple of inches to the other, or a couple of inches below, and we wouldn't be sitting here talking now.

'That's the difference between you and me, eh, Angus? The inches were in my favour.'

Blink used to complain about the way politicians and commanders spoke about war as if it was a single entity.

'They'd know better if they'd been up at the pointy end,' he said. 'They forget about the bits and pieces, the individual parts. I suppose it makes it less personal. It must make it easier to send more young fellows away if you don't make it personal. That's right, isn't it, Angus?

'Maybe that's how you have to think to be able to live with a decision like that. A gardener, at least not one worth his fertiliser, can't think that way.

'I mean, if you stand up there on the top stair and look over this garden, you can see the patterns and colours. You can see where something is and know that it fits.

'But down here, close to the ground and in amongst it, down here you can see the real story, you can see all the tiny things that come together to make the garden what it really is.

'It's the same with war, Angus. When you're in amongst it, you see it for what it really is. Those blokes in charge should have spent more time with us. Come down from the top stair. That might have changed their thinking.'

Blink loved to use a line from a 1950s Hollywood western and he loved to use it on occasions like Anzac Day when platitudes were so plentiful.

'They were so young,' someone would invariably say while reading the names on the cenotaph's roll of honour.

'Yes,' Blink liked to respond, the cheeky bugger. 'But they're dead. And you don't get any older than that.'

He'd say it with a drawl, as laconic as John Wayne, whom he adored and always refused to believe was really named Marion.

For all the time Blink had spent in France during the war, he had picked up only a smattering of the language. What he heard most was English, then German.

Nevertheless, his rudimentary French was enough to thrill Stevie and me when Blink would count to ten.

He did so with an accent we considered exotic, but which high school French lessons later taught me was lacking in every department.

'Unn. Der. Twar. Katra. Sank. Seas. Set. Wheat. Nerf. Deece.'

Some of the numbers sounded more like nicknames.

He had also learned to say "Parlez-vous français?", which came out of his mouth as "Paar-lay vooz fronsayz".

He liked to sing "Mademoiselle from Armentières". Unfortunately, these were the only words of the song he knew. Even more unfortunately, Blink was tone deaf and those three words never came within cooee of the melody.

But he made up for it by dancing a jig, clomping his boots on the floor until Isobel told him, 'Keep it down, Blink'.

It was at that Anzac Day dawn service when I was a kid that Blink's body stiffened and his hand squeezed mine hard when the mayor of Launceston mentioned France and places like Pozieres, Bullecourt and the Somme.

Now that I think of it, I remember I wasn't Angus that day at all. That day was one when Blink knew me as his grandson.

A skirl of bagpipes split the cold morning air and the strains of the piper's lament were stirring. As the sun came up, it glinted off polished medals and bugle brass and gave lustre to badges and ribbons. The flags were at half-mast and waiting for a breeze. Wreaths had been laid and prayers said. All was sombre and dignified as the bugler began the "Last Post".

To my left, a small boy, younger than me and who had been hidden behind a blanket and duffle coat, sniffled and moaned, asking when it was time to go home.

'Quiet!' clipped his father. 'This is not about you.'

Blink released his grip on my hand and took a step closer to the man and his son.

'Excuse me, sir,' he said. 'You're wrong. Otherwise, what on earth was the point?'

Today, when I read the roll of honour on the Anzac cenotaph in Launceston, I see men I never knew, but names I recognise.

I went to school with a Bartle, a Brand, a Briggs, a Cheek and a Collings. I knew Driscolls and Friths, Howells and Jessops, Lucks and Machins. I have worked with a Ratcliff, drunk with a Shegog, argued with a von Bibra and kissed a Webb.

These are northern Tasmanian names. And all these northern strangers are close to me. Blink made them so.

Late April is an important time for Tasmanian gardens. Winter is picking up speed and there is much to be done before it bites.

As Blink grew older, and less able to spend a lot of time on his feet, he gave up attending the Anzac Day ceremony.

If it was a fine day, he would spend the time in his garden and, at some stage of the morning, he'd knock the top off a tallie of Boag's draught beer and pour some into a cup. Then he'd raise the cup to the sun, just for a second.

He said nothing because he knew the gesture said, and meant, everything.

It was another measureless inch.

chapter 22

Isobel was in the kitchen, cleaning up after lunch, and Blink had made his way to his chair in the main room.

I was having a day off school. My tonsils were infected and Mum had taken me to the doctor and the chemist, before dropping me off at Raymond Street while she went to work.

'I don't know why your parents don't have those tonsils of yours taken out,' said Isobel.

My backside was sore from the penicillin shot and my throat hurt every time I swallowed. There was no cooling ice-cream in the house and so I moped about feeling sorry for myself. I had a temperature and during the previous night, when it was at its highest, I had hallucinated for hours as my mother kept a vigil over me and dabbed a cold flannel on my body.

I was miserable and made sure Blink and Isobel knew it.

'Come on,' said Blink, hoisting himself up and grabbing his cigarettes and matches. 'Come with me.'

'I don't feel well. I want to stay here,' I said.

'Come on, you can help me. No arguments.'

He put his hand on my shoulder and it was gentle and firm at the same time. I had no choice, although I made my discontent perfectly clear.

'Pick that lip up,' said Blink. 'Any lower and you could get it caught in the rake.'

'I don't want to be in the garden, Blink. I don't feel well enough today. I want ice-cream.'

'Well, how about we just give it a few minutes and we'll see how it goes?' he said, pushing me out the back door.

Blink was old by this time, slower, but he got about okay. He still loved a smoke but had trouble working his fingers around the paper and tobacco to roll his own. He smoked filters now and shoved one into his mouth as we walked into the heart of the Raymond Street garden.

'Over there, over to the stump,' he said and I made my way through the vegetable rows. Blink slowed behind me.

By the time I reached the stump, I was gone. The grandson who'd been leading Blink into the garden had become Angus. Blink sat down.

'Angus,' he said, with surprise in his voice, 'what are you doing here?'

I heard Isobel walking down the back stairs into the laundry and when she emerged again with a heavy basket of washing, which she dropped underneath the clothesline, Blink was well away.

He told me that I didn't look too well, but not to worry. We just had to get through the next couple of days and we'd be right. He told me that the Hun must be on the verge of surrendering and that there was no need to shit bricks because a man shitting bricks is carrying too much weight around and makes an easy target.

'I'm not shitting bricks,' I said, revelling in the bad language. 'I've just got a sore throat and a temperature.'

But that was me talking and Blink wasn't seeing or hearing me.

I called towards the line and my grandmother, 'His mind's gone again.'

'Just go with him, love,' she said. 'It can't hurt.'

She pegged the last of the load and went up the stairs and back inside the house.

Another day, again out in the garden and with a shower approaching, Blink and I had our trowels and forks in the earth, making space for carrots.

'When I came back,' he said suddenly, 'I swore I'd never dig another bloody hole ever again.

'You remember, Angus? Sometimes it felt like we were digging our way across Europe. Foxholes, firing trenches, forward trenches, reserve trenches, covering bloody trenches, communications bloody trenches, support bloody trenches.

'Those blokes who flew over us must have looked down and seen the ground wriggling, like it was full of tunnelling worms.

'You have to laugh. Here I am, a gardener for Christ's sake, trying to swap my spade for a rifle and bayonet and when I get over there the first thing they do is take the rifle and bayonet off me and give me a bloody spade and a pick.

'Do you remember that day outside Lagnicourt, Angus? That day I put the spade right through my boot and almost right through my big toe? I know a lot of blokes did that sort of thing to get out of the fighting and you couldn't blame them, especially after what some of them had been through.

'But mine was an accident through and through, the records show it. Just one of those things. I lost concentration or something in that bloody mud and nearly lost my toe.

'I'm no Charlie Forster but. You never knew him did you, Angus? Chopped his foot clean in half to get out of the war. I used to work with Charlie for a while.

'I was lucky but. Nothing went septic. They just stitched and bandaged me and sent me back to the lines. Nice for a while, though. Warm. Rum in the tea. Hot stew. Pretty clean and comfy in those field hospitals when you compare it to the trenches. Bit of a stench from some of the crook blokes, but on the whole it was a bloody nice change.'

There was no stopping him.

'Mind you, they got me back to the mud and shit in time for the fight, bless 'em. Eh, Angus? Eh? And all they did was give me a brand new spade and a brand new pick and I started digging like nothing had changed.

'To tell you the truth, Angus, if there's one thing can be said for all the digging, it kept your mind off what was coming.

'Over the other side, those blokes were doing the same thing for the same reasons. Probably some German bloke almost chopped his toe off too, like me.

'Strange thing, all that. We dug up the ground to protect it. Pretty silly, eh? We dug it up and blew it up and bloodied it up to keep it safe from each other. What a bunch of silly buggers. You've gotta laugh. Eh, Angus?'

I had nothing to say.

'All that digging kept your mind off shitting bricks. For a while anyway. Because it was just too much hard work digging to bother your brain thinking about anything else. It was too hard. You'd dig for a couple of hours, wait for the rain to cave the walls in, then start digging again.

'And then it'd rain again and it didn't once seem to occur to the top brass running the show that shovelling water while it was raining didn't actually achieve very much.

'I swore and vowed and declared I'd never dig another bloody hole, swore and vowed and declared. And when I came back I went back to work as a gardener and started digging holes again.

'Still, you were never shitting bricks when you were digging the trenches, foxholes and gun placements. Eh, Angus?

Blokes'd get angry, frustrated, impatient, all those things. But not frightened.

'Plenty of time to be frightened after the trenches and holes were dug and you were sittin' in 'em waitin' for the order to go or for the bombardment before the push.

'Then you'd be frightened. Eh, Angus? Real scared for a couple of seconds or minutes, fear like you wouldn't believe, and then it'd go because you'd be into the fight, into the thick, and you knew after a while that blokes who stayed scared usually got knocked.

'It's like they drew attention to themselves. Christ, that was the last thing you wanted.

'It's like footy, I reckon. Go in hard and you'll be right. Go in timid and you're vulnerable. You stand out. You've got to go in hard, hard as you can.

'Brave men coming. Remember that, Angus? Brave men coming. Out they came, waves of them, all running, falling, dodging, tripping, stopping to check on mates. Brave men coming.

'Remember that? Angus, remember that? No time to be shittin' bricks then. Not in the thick.'

Blink spoke often enough for me to discover what he had feared during the war.

He told me that at the front everyone feared dying because the likelihood of it happening to an Australian was one in three, a number not helped by the British command's tendency to send the Australians in first.

'I'd never fight for Mother England again, that's for sure,' said Blink. 'The Pommy blokes were all right, but their officers...I had no time for them.'

More than death itself, Blink said it was the manner of dying that men feared.

'Once you're dead, you're dead,' he said. 'We know that, don't we, Angus? Saw blokes get killed every day, but at least you can't get hurt anymore. How you go, that's another thing.'

He said blokes weren't too concerned about being shot.

'No, hang on, that's wrong,' he corrected himself. 'No one wanted to get shot but, if you had to go, then that was the way to do it. Quick and clean, through the heart or between the eyes. If you were lucky. Done in a flash.'

'But you know all about this, Angus,' he said. 'We were there, saw it up close. Don't need to tell you any of this.'

I nodded. My throat still hurt and I rubbed at it. But I didn't want to go inside anymore. I wanted to listen to Blink.

And for once he went beyond assumption.

He said plenty of men worried about being shot in such a way that they'd lose a limb or part of their faces or their balls and be left out there, alone; knowing that every second meant a greater risk of infection, and that meant rotting to death with nothing to do but wait for it to happen.

He said other men were frightened of being bayoneted out on the battlefield, because it seemed such an old way to die, like an act of past wars, not this new modern war they were fighting.

He said that, for some soldiers, nothing compared with the fear of freezing or drowning in your own muck as pneumonia or influenza gradually filled your lungs.

'I knew one chap,' said Blink, 'and he was frightened of being killed and the war ending the next day. Odd thing to think about, if you ask me.

'And you and me, Angus, we know what we were frightened of. We were frightened of the wire and being left behind, eh, Angus?'

I said yes. I rubbed my throat again.

'Because some nights you could hear them, blokes on the wire or on the ground, wounded and whimpering, and you couldn't do a thing for them because if you popped your head up out of the hole some bastard across the way, who could hear his own blokes crying and wailing, would try to shoot it off.

'That's what we were frightened of, eh, Angus? Being one of those men, strung up and stranded, like a bloody Christmas decoration, unable to get back to the lines or understand why no one was coming out to get them.

'I was terrified of being left, I admit it. Shit bricks at the thought of it. And you were terrified of being left, Angus. Of being one of those blokes yelling out "Don't leave me here, boys. Bring me in, boys".'

Blink's voice caught. He took a sip from a glass of water and closed his eyes. There was a wetness beneath them.

He leaned back in his chair and the calendar dropped from his knees and fell to the floor.

'You rest now, old fellow,' I said. 'Nothing to be frightened of. Not anymore.'

Blink opened his eyes and what he said next came in a whisper. A bubble of drool formed at the side of his mouth, growing and shrinking as he breathed.

'I left you, didn't I, Angus? Eh, Angus? I left you.

'Up on the wire for all to see. Like a bloody Christmas decoration.'

chapter 23

'Everything we are has a colour,' says Blink, chatting as Gemma and I wash up the dinner dishes. 'You know what I mean? If we're happy we're in the pink. If we're sad we're blue. Or we're red with anger or green with envy. White for good. Black for evil. And scared? Yellow.

'Right now, I'm in the pink. Happy as a clam.'

I don't know what's brought this on, but colour has always been important to Blink, as it is to any gardener.

And I know Blink has seen all these colours at the front.

What he was not prepared for was those men he says had been drained of all their colour.

He tried to understand them. He searched so he might learn what it was that they had lost and where it had begun; so he might know whether it had begun to happen to him.

He's told me of how he watched them prepare for battle, taking hours to polish and hone their bayonets, then holding them to the light on those nights when the sky was clear and the moon was out.

'The light hitting the steel could be beautiful,' he says, 'but those blokes' eyes were narrow slits.'

He thought them men without reason, men who had fallen too far.

It disturbed him that when one was killed it gave him a sense of relief.

He told no one this at the time but continued to observe and mull over whether this lack of compassion was, in fact, his own colour being drawn away from the surface.

'I never had much cause to hate anyone, not even the Germans,' he says. 'I hate turnips more than I hated Germans.

'I figured the German army was full of blokes all pretty much the same as me and the rest of us. Young blokes. Bum-fluff battalions.'

Apart from when his father died, Blink had never had much cause to think about death. Certainly not his own.

But in France, death was all around him. He saw it, caused it and fought it each day.

'You know, I reckon what I've noticed most on the faces of dead men is surprise,' he said one night as he and a group of soldiers prepared their evening meal. 'Why do you reckon that is?'

'It's supposed to be the prime of our lives,' said Private Angus Bain. 'We're supposed to be bulletproof.'

Every soldier knew about the bullet and the bayonet, but the western front offered any number of options.

You could drown, sucked down into the slush by the weight of your own gear, your last meal all grit and foulness.

You could be poisoned, as filth found its way into small cuts and deeper wounds and, slowly at first, then with gathering speed, bits and pieces of flesh rotted away.

You could die by shellfire, by bombs and mines that blew a person apart and left nothing to indicate that anyone had been there at all.

You could slip in the mud and fall on your own bayonet.

The puttees that were wrapped around your lower legs to keep out the water could unravel and catch on wire and leave you stuck there, a sitting duck for machine-gunners.

You could be gnawed at by rats until you didn't care anymore. You could freeze. You could die of waiting to be found. You could die of heartbreak and exhaustion. You could die quickly and slowly on the wire.

You could even die of sheer relief at having been found, beyond salvation, but at least not alone for those final moments.

You could die of courage and of cowardice, of stupid mistakes, idiotic orders, bad luck, panic and terror. You could be blasted into the air, buried undergound, taken quickly thanks to a clean shot or clean thrust, or go in some miserably drawn-out affair with agony and inevitability.

You could die in the hospital as wounds went septic faster than they could be dressed, or when gangrene set in and bandages and ointments and knowledge ran out. You could die of the damp that turned your sniffle to a cold to influenza to pneumonia.

Blink says some men died of pleasure. They so loved the war and its simplicity of order followed by action. Kill or be killed. Advance. Retreat. March. Rest. Dig. Eat. Sleep. Not much to leave a man confused.

You could be killed on an offensive or a retreat, on the day you arrived at the front or the minute before you were to leave.

Blink hated it out in the open ground but never shirked it. Out in the open, he knew it was a case of moving, ducking and weaving, cutting and thrusting, forging on and on, with his helmet clanking around his head and cutting at the rubbed raw bone behind his ears. Just keep moving.

The sweat dripped into his eyes and turned the landscape into a bleak blur of clouds and a series of dark, running, falling, yelling, crying, slipping, moaning shapes.

On one push, Blink swallowed the blood from where he'd bitten through his lip and he ground his teeth and bit his tongue and chewed chunks out of the inside of his mouth.

All the time he was running, stumbling forward, with smoke and fumes and sweat in his eyes and throat, and with friends and strangers falling either side of him and up ahead. He thanked God it wasn't him and then immediately felt selfish.

Another time, as he was taking cover, the sound of bullets and bombs all around reminded him of the sounds from the showgrounds at home every October when he was a boy.

He was reminded of bonfire night, with all the family gathered around, chucking timber on the pile and watching as sparks fizzed skyward and the green wood spat. Young couples held hands and sneaked kisses while Stocky stoked the fire, Elizabeth made tea and someone took the top off a bottle, using an opener they always kept hooked to their belt.

He remembered all that in a flash until he was brought back to the here and now by an order shouted in his face, a bomb blast too close for comfort, a bullet whipping through his sleeve and a tumble into a waist-deep puddle he didn't see and that wedged him there like a coconut at a shy.

He tried to thank the ruddy-faced sergeant who pulled him out by his underarms but he didn't have time because the sergeant fell dead before he could say anything or ask 'What's going on?', 'What's the story?', 'How's the push going?'.

Blink looked at his fallen saviour for longer than he should have, transfixed by him until someone else rushed up from behind and yelled, 'Come on, come on, forward, forward, go forward, man!' and off he tore once again.

The next thing he saw was soldiers running towards him and he held his bayonet out in front and ready until he saw the men were his own and this time the order was, 'Go back, go back' because the Germans had counterattacked.

So he turned tail and ran back towards the place where the day had started. He could hear the sound of his breath, grunting with the effort of running, and he took his helmet off and ran with it in his hand because the bruising and bleeding around his ears hurt as much as the cacophony inside them.

He jumped over holes and puddles and bodies and parts of bodies and wire and markers and he tried to concentrate on keeping his footing, on staying upright enough to run and stooped enough to reduce his own target area.

Finally, after all this exhausting waste of time and effort, he fell back into a trench with all the others and leaned his back against the wet wall, sucking in air that tasted of smoke and fired ammunition.

When the action was over, he chewed on a piece of hard biscuit, wiped his brow, checked himself over for nicks and holes and tried to relax.

But he couldn't seem to close his eyes and for hours into the night, as the flares lit the sky, he tried to take his mind off the war by thinking about that girl. What was her name?

She was the one he met at the showgrounds and kissed behind the railway sheds.

What was her name? Not Isobel. Isobel's his girl now.

Who was that other girl? Ruth. Ruth Collins. That was it.

The memory of her was like a beautiful dream.

As Blink finally dropped off to a soldier's sleep, he wondered whether Ruth Collins ever thought of him and that day at the showgrounds and that one kiss behind the railway sheds.

And the last thing he wondered was whether Ruth Collins had any idea how much she meant to him right now.

chapter 24

Blink was frightened almost out of his wits on his first few days at the front, by the noise, the sight of men there one second and gone the next, the confusion and turmoil of fighting.

He was no student of military history but knew this was a different kind of war, one writing its own new history.

He pushed forward and pushed back, part of ascendencies gained, relinquished, regained and relinquished once more.

His first battle was in July 1916, at Fromelles, a village in northern France and the first taste of the western front for many of the Australians. Blink was dirty and wet and weary as he made his way back to the lines with a ragtag bunch of other soldiers.

During the fighting, the familiarity of the ground, something on which he used to be able to depend, left him.

He skirted around, jumped or tripped over bodies of his own men and the enemy. Often it was impossible to differentiate between them.

'How'd we get out of that little lot, digger?' a buck-toothed private asked Blink as the pair of them slumped into a trench after yet another attack had ended in stalemate.

'Buggered if I know,' Blink replied. 'All I'm worried about is getting a cuppa in before the silly buggers send us out again.'

A few days later they were at Pozieres.

The battle began with Blink among those Australians ordered to secure the devastated village and hold the main road.

At one stage, he took cover in what had been a shop, crouching behind what remained of a bakery counter. He rubbed and stretched his neck and, seeing where he was, tried to conjure up the smell of bread baking.

With both their forward trenches and the village taken, those Germans not killed, taken prisoner or having fled, retreated to a second line of defences, Pozieres Heights, from where they mounted a fresh assault.

The German bombing was like the pounding of a migraine and Blink thought it might never stop. For three days, it didn't.

The number of casualties became ridiculous and the constant toing-and-froing of gains made, and then lost, wore Blink and the rest of the men down to their nerve endings.

Some were reduced to tears, others to rage. More than one felt the cold piss of panic running down their trousers. The trenches reeked of vomit and shit.

Blink smoked and took swigs of brackish water from his canteen. He held his hands before his face and saw that they were bleeding and trembling.

When the order came through shortly after midnight to attempt another push to capture the Heights, Blink thought of Isobel and Elizabeth. He willed himself to move.

The Heights was a ridge not far from the village and the way there was heavily protected by entanglements. The object of the advance looked as attainable as the moon but the command hammered home to the Australians the urgency for the Heights to be taken. The attack was founded on miscalculation and the German retaliation was brutal.

'How many did we lose?' asked Blink later that morning, amazed that he had not been one of them.

'I heard more than a thousand,' said a sergeant.

'More like two thousand, the Aussie brass is saying. I spoke to a communications bloke,' said another soldier.

'That probably means three thousand,' said yet another.

However many there were, Blink knew he would never forget how some had fallen. He had seen one soldier shot dead as he tried to disentangle himself from a strand of wire. The panic ignited in the soldier's mind spread down his arms and into his hands, refusing to allow his fingers to work around the metal and cloth. He saw other men die, flung backwards in a staccato dance or thrown high into the air. Some fell in one piece, others in several.

The vision of the battle came to him in flashes. Nothing was sustained except grimness and fear, and the need for him to keep moving, to find cover in the dark. At times he lay flat on the ground, writhing his body, trying to carve some pathetic trench for himself and a few seconds of relief.

What he couldn't see, he heard and he heard nothing sadder than a boy's voice calling for his mother, trying to understand what was happening to him and why he was so cold.

Later, Blink sat with soldiers whose faces told of their dismay, despair or detachment. A smoke was passed around.

'What a bastard of a day,' said one.

'Yeah,' said another, 'and there's more to come.'

When the sun did come out, so did the shovels and the monotonous routine of digging began anew.

'Angus, what was the most important weapon in that war?' Blink asked me, as he rolled a smoke on the stump in the Raymond Street garden.

'The rifle?' I said. 'The bayonet?'

'No, Angus. The spade. Without it, where would we have been? I know where we would have ended up, that's for sure.

'To think, off we went to experience the Great Adventure and it turned out to be the life of a mole or an earthworm.'

The digging of new trenches at Pozieres delayed the next push, but when it came it did so in a storm of violence.

Blink and the rest of his battalion had been hastily assembled before dark and they were ready to go, geeing each other up, slapping each other's backs and grinning. They waited another four hours before any move was made, which was a cruel punishment because it was time that allowed men to lose their fighting edge.

Finally, seven battalions attacked in four waves and secured the Heights, with the infantry sweeping over the crest and raining down upon the Germans.

Blink was in and out of holes and trenches, the action of firing and thrusting and running a blur, except for the odd scene that registered with exceptional clarity—a German pinned to a trench wall by his own bayonet; an Australian private and a German corporal both fallen, their hands touching.

In a dugout hit by the full force of the artillery barrage, Blink saw men who had been pulped, as if blown inside out. He saw a dead dog, its pink tongue hanging slack from the side of its mouth, a dribble of shit near its tail.

Not far from there he saw an Australian captain, smiling and peaceful, with nothing below his waist.

The Germans retaliated the following day with a fearsome, final and failed bombardment. Then it was over.

Blink rolled a smoke and drew back on it. Exhausted, he closed his eyes but opened them soon after, when he was tapped on the shoulder.

'Got a smoke for a digger?' asked Angus.

chapter 25

Blink Johns and Angus Bain had met in a hospital tent in Etaples, an Allied disembarkation point on France's west coast.

It was a pretty place, or would have been under normal circumstances, when boats bobbed in port and narrow streets were left to the villagers, not armies. It was easy to imagine the thickness of coffee, freshly baked bread and idle chatter.

Before making landfall, Blink had scanned beyond the coast and was pleased to find the distant ground a lush green. He thought that flowers and plants could grow well on ground as green as that, after the soldiers had left.

The coast did not offer him the same sense of optimism. The ground wasn't up to much and any goodness that may have existed had been crushed beneath heavy boots and machinery.

The reason for Blink's hospitalisation, before he had seen any action at all, lay in the form of a mild bout of influenza.

Still naive to the ways of armies, he had thought it a gross overreaction when Sergeant Edward Miller had heard a thick cough one morning at parade and, investigating, caught Blink as he hoicked up a glob of greenish phlegm.

Bemused by the order to take himself to the medical tent quick-smart, Blink was even more surprised when, within the hour, he was lying on a stretcher with clean, white sheets over him.

'Geez, love,' he said to the nurse monitoring his progress, and that of the other twenty or so men in the ward, 'if this is the way you treat a bloke with the sniffles, how are we ever going to win this war? We can save our bullets because if the Germans find out about this they'll kill themselves laughing.'

Nurse Pearl Stone set him straight.

'Not if they've got any sense, they won't,' she said. 'If they know anything they'll be doing exactly the same thing.'

Nurse Stone was plain and friendly. Blink and the other men liked her forthright manner.

'There's nothing can rout an army faster than influenza,' she continued, fluffing his pillows. 'It may not be as quick or as exciting as a bullet or bomb, but it is every bit as deadly.

'And I don't know about you—Private Johns, is it?—I don't know about you, but it would seem to me to be a waste of everybody's time to have come all this way from home to defend all this,' she waved her arm in a half-circle and there was no doubting her derision, 'only to give it all up because we didn't take care of the sniffles.'

Private Angus Bain did not have the sniffles but wished he did. He was in the bed next to Blink and was waiting his turn with Nurse Stone, his mind very much on the wording of the communication to be sent to his parents in Queenstown.

'I can understand the need to keep families informed about our health and wellbeing,' he said to anyone who would listen, 'but do they have to do it every time we get laid up for the slightest problem? Especially something like this?'

At Raymond Street, Elizabeth Johns received so many telegrams in the first few months of Blink's absence that she began to fear for her sanity. Yet each one reported that her son had been admitted only for minor problems.

Isobel came round every Sunday after church and Elizabeth would pass on any news. She stored any correspondence in the back of her diary.

'And how is it this morning, Private?' asked Nurse Stone of a sheepish Angus Bain.

Diagnosing the medical status of others in the hospital was relatively easy, thought Blink, because there was no concealing 'flu or fever, combat wounds or broken bones.

At first, however, he could only hazard a guess at the nature of his neighbour's problem. He felt another cough coming on and reached for the jar beside his bed.

All became clear as he watched Nurse Stone go about her work, peeling back Angus's sheets, taking a tongue depressor from her uniform pocket and lifting and manoeuvring Angus's penis.

She flopped it this way and that and peered down its murky eye. Angus looked mortified as she went about her work.

'Still weeping, Private?' she asked.

Angus knew the question was coming because it had done so for the past few days. And with it came the usual salvo of sniggers throughout the ward.

'Yes, Nurse,' he replied, 'and do you think you could possibly ask that any louder? Some people in Berlin couldn't hear.'

One patient, who was covered in red and angry sores, had taken to calling Angus "Willow".

'Still weeping, Willow?' he'd say when Nurse Stone was gone.

Another made fun of Angus's gullibility.

'What did you think, Bain: that the clap was a round of applause after you'd finished with her? I hope she was worth it.'

The soldiers joked whenever Nurse Stone approached them and took out a tongue depressor.

'That's not the one you used on Willow, is it?' said one, who had both his arms in splints and was strung up as though he was still caught on the wire.

'I hope you don't just wipe it under your arm and use it again. Times are tough but the army can't be that hard up for medical supplies.'

Angus would slink further into his bed, the pain in his very public privates no match for the pain of his humiliation.

And as he lay moaning quietly in his hospital bed, Angus gave up trying to earn any sympathy from those around him.

Instead, he focused his attention on cursing the woman, who had had such lovely hair, lovely eyes and lovely curves, but who had, in his mind, turned out to be an enemy every bit as dangerous as the Hun.

'I'm a gardener in Launceston,' said Blink as he and Angus strolled in the late afternoon sun. The camp bustled with activity. Orders were barked and obeyed. Ships unloaded troops and equipment, then steamed away to fetch more supplies.

'They reckon there's a hundred thousand or more of us over here now,' said Blink.

'A hundred thousand, eh?' said Angus. 'That'd explain the trouble we have getting dinner on time.

'I was a miner in Queenstown,' he continued. 'Never been to Launceston, never seen much else of Tasmania bar Queenstown and most of the time I was there I had my head down. Didn't see much apart from rock.'

They walked a little further. In the past few days, their various forms of treatment had begun to work wonders and both Angus's dick and Blink's chest were becoming free of infection. Soon, both would be heading inland to take their places at the front.

For Angus, the wait to join the action had been a protracted one. He'd enlisted with the other Mount Lyell boys almost a year ago but a series of setbacks had nearly convinced him he would never make it to the fight.

'First up, I got knocked back because of my teeth,' he said. 'Half the Queenstown intake had rotten gobs and had to be rejected or get them done.

'I got mine done. Dentist in Burnie yanked 'em out and whacked in these beauties.' He used his tongue to push forward his dentures. 'Not bad, eh? They wobble about a bit but they're not bad.

'Then, not long after that I'm in Melbourne waiting to board the ship and we're all standing by the dock in our lines and the next thing I know I'm in the bloody drink.'

'You're having me on,' said Blink.

'No, true as I'm standing here with an itchy dick. It must be getting better but I've got to stop scratching it.

'Anyway, not only did I go overboard without even being on board in the first place, I somehow managed to hit something and break my leg on the way down.

'It kept me out of uniform for nearly six months but it came right in the end.

'Of course, I had to do my basic training again and that was a bastard, but I knew I'd be needed. No way was this war going to end early.

'That's why I wasn't too worried when we got over here and they split up my company and sent us here and there. That's how I ended up with your lot. There's a couple of others, too. I'm just glad to be here. Any idea of what to expect?'

'Not really,' said Blink. 'But looking at some of the blokes in the hospital, I'm not sure I want to know.'

'Nah,' said Angus, 'mostly training accidents, measles, 'flu like you. That's nothing. I've talked to some of the blokes who were in Turkey. They've got some stories. But I reckon they bullshit us new blokes a bit.'

'I hope so,' said Blink. 'I've talked to them too.'

'Nah,' said Angus again. 'I can't wait to get stuck in. It's why we're here and it's got to be better than mining. Got to be.'

As much as they had heard about the fighting so far, and as much as they were ready to take up the fight in France, combat meant little to them. So far, Angus and Blink knew only how to march in a straight line, shoot at targets and bayonet hessian sacks filled with straw and sand.

'I wouldn't mind a few days in Paris,' said Blink. 'I've heard about the gardens there. I've heard there are flowers that leave ours for dead.'

'I'd be happy to join you,' said Angus, 'except I don't think flowers will do much for me.

'I was talking to Mackie the other day, you know, the bloke with the busted arms—apparently he fell off a donkey—and he says he's been to Paris and has never seen lights or ladies like it.

'He says that the middle of the night in the centre of the city is as bright as daytime everywhere else in the world. I could do with seeing that.'

'I don't know about the lights but I would have thought you'd have had your fill of the ladies for the time being,' said Blink.

They took a break to roll smokes. A company of soldiers approached in four lines.

Pencil straight, they marched past, hup-twoing.

chapter 26

After Fromelles and Pozieres, the Australians strove gamely along the front, making it into the German lines time and again, only to be forced back.

Too often, artillery support failed and the new tanks were next to useless. Advantage was only ever fleeting. The gardener and the miner were surviving but wasted little effort in asking how or why. What they did discuss, as did most of the Australians, was the British command.

'I don't mind fighting. That's what I came here to do,' said Angus, taking off his helmet and running a dirty hand through his sweat-soaked hair, 'but I'd like to think the people we're fighting for are actually on our side.'

Blink agreed. Nothing had been as expected.

'This is a farce,' said Angus.

As the months passed and the ferocity of battle and the extent of losses showed no sign of easing, the effect told heavily on the men.

Between attacks, they descended into a kind of stupor and either stumbled along the trenches muttering inanities or stood stock-still and vacant-eyed, resting against their rifles. For many, comprehension was now just a weary shake of the head.

Men chewed at their cigarettes, squeezing the smoke into and out of their lungs and mouths, because the feeling and sight of it reminded them they were breathing and alive.

'I hear we're heading for a farming district,' said Blink to Angus as they marched. 'Or what was a farming district. Christ knows what it will be after we're done with it.'

'That must be the farmhouse,' said Angus a day or so later as they dug in.

'How can you tell?' asked Blink, looking at a pile of rubble in the distance.

'Because it has a chimney,' said Angus. 'In fact, that's about all it has now.'

The battle began and then typically ebbed and flowed, the only constants being impasse and heavy casualties.

'I'm not afraid,' said Blink. 'I'm just so buggered. All this bloody back and forth.'

It took all of Blink's energy to keep going. Night raids, dawn patrols, skirmishes, charges and bombardments so rattled him and the other soldiers that some began to speak, quietly, of death as a welcome relief.

The fighting around the farm continued for weeks. The punishing rain and impossible mud only made things worse.

Angus told Blink he'd overheard a couple of officers saying eleven thousand men had been killed.

'Imagine that, Blink,' he said. 'Eleven thousand. It'd take me a week to count that high. And all for a few yards of mud.'

'Maybe they're the ones who are better off,' said Blink.

During one advance, Blink was momentarily taken aback by the sound of laughter. Risking his head, he peered over the top of a foxhole and saw a delirious British soldier standing in the open, cackling like a lunatic. A hail of bullets stitched a line across his chest and the soldier fell backwards, smiling as his body splashed and then sank into the mud.

The drenching rain was growing ever more depressing. In the trenches, the men appeared old and resigned. Blink had no desire to see how he looked himself.

He sat with Angus and ate cold meat from a tin and they were quiet as another chilly night began to fall. There was not much to talk about and they had little energy to do so. Their focus was not on what was to come or what had been. The effect of the past few months had honed all concentration on the now.

It had been another miserable day, the clouds low and forlorn, though the fighting had been minimal, particularly for Blink and Angus, who had been kept back in rear trenches with a company of others.

About six o'clock, with night sapping the last of the twilight and the cold etching its way through his uniform and under his skin, Blink was scraping at the last dregs of his dinner when a captain approached.

The men were called together. Blink and Angus stood and awaited Captain Steve Hart's orders.

'Any relation to Ned Kelly's Steve Hart?' cracked a soldier. 'Because you know what happened to him, don't you?'

Night raids were not unusual; all soldiers had been on them. On this night the command planned to flank west of the German lines, separate and then rush forward on two small fronts.

'Our goal is to cause enough trouble for long enough to enable other companies to assault front-on, to secure the land around the farmhouse and further ground if we can,' said the captain.

Blink checked his rifle and smeared mud over his bayonet so that it wouldn't glisten in the moonlight. There was no sign of the moon but he went through the routine out of habit.

He tied his boots and tightened his puttees. Angus did the same.

For the first time in a while, Blink thought of home. Concentrating, he tried to remember faces and places; to see himself on Windmill Hill, taking in the views; to see the garden at Raymond Street.

The order to move snapped him from his reverie. The rain started again and dripped from his helmet. Angus scanned the sky.

'Fancy a stroll, Blink?' he said.

Out they went.

It poured, turning the ground to slush and the duckboards in the trenches to slippery slides. Visibility was a joke.

Making their way out of the trenches, the patrol sloshed in puddles, their boots making ugly noises as they trudged in and out of the sucking mud.

Blink wiped his face with a wet hand. Angus, crouching, tasted the rain on his tongue.

'Just like home,' he whispered.

'Where are we?' asked Blink.

'In France, you dill.'

Blink tried not to laugh, but the situation was laughable. He thought that if the enemy appeared now he might put down his gun and ask for a towel. He didn't feel in the least like fighting tonight. Tonight, in all this rain and muck, it all seemed more pointless than ever.

Down it poured, gathering strength and sweeping through in blankets of saturation, and still the men plodded on, each one trying to keep sight of the one in front.

It took a couple of seconds for Blink to work out that the soldier nearing him was the young captain, who gathered the men around him and signalled for them to crouch, be quiet and listen.

'This rain has thrown us,' he said. 'I think we should sit tight for a bit. Get our bearings before we move on. It seems safe enough. No sign of the Hun as yet.'

An arc of light from a German flare revealed the folly of the captain's words. Hopelessly out of position, he had led the patrol not to the west of the German lines as planned, and not behind the German lines. They were between them.

The flare exposed them like shooting-gallery ducks. Fat raindrops shone in the light.

Captain Hart was aghast but only for a second. 'Retreat! Retreat!' he yelled, but the second word was cut short and he fell to the wet ground.

At Pozieres, Angus had seen men caught in crossfire and knew the panic that could result. He grabbed Blink by the belt and yanked him down. Bullets pinged above their heads and Blink heard the anguish of shot men. He felt them fall about him and was splashed by their landings. The ground was sodden and stinking and the only voices he could make out were German. Another flare illuminated their position again and Blink saw how many had been killed so quickly. He was sad and furious and thrilled to be alive, for however long that might be.

He and Angus crawled, like excited babies, through the mire, under and around bodies and away, with luck, to where they were supposed to be.

The Allied barrage began and Blink's head throbbed with every *whomp, whomp, whomp* of shells fired and exploding.

He held his hands over his ears. A shell landed close by and stunned him. His senses danced and his helmet was gone. He rocked from side to side, desperate to gather his wits, then resumed slithering forward and away.

Blink was used to the slow, methodical transformation of the earth as it turned from soil to green grass or orchards or gardens. It was a gradual process and one he could understand. But here the land was being wrenched apart and reshaped in seconds. One blast could put a hill where level ground used to be, another could make level ground of a hill.

He was tired of not being able to count on anything and he wanted to sleep, to wake up in a few hours, roll a smoke and ease into a new day.

A surge of foul water burst over his face and down his throat and he gagged and spluttered. He was moving despite himself and wondered how that could be until he realised Angus still had him.

Blink waited for the rip and burn of bullets, but they didn't come. The two friends snaked their way over the wet ground, side by side, inches at a time. They were saturated by rain, mud and sweat and they were heavier because of it. Their breathing came in groans and the effort of it seemed to make them weigh even more.

Blink rolled onto his back and the position offered him a new perspective.

The clouds he saw were of smoke and fumes and the rain turned brown as it passed through them. In his mouth, he could taste oil, mud and minerals.

'Blink, keep moving!' shouted Angus, now a little way ahead and to the left of what Blink saw was a coil of barbed wire.

'I can't. Just give me a second.'

He was dazed. He desperately wanted to sit up, to untie the dark metal top button of his tunic, to unfasten his belt and loosen his puttees. He was breathing so hard. Of all things, a fly landed on his cheek and he waved it away.

'Blink! Come on! Move! Now! Blink!'

Blink heard Angus but didn't heed him. Lying prone in the mud, he had opened his mind to other things. Shells and flares flew back and forth.

Flying above and through the garden, bees and butterflies use, and are used by, imperceptible currents of air. The bees are sticky-legged and noisy, darting from flower to flower, while the butterflies are skittish, as if conscious of their frailty and brief loveliness. Blowflies land in the strawberries or sit on the stakes training the tomatoes. Mosquitoes fizz.

On the ground, a grey snail leaves a slimy trail and makes slow progress out of the sun. Above it, a stick spider takes its daily rest among leaves, its head down and its body perfectly still. It resembles a few loose and light twigs but tonight, after dusk, those twigs will spring to life and begin weaving a net. Then the spider will wait, holding the four corners of the net in its second and third pairs of legs and, like a fisherman casting into the ocean, the stick spider will cast its net when a meal moves into range.

A colony of ants marches back and forth, toting scraps of leaf, stick and food.

A brown slug, which seems to do nothing with any ease or willingness, seeks shade, damp and a spot away from the quick eyes of birds.

The sun moves faster than the slug and gives its presence away. A sparrow swoops, picks up the slug with its beak and tosses it back into its tiny throat.

Under the ground, worms writhe, trapdoor spiders are waking, more ants are moving to-and-fro. Birth and death continue.

In the course of any day, a million and more subtle changes occur in Blink's garden and when people ask him, 'How do you keep it like this?' he always answers, 'Hard work, and hardly any of it is mine.'

Blink heard the gentle flutter of butterfly wings, but was confused by the way the sound then changed to the high-pitched whine of a mosquito looking for a patch of soft skin and a purple vein. Then lowered in tone to the thrum of a march fly, then the angry drone of a wasp as it hovered and darted around his face.

Then the wasp went away and in its place came the guttural growl of a dog and Blink was struck with fear. The dog gave a warning bark, and another, before erupting into a barrage of noise close to his face. The dog sank its teeth into Blink's arm but no, that couldn't be, because he could still see the mouth and teeth so close to his own face. And he could hear the barking and barking and barking.

And when it struck out, hard across Blink's chops with what must have been its big paw, Blink opened his eyes and stared straight into Angus's dirty face, at his yellow teeth, cut lips and wild eyes. He heard Angus barking at him, 'Blink! Blink! We have to move! Now! We have to keep going!'

'Angus?' Blink rolled back onto his stomach and began to move. They slid away on their wet bellies, not to any place they knew but to any place away from where they were.

Blink had no sense of time, no real sense of anything but the need to stay with Angus.

Angus had him by the collar, until a shell blast rocked them loose and Blink lost him. He felt around, swishing his arms in the ground to try and regain contact and to continue their strange journey.

Digging his knees into the mud, Blink lurched forward until the ground disappeared from beneath him and he felt himself tumbling, out of control and splashing down hard, his back half-hitting the duckboards, half-hitting the muddy trench floor.

Frantically wiping the grime from his eyes, he saw beside him the bodies of two soldiers, one face up to the rain, which was bubbling from his open mouth. Blink couldn't tell if they were German or Australian, but thankfully neither was Angus.

Then he saw Angus, on his knees, breathing hard, and he yelled to him, 'Angus! Angus!'

The shelling continued overhead as the two men caught their breath and fought to regain their composure. At least they were out of the line of the machine-guns.

Blink rose halfway to his feet and a jolt of pain wracked his muscles and bones. His arm hurt and he saw that it was cut open.

They were safer here than in the open, but they were also still lost and the contours of the trench only added to their confusion. They could go left or right and either might be the wrong way.

The rain beat down.

'You know what?' said Angus, still puffing.

'What?'

'If someone said to me that they could get us out of this as long as I went back into the mine for the rest of my life, I'd take them up on it. In a flash.'

They headed left for no good reason, arms and legs flailing as they tried to keep their balance.

Rounding a curve in the trench, they took it together and at speed, ploughing into two soldiers at the head of a company coming the other way.

Behind them, men limped or supported others between them. All looked like drowned rats.

'You're game going that way,' said a soldier, who seemed so young and small that his uniform didn't fit, as if he was larking about in his father's clothes.

'We don't know where we're going,' said Blink. 'We don't know where we've been.'

The sergeant wiped at a splash of mud on his sleeve, as if it made any difference. A man moaned and others kept glancing back at the way they had come.

'Have we taken the position?' said Angus.

'We should have done,' said the sergeant, and he spat into the trench wall, 'but something went wrong with the first patrol.

'Christ knows what can happen in this weather. We're back where we started. Stalemate. We've been ordered back to the lines and, unless you're Jesus Christ or God Almighty and have nothing to fear, then I'd suggest you two come with us.'

The farmhouse was never taken. At times, the Allies had the upper hand but they could never quite maintain it.

For Blink and Angus, momentarily safe back in their own lines, soaked to the bone and shivering, it was the next day before they were to realise the expense of the previous terrible night.

An apologetic sun broke through and helped disperse the thick clouds that had dumped so much misery. The dribs and drabs of men in the lines told the story of how many more had not made it back.

A communiqué was issued to the German command requesting a ceasefire to allow both sides to recover their dead and any wounded.

Men from both sides emerged timid and watchful out of trenches, ditches and foxholes, without weapons or anger. They stared at the scene before them. The ground was littered with bodies.

Blink thought it the strangest dance as men stalked and skirted each other, uncertain of reactions or responsibilities.

After a few minutes, however, the tension eased. Some soldiers shook hands or traded cigarettes. Some strolled the field together, bending to check on men.

Blink looked upon the faces of the dead, contorted by fire and metal, and recognised Captain Hart. He saw Angus off to his right and whistled.

Angus shook hands with a German private then turned away. The German stood still, raised his eyes to the sun, then also turned and walked away.

Stretcher bearers and wagons were used to cart off the bodies and it was slow going.

Wheels stuck in the mud and the wagons were weighed down further because of the numbers of casualties they had to bear. Every now and then an arm or leg would flop over the side of a stretcher or wagon and jerk with every bump or hollow, moving as if it was still alive.

'You might need this,' said Angus, handing over Blink's helmet. It was full of brown water.

Blink took it and emptied it. It felt as cold as ice in his hands. He wiped the helmet with his sleeve.

'Thanks,' he said. 'But what I really need is a hot bath and a clean shirt. I could also use some dry scratch and new smoke papers. Couldn't organise that, could you?'

'I wonder how far we got,' said Angus.

'Probably not far,' replied Blink. 'Maybe a couple of hundred yards. It still felt like a couple of hundred miles. I wonder if I'll ever feel warm again?'

They said nothing for a few minutes, taking in the scene.

'Thanks again,' said Blink. 'I owe you one. I don't know what happened to me out there.'

Blink Johns had never been one to shirk on his debts.

He knew that without Angus that night he would most likely have been killed and his mother Elizabeth would be receiving the telegram every mother dreaded.

That debt became embedded in Blink's heart and mind, like the image of Angus's face so close to his, yelling at him to move, urging the sense back into him. He'd thanked Angus, sure, but his friend had waved it off.

'Nah,' he said, 'I'm just more used to the dark, the wet and the noise. Water off a duck's back, to me.'

The two Tasmanians had become friends and that was a dilemma because, on the battlefield, friends could be gone in seconds.

Yet Blink and Angus were a pair and for a long time, and through many fights, they were equals, until Blink began to feel his debt to Angus gaining interest with every day.

chapter 27

It was when Blink's mind started to close down on him that his conversation opened up. It was most unJohnslike.

I was the fortunate one because of the person he saw in me. He could speak to me and did so abundantly and almost exclusively. Through our discussions I discovered that Blink's emotions were not completely buried.

I say "almost exclusively" because Blink also had a connection with Mick. They had common ground, both understanding growing and balance, about the worth of the earth and what it could yield.

Down at the orchard, the two men would find time for just themselves and Dot would let them go, watching them head up the small hill past the driveway, disappearing into the orchard, Mick's hand at Blink's back.

During our Christmas and Easter family gatherings at the orchard, all the men would go fishing on the second morning.

A good-sized stream flowed through the property and in summer we kids would head upstream away from the men. The sound of our splashing and squealing would filter back to them.

We could fit three of us at a time on a thick branch that stretched out over the swimming hole and Dot and Mick's boy, Terry, loved to tell how he was floating in a rubber tube one day, lapping up the afternoon sun, when a fat black snake casually swam by, its head out of the water, tongue flicking.

'Near shit meself,' said Terry every time, and we'd fall laughing out of the tree and into the water.

Fish jumped and we'd gulp big breaths of air and dive under to seek them out.

There were some mornings when the men also dipped their heads in the cool water. With the effect of the previous day's drinking pounding in their skulls, the stream was medicinal.

They'd flick back their dark hair and sprays of water would plume behind them. Refreshed, they could then concentrate on the fiddly business of rods, reels and flies. Fishing was a way for the men to keep from getting under the women's feet as they prepared the big lunch.

'If we don't get away from the house,' said my father, 'they'll have a tea towel or a scrubbing brush in our hands before we know it, or we'll be running errands for missing ingredients and other stuff.'

Easter in Tasmania was too cold for swimming but it was best for fishing and we headed out each Good Friday morning to do what Isobel called God's work. She and my mother were sticklers for the tradition which demanded that no red meat be eaten on Good Friday. To them, the day was for white meat and the only suitable white meat was fish.

In the dark and numbing hours, my father, Blink, Mick, Rex, Phil and we kids would dress in our warmest clothes, fetch the rods and tackle boxes from the downstairs cupboard and head for the stream.

There was a spot where it flowed gently and offered plenty of room on the bank for the men to find the fish and cast their lines. Getting there was a slippery stroll at that dewy time of the morning and it was often so cold we would blow on our fingers to try to keep them warm. Once at the fishing spot, we'd lay down plastic sheets and blankets, open a thermos of hot tea and get down to the business of preparing the rods.

Normally, this was as far as Uncle Phil got. The earliness of the hour, the rigours of the walk and the need to concentrate his bloodshot eyes on hooks and flies would take its toll on him and most times he would put down his rod, stretch out on a blanket and go back to sleep, snoring and farting.

In the others, there were degrees of angling expertise.

Mick and Uncle Rex were so adept that we kids believed they could whistle fish into their baskets. Blink was also a deft and deliberate fisherman, but as he grew older the cold took longer to leave his body and he caught fewer fish and bothered himself less about it.

What was obvious was how much he loved those mornings, even if he never said as much. It was always Blink who woke us and on the way to the river it was always Blink who urged us on.

My father loved fishing and never let his complete inability to master it affect his enjoyment of being out. Give him a hammer or saw and he was a tradesman's tradesman. But he couldn't catch fish with dynamite and a trapeze net.

The lack of conversation on the riverbank was neither a ploy to lull the fish nor a symptom of discontent with each other. It simply conveyed the Johns' natural solitude and their ability to be together, yet somehow totally alone.

I liked to watch the morning air billow from Uncle Phil's mouth and nose as he snored. I loved waiting for the long sound of his next fart.

I loved the flick and flash of the fishing lines, swirling like lariats in a cowboy movie, before they dropped daintily on to the surface of the water.

I loved the loop of the line in the air, the rhythm of it. I loved the calculation of the cast and the patient wait for a bobbing fly to suddenly drop beneath the water, taken by a trout fooled by string, wire and colour.

We'd start to pack up about 10 a.m., after five hours or so of being out, with the sun still battling to shrug off the night's chill.

We kids would count the fish, touching their slippery sides and poking at their dead eyes till the mush oozed out.

Back at the house, we'd kick off our gumboots and hang our coats and jackets on nails hammered into the shed wall. We'd jostle for a place in front of the fire and feel the weird pain that signalled heat returning to our bodies.

My mother, dressed in her church clothes, would have the kettle boiling and there'd always be a drop of Mick's rum in the bottom of every cup.

Mick said that you didn't breathe the air in the orchard as much as you tasted it. It was sweet with the mix of fresh apples and pears on the trees, and sickly with the rotting fruit on the orchard floor, some already pulped, some still with the teethmarks of possums.

A couple of times a week, he would head out after tea to shoot rabbits.

Dot would kiss him as he left. He held his rifle crooked in his arm and carried his rabbit sack and an old TAA flight bag.

Inside the bag was a thermos of tea, a sandwich and an apple. Mick never asked why Dot felt the need to pack fruit when he was going to be walking among trees groaning with it. He accepted it as one of the quirks he loved about her.

Under his belt he had a knife he used for skinning the rabbits or for finishing off those that his shot hadn't killed outright.

Mick could be gone for hours, even the whole night, but he didn't shoot the entire time. Sometimes, the same cartridges he'd loaded before leaving the house were still there when he arrived home.

He liked it out in the orchard, in the dark, in the quiet among his trees, hearing the rabbits but not always concerned with them.

On those overnighters, he'd wait until the sun was just appearing and the darkness was peeling back. The orchard brightened before him. Then he'd eat the sandwich, drink the tea and toss away Dot's apple.

When he was shooting, Dot could hear it from the house, cracking through the trees. She'd grown accustomed to it and was never anxious about any longer than usual absences. If he wasn't home by midnight, she knew he was staying out.

He'd come back in the morning, right after first light, with the rabbit sack either full or empty or inbetween and with him saying, 'Love, I could murder a cuppa.'

Dot would bring it to him, out to the big table, and sit with him as he asked her, always, how she'd slept and whether the shots had kept her awake. They'd stay out there together, talking quietly, and Mick would blow on the cup to cool the tea, the steam rising. Though they touched only occasionally, there was an intimacy to every brush of a hand or shared smile or nod of understanding as they mentioned the kids or the day ahead.

Sometimes, they'd shock the air with a hearty laugh.

'What's so funny?' one of the kids would say when Dot and Mick came back inside.

'Nothing. Don't you worry about it. Just finish your breakfast. All of it. Back you go.'

When the kids had left the table, Dot would fix Mick's breakfast. He ate slowly and plenty, dipping his buttered toast in his second cup of tea. He liked his eggs soft and salted.

Breakfast had to carry Mick through until evening and he was hungrier than ever after an overnighter.

'You should eat something through the day,' said Dot, more often than she could remember.

'Dot, love,' said Mick, 'I've got a bloody orchard out there full of food. Bloody full of it.'

Dot would tell him not to swear.

Soon he'd be gone again, into the trees, leaving her to deal with the skins and meat.

'I know they're a pest,' she said to Mick one morning, 'and I know that once you've got one rabbit on your land that means you've got a hundred or more of them. But I could do with you bringing a few more home.'

'Geez, woman,' he said, 'how much rabbit pie, rabbit stew, rabbit soup or rabbit mince do you expect a family to eat before we all start growing ears and buckteeth?'

'I don't want the meat. I want the feet. The fur,' she said.

Like most of the orchards and farms in the area, Mick and Dot's had bags of apples and pears, bottles of juice, and cakes for sale if Dot could be bothered baking, from a small roadside stall. All the stalls worked on an honour system. Drivers would stop, leave their money in a wooden box and take a bag of fruit or a bottle of juice, whatever.

'I want to use the feet to make lucky charms and flog them on the stall,' said Dot. 'And I want the fur to make little purses to sell.'

'Will people go for that? How much do you plan on charging?' asked Mick.

'Fifty cents a foot; a dollar or so for the purse. Mavis down the road and I have got it all planned. We'll share the takings, half and half, because we're supplying the rabbits and she's going to do all the sewing and clasp-work for the purses.'

'What about the feet?' asked Mick.

'What about 'em, Mick? They're feet. You know, a rabbit's foot is supposed to be good luck.'

'Not for the rabbit,' said Mick.

'Shut up. If we only sold a few each week it'd pay for the bullets you use up.'

'Depends on how good a shot I am.'

'Well, get better. Less overheads, greater returns.'

'Where do you come up with words like "overheads" and "returns", woman?'

'I'm a smart woman, Mick. I keep up.'

Mick didn't mind. The orchard at night was beautiful, spending an extra few hours out there was no burden to him, although he didn't take much notice of Dot's shooting instructions.

'Pop 'em between the eyes, Mick,' she said. 'That way the money-making areas won't be damaged.'

'I'm a fruit grower, not a bloody sniper,' he said.

One night, Mick killed a wallaby and brought it home at first light. He draped it across his shoulders and behind his head.

'What am I supposed to do with that?' asked Dot.

'Look at the feet, love, imagine how much good luck a foot this size could bring.'

'Somehow,' she said, 'I can't imagine anyone tying something that size to their car mirror or carrying it around in their pockets or handbags. Bloody fool.'

Mick told her not to swear, adding, 'They reckon a wallaby's ball-bag makes a good purse.'

Dot shook her head and went into the kitchen to put the kettle on. She watched out the window as Mick unloaded the wallaby onto the ground and grabbed his skinning knife.

As the dogs tried to break off their chains to get at the fresh meat, Dot couldn't wipe the smile of her face.

'They reckon a wallaby's ball-bag makes a good purse,' she muttered to herself. 'Bloody fool.'

chapter 28

Blink spent other times at the orchard, with and without Isobel. Dot would drive up to Launceston, never knowing whether she was bringing back one or both parents.

After Blink retired, she had a room set up for them at the house and they had the run of the place.

It was during one visit that Blink made a start on a garden.

There was good soil at the rear of the main house and all the way to Mick's machinery shed and the work kept him occupied while the women were inside and Mick was running the orchard.

Blink settled easily into it, working in the mornings when Dot's hearty breakfasts gave him energy. She had a brew ready whenever he took a break for a smoke.

The plot basked under plenty of sun and was well-drained. Dot thought it ideal for vegetables.

'Flowers, Dot,' said Blink. 'What you need is flowers.

'You've got fruit growing by the ton out there on the trees and you've got a decent enough veggie garden round the other side of the house.

'You need something you can just look at and like. You don't even have to worry about it. I'll take care of it for you when I'm down.'

He opted for roses as the main feature—gallica, damask, bourbon—and knew they would flourish in the cool climate and pretty much look after themselves.

He dug the soil and chucked any weeds he found into a wheelbarrow. When the ground was ready, he spread the stinking blood and bone which drove the dogs mad.

He also planted carnations and gypsophila, with flowers so tiny and fragile that if you touched them roughly, their petals threatened to melt between your fingers.

Blink kept a set of gardening tools in Mick's shed and made sure the blades were honed and the handles were secure. With a smoke in the corner of his mouth, he would sit on a bench, pick up each tool and give it the once-over. Dot bought him a pair of gardening gloves for his birthday but he never took them out of the packaging, always preferring to feel the earth in his hands.

By lunchtime, the aching in Blink's back and shoulder told him it was time to quit and he would stow his tools, make a quick inspection of the garden and then come in for a feed.

Much of the afternoon he spent walking in the orchard, gradually returning to a reasonable straightness.

He enjoyed the scent of the fruit and the goodness of the ground.

He'd meet orchard workers—Mick had told them it was fine to take a few minutes off for a chat with the old man.

'Not too long, though,' said Mick. 'There's still fruit to pick.'

As his mind increasingly failed him, however, Blink's afternoon strolls required closer monitoring. Isobel tried to walk with him but she always struggled to stay with his pace. And when Dot walked, it was never long before she began to worry about her mother back at the house and she'd also call a halt.

Eventually, the greatest concern had to do with the now regular change between Blink in the morning and Blink in the afternoon. In the morning in the garden, he was the Blink everyone knew, focused on the work before him and familiar with his surroundings. Later in the day, and sometimes as soon as he'd washed for lunch and sat down with Isobel and Dot in the kitchen, he seemed a stranger.

On the good days, there was a jauntiness to him and he could talk freely with Sam on the tractor or with a couple of young fruit-pickers or Mick, who'd pour Blink a cuppa from his thermos. On the good days, Blink floated through the orchard and knew it as well as he did the cut of roses or the fragrance of lilies.

But there were bad days, when his disorientation meant that places like the fishing spot, the storage shed and the big oak he used to sit under to have a smoke were new discoveries for him, offering no clue to his whereabouts as he wandered. On the bad days, the branches of the trees hung like German entanglements reaching out to snag him.

The sound of the tractor frightened him and he would hide from it. Pickers would see Blink behind a tree and they'd wave and laugh at the game they thought he was playing, not knowing that their presence terrified him.

He slipped on fallen fruit, cutting his palms and knuckles on the knotty roots of the trees as he tried to break his fall.

On the bad days, Blink surrendered, sat hopeless on damp ground and waited for the end to come. Someone would find him and bring him to Mick, who sat him down and helped him recover his senses.

On the worst day, a picker entered the storage shed where Mick was making notes on a clipboard and counting apple crates.

'There's something wrong with the old gentleman,' he said and Mick, immediately passing the clipboard to another worker and pointing out the tally, followed the first man out.

They found Blink sitting with his back against an apple tree. His boots and socks were off and, as Mick pulled Blink to his feet, he noticed how the old man's back was covered with leaves, grass, twigs and dirt and stained with squashed fruit. Dirt and fruit smeared the soles of his feet and squeezed up between his long toes. There was blood from small cuts on his heels and elbows.

'What have you been up to, Blink?' said Mick. 'Don't worry, it's only me. What's been going on, old fellow?'

Blink was silent. A bubble rose and fell in the corner of his mouth and his eyes were fixed on something far away. There were tiny pieces of wood and grass in his hair.

'You're a bit old for a roll in the hay,' said Mick. 'Who's the lucky lady?'

Blink turned his gaze towards Mick and stared right into his eyes, reliving what he had seen before.

'I felt like a movie projector or something,' Mick said to Dot in bed that night. 'I felt like he was watching something through me. Right through me.'

Through Mick's eyes, Blink had seen signposts bearing names like Noreuil, Mouquet, Lagnicourt, Pozieres, Bullecourt and he could make out young men with dirty and drawn faces.

He saw furrows dug too deep for flowers, filled with moving men.

Ponies caked in mud collapsed from exhaustion. Clouds of dark smoke rose and spread. Blink heard pitiful moans coming from where those same clouds had formed.

He saw wire, great spools and strands of jaggedness, and men caught on it.

Then he saw himself, running through the streets of a battered village, his rifle and bayonet pointed forward.

He leapt and dived for cover, first behind an upturned barrow, then into a hole in the ground, then behind the one remaining wall of a patisserie and into the interior of a bar where everything was smashed to pieces except, miraculously, a single champagne flute, which was defiantly intact, its crystal ringing to the impact of the shelling.

Blink saw other men doing the same as him and he heard shouts to press on, to advance at all costs.

Five men crossing a muddy road were swept from his view in a flash. Smoke rose to reveal a crater where they had been.

Then others leapt into that crater to take cover, their guns aimed up the street, firing as the men tried to keep their footing on the slippery remains of the new dead.

Blink saw himself again, and then Angus, crouched behind a slab of concrete blasted from a beauty parlour and falling to rest in a closed alley. They looked at each other and winked.

Then out they went into the open, running and firing, searching for the next barely safe haven behind which they could shelter for a few breathless seconds.

Blink saw Angus trip on a chunk of rubble and he saw himself pause in the middle of the street, then go back to see if his mate was all right. Angus gave the thumbs up.

Then Blink saw himself facing up the street and there were soldiers there, racing towards him and Angus.

Then he was flying, backwards, and he couldn't work out how this could be or why he was unable to find his feet or something solid on which to place them.

He landed on his back and, when he tried to brush himself off, he felt something sharp and painful in his left shoulder and, looking, he saw that it was bone, and that the bone was white and broken and his.

He tried to sit up, but immediately felt a dulling in his head that plonked him back down.

As he fell backwards, he saw the world in an arc, from the German soldiers up ahead of him, then above them to the ruins of buildings and to the wide sky, then to the ruined buildings behind him and then nothing, just a blackness that wasn't death but he felt had to be something close to it.

Mick, frightened, tried to break through to Blink. He shook him there in the orchard. Tears fell from Blink's staring eyes and Mick felt the sting of his own tears beginning to build.

Still staring, Blink looked into and beyond Mick's eyes again and saw himself take a small knife from the leather sheath on his belt and, as he lay wounded in the middle of the road, he lifted one knee so he could reach his boot. Then he started cutting at the laces and prising the boot from his foot.

The boot plopped into the mud and Blink lifted his other knee and started to work on the other boot.

His left arm hung slack and useless.

He cut away his puttees next, relieved as they unravelled and fell to the ground.

He hooked his left foot into the top of his right sock to peel it down and over his ankle and heel, over his toes and off.

He did the same with his right foot to remove his left sock.

Through Mick's eyes, Blink saw that he was on the ground, his feet were bare and bullets and shells were flying above him.

As German and English voices blended into a babble, Blink rubbed his feet into the mud of that road as he loved to do on the lawn back at Raymond Street. He tried to imagine himself there, or at Windmill Hill, or with Isobel.

He scoured and tore at the road with his feet and fingers, hardly feeling the fingernails pulling loose or the sharp stones and broken glass gnawing at his feet.

He was on his back, writhing, like other men in their death throes, except Blink was scrambling in search of life from the one place he had always found it. But the more he dug in with his feet, or grabbed with his hands, the less life he found and, still through Mick's eyes, he saw himself lose hope.

And then he was being dragged. He was being pulled away and he tried to discern faces and places until the pain in his shoulder sparked anew and became the only thing on which he could concentrate.

Then even that faded and he could no longer make out anything. The only sensation was the wet of the blood seeping through his uniform and the agony of bone blasted out of place.

The scene blackened, the sound dimmed and all diminished to a dot that became the pupil in Mick's eye.

'It's only me, Blink,' said Mick.

'Angus?' said Blink.

'No, Blink. It's me, Mick.'

Blink took a deep breath and the bubble of saliva popped and dribbled down from his bottom lip.

It was after this that Mick began to take an evening walk with Blink, ruling that if the old man was to walk during the day he had to be accompanied.

Many times during those walks, if Blink seemed fine, Mick would ask him what had occurred that day in the orchard.

But Blink mostly talked about the garden and what would need to be done the next time he and Isobel were down.

chapter 29

It's the first day of a long weekend and nothing seems able to stop Blink from shivering, not a blazing fire nor a hot tea. He says he's fine and still wants to go out to the land. I think it might be best if he stays with Gemma for the day, recovering by the fire in the lounge.

Determined, Blink wins out. Gemma hands over two packed lunches and two thermos flasks and I strap Blink into the car. He's quiet on the drive out, timid even, and I wonder whether the effort is getting to him, whether the new lease of life he has shown since we started digging has finally begun to wane.

We've been in the newspaper again, but the pictures are smaller and I allow myself some vain hope that this means we'll be more difficult to identify.

Gemma has done her best to shield us from her other guests, but it's not always possible. Most have been one-nighters, eager to leave, apparently content to tick off Queenstown as another checkpoint on their journey, a minor contribution to their travel stories.

Even so, I know our anonymity cannot last and I am becoming more certain of the need to go to the police.

That need has been steeled by an inclusion in one newspaper article of another quote from Isobel. It's nothing inflammatory or panicked. It merely reveals a longing that I know I am callous to ignore.

Of anyone, it should have been Isobel I told what I was doing. I know that now and suspect I've known it all along. Yet when I ask myself why I have treated her so disrespectfully, I have no answer and those I try to muster seem wretched and false.

Driving, I mull over what I might say to the rest of my family, what might convince people that my actions have always been reasonable and well intentioned. The more I consider the events of the past few weeks, the less reasonable everything seems to be.

I suppose what has stopped me from owning up is Blink. When I watch him working, watch him eating his lunch at the gravestones, bending like a supple young man to draw diagrams in the dirt, I see him gaining strength, not lacking it. I have loved that.

I turn the car off the main road and head up to the land.

'Are you sure you're okay?' I ask him.

'Never better,' he says. He's stopped shivering and looks ready for the day.

Cassidy and Alex have broad smiles as they stand by the trucks. There are six young people with them, who turn out to be students, and two other adults.

Blink is troubled by their presence.

'Who are all these people, Angus?' he says.

'Do you remember Cassidy and Alex? From the farm? The good soil?'

The names mean nothing to him and I can see he is annoyed by it. I feel a weight of sorrow for him because I know how much he enjoyed the time at the farm.

Alex approaches as I help Blink out of the car and she kisses him on the cheek. His face brightens and he points to her.

'Alice?' he asks.

'Close,' she says. 'It's Alex.'

'That's right, Alex, that's right. I remember now. Where's the big cow?'

Alex grins. 'We couldn't fit Frolic in the trucks, not with all this other stuff we had to bring down. She's back at the farm, grooming the top paddock.'

'Good soil up there,' says Blink. 'Grow anything you want up there, Alice.'

Leaving them, I move to where Cassidy is talking to a couple of the others. I shake his hand and shake my head.

'What the hell have you done here?' I ask. 'I thought *I* was the kidnapper.'

'Rural studies,' he says. 'A weekend field trip to examine the re-emergence of vegetation and soil on the west coast mining hills. Extra credit towards end of year marks.'

How young and smooth the students are.

'You've been cheated by your own teacher,' I say to them and they glance nervously among themselves.

'Not at all,' chips in Cassidy. 'What better way to gain insight into the changing environment than by getting in amongst it? That's the point of environmental studies.'

'I thought you said it was rural studies.'

'Same difference,' says Cassidy, 'and anyway, if you think I'm shovelling tons of soil by myself you've got another think coming.'

Cassidy makes the introductions and Alex and Blink join us. They are as close as kittens in each other's company.

'This is my grandfather, Mr Johns,' I tell the group. 'Everyone calls him Blink. Usually, he lives in a nursing home in Launceston—although I understand you already know that—but before that he was a gardener, and that's why we're here. To create a garden on this piece of land. Try not to laugh.'

One of the students raises his hand as if he's back in class. 'Nothing grows here,' he says after re-introducing himself as Barry. 'Nothing's grown here for donkey's years.'

'I know,' I say. 'I don't mean it's going to be easy or even possible. But we could try. It's very important to my grandfather that I try.'

A girl speaks next. 'What sort of garden, sir?'

This time Blink steps forward. 'A flower garden,' he says, 'and I think it could be beautiful. I think Angus will like it. It's for him.'

Blink wanders away. He kicks his boot into the ground. All attention is back on me.

'I don't know exactly what Cassidy told you,' I say, 'but Angus died in the war and my grandfather was able to live because of him. He wants to honour him.

'And even though I'd really like to thank you for coming all this way, I wouldn't blame you if you decided to leave.'

No one moves.

'Thanks again,' I say, then Cassidy chimes in.

'Now, it's been a long, slow and early drive down so who fancies a cuppa before we start?'

Hands shoot up.

'And after that, Blink will tell us what he wants us to do. Is that fine with everyone?'

A girl approaches as we drink. 'I'm Stephanie,' she says. 'Are you named after the other Angus?'

I think about this for a few seconds.

'Yes and no,' I tell her.

'Don't worry about me, people, I'm fine,' yells Cassidy, sarcastically, from over at the trucks. There are four in all,

Cassidy having driven one, Alex another and Dave Atkins, who turns out to be Barry's father and a mate of Cassidy's, the third. Dave's wife Denise was behind the wheel of the final, smaller truck.

'I didn't know you had a heavy vehicle licence,' I say.

'I got mine the week after Alex got hers,' says Cassidy. 'The smartarse. It's good for school, to drive the buses. And at home we're always on the tractor, the bobcat, that kind of thing.'

'But you grow proteas,' I say, gently mocking him.

Three of the trucks are piled high with soil. It looks like thick chocolate, like good turds, as Blink says, and has been covered and held firm for the trip down by canvas tarps.

A bobcat and rotary hoe have been chained onto the fourth truck and take up most of the available space, although all the trucks have a plentiful supply of shovels, forks, wheelbarrows and sundry other items, including bags of fertiliser.

'How are you going to water it?' asks Cassidy.

'It rains every other day down here,' I reply. 'That's our biggest problem. Too much rain and we'll be washed away. I just have to hope. We've been lucky so far.'

We unload two steel ramps and put them in place at the back of one truck. Once we've confirmed the ground is stable, Cassidy releases the chains, jumps into the bobcat starts it up and guides it carefully down the ramps.

Not far away, Blink is draining a second cup of tea and gabbing easily to Alex and the students, a couple of whom move towards us.

'Blink says we need shovels,' says Linda, a largish brunette. Cassidy passes them out and the students return to where Blink is waiting. He leads them up the rise.

'Where'd you get the trucks?' I ask Cassidy.

'Well, the three big ones belong to the school,' he says. 'The fourth one is hired for the weekend and it's going to cost you a fortune because I've reserved it and the other trucks for next weekend as well. The rotary hoe and bobcat are mine. Need a shovel?'

I leave Cassidy and walk to the others. Once at the gravestones, Blink, touching people on the shoulder, directs them to specific areas of the field. Alex is with Barry and Linda chopping their shovels into the ground, churning it just as Blink and I have been doing for days. There is no question as to who is in charge. Blink has complete control and moves between the various groups, instructing all the way.

Cassidy is on the bobcat, further levelling the ground, and Dave is working the rotary hoe. They can work many times faster than the rest of us and the field quickly changes texture.

I can see groups of two here and three there involved in their work. There is laughter, the odd swearword. It feels good to be here. It feels real and possible.

The unease I felt at the involvement of the students is still there, although I trust Cassidy's judgment and am buoyed by their ready acceptance of Blink and the way they seem to hang on his every word.

To them, there is none of the frailty that I have seen in him.

He kneels and picks up lumps of earth and he points out its strengths and weaknesses. He is convincing them, showing them the earth recovering and, just as it inspires him, he uses it to inspire them.

Nevertheless, there are occasions when I see Blink move away on his own.

At first, I mistake it for fatigue and, at one such time, I too take a break from my digging.

'It's not a bloody chain gang,' I say, and Cassidy laughs.

'Tell that to Blink,' he says.

We both look up and catch Blink studying a sheet of paper and pointing out areas of the field. He scratches his head, then turns a full and slow circle before returning his attention to the paper.

It occurs to me late in the afternoon that Cassidy, Alex and the rest of the group will need somewhere to stay.

They can't be expected to drive back up the main road in the dark and return again early tomorrow, then repeat the process on the long weekend Monday.

Fortunately, Cassidy has everything planned.

'The Education Department has a camp on the other side of town,' he says. 'All the schools use it. It's not the flashest place in the world but there are dorms, bunks, hot water, a kitchen. A van for excursions. We'll be quite comfortable.'

'Do you want to come around to Gemma's for a few drinks?'

'Love to,' he says, 'but we can't. Teacher's responsibilities and all that. Anyway, Bill will have brought something down, just to keep out the night air. I'll be right.'

Clouds darken over the mountains and the light of day is fading fast. Blink puts his shovel down and wanders over.

'As long as it doesn't hammer down tonight, we should be able to spread that soil tomorrow. A nice shower won't hurt but no storms, thank you very much,' he says.

That night, Gemma comes up trumps with the evening meal.

Vegetables steam on the plates and there is a juicy roast in the centre of the table.

A young couple join us for dinner. They're holidaymakers from Melbourne, doing the cliché "around Tasmania in a week" trip. They'll go home in a few days believing they've seen all there is to see of the place. They seem decent enough. He's a builder and says this is his first break in two years. Even then, he says, it'll only be for a week, ten days at the most, because there is so much work to be done at home and plenty of competitors happy to take it off him.

His wife is a school teacher, or had been until a week or so ago when she entered the final month of her pregnancy and began maternity leave. She doesn't eat much and is content to pat or stroke her big belly after every small bite. Her husband downs his food as if he is the one eating for two.

Blink eats quietly, uncomfortable with the presence of the newcomers. I wish they were staying somewhere else.

Gemma plays hostess with practised ease, serving extra potatoes to Mark—that's his name—and pouring water for Eloise, the wife. The conversation comes around to what Blink and I are doing in Queenstown and I say we're here for a few days revisiting places Blink had known as a child. They're happy enough with the explanation and the talk turns to lesser things, like the weather and the football. Finally, they excuse themselves.

'How did it go today?' asks Gemma as she packs up the dinner plates and stacks them beside the sink.

'It went well,' says Blink, although Gemma had been talking to me, 'but we've got to get all that soil down and then get more of the stuff to finish the job.'

'More?' I ask, picking up a tea towel as Gemma fills the sink with water.

'Those truckloads will do for some of the job,' says Blink. 'It's good soil, but we'll need just as much again to make sure, to really give the land, all the land, all it needs.'

He yawns and it sets off a chain reaction.

'Why don't you two head up as well,' says Gemma. 'It sounds to me as if it was a very busy day and you'll face the same tomorrow and Monday.'

Blink wants a whisky and, to be honest, so do I. Bed can wait.

I lead the old man into the lounge where a fire is crackling and the big chairs look as soft as spring clouds. I pour three drinks and pass them around.

'The police paid me a visit today,' says Gemma.

I put down my glass. From her apron, she takes a sheet of A4 paper. A photocopy. It's not a "Wanted" poster, like in the cowboy west, but may as well be. Blink and I are listed as missing persons, but our images make me feel like an outlaw.

'Jesus,' I say, 'did they suspect anything?'

'No, I don't believe so,' says Gemma. 'The posters would be in all the police stations. I don't think they know you're here.'

'What about the door-to-door service?' I say.

'Don't worry,' soothes Gemma and she pats my arm, 'that's just Morrie's way. There's not much for a policeman to do down here these days, so he fills in the hours with the odd personal visit. Don't get in a pickle. I just thought you'd better know.'

I get up out of the chair and move in front of the fire. Picking up a poker, I nudge the logs and a few sparks shoot out. Black marks on the rug show it is not the first time.

'Morrie likes a chat and he loves a sly drink,' says Gemma. 'He would have had the same conversation with many others in town, especially those of us who run the B & Bs and the hotels. It stands to reason.' She is trying to placate me but the news has stirred me from my weariness. I know I won't fall asleep easily tonight.

Blink carries on as if nothing is out of the ordinary.

'Early start tomorrow, Angus,' he says. 'I'm tired now.'

He tries to hoist himself from the chair but his bones and muscles seize on him. He falls back and chuckles.

Gemma and I take an armpit each and lift Blink to his feet. He can walk but it is an ungainly style and his joints click as he goes. He looks at the stairs as if they are Mount Everest.

The rain comes during the night and when we arrive at the land the next morning we are greeted by Cassidy's team and a lot of mud. The ground needs time to settle and then we, or Blink, can assess the damage.

Blink doesn't seem too fussed. Whether friend or foe, he says, rain is a part of gardening and it's up to the gardener to make the best of it.

The new soil is still secure under the tarps and Blink reaches his hand under one canvas and pulls out a clump. He studies it for a second then carefully puts it back, as if not a single handful can be wasted.

Another shower, not too heavy but decisive enough, makes up our minds. Today is a write-off and we must hope for better luck tomorrow.

Gemma is still in her Sunday best when Blink and I pull up outside the house. She says Mark and Eloise are still there. The weather is keeping them off the west's treacherous roads. They're in the lounge and I say hello. They return the greeting but I notice how their eyes fall. Over the next few minutes, I come to feel more than their suspicion. I feel their knowledge.

'Please don't say anything,' I say. 'We just need a little more time.'

Monday is bright. For the west you could even go so far as to say it is balmy.

Blink is up before me and already half-dressed, needing my help only for his boots and the fiddly shirt buttons.

He has energy. The longer we are here and there is work to be done, the more he seems to be improving.

I, on the other hand, feel more uncertain. There is now not a skerrick of doubt that Blink and I will be found. I must call my family soon.

Cassidy has the trucks parked at the edge of the land.

'How'd you get them up the slope?' I ask him.

'It was okay. Not as bad I thought. It's quite firm underfoot, despite the rain. The ground has absorbed the water, not been drowned by it. Must be a good sign, I reckon.'

'What did you do yesterday?'

'Excursion,' he says. 'Took in the mine, drove around to look at the hills, that kind of thing. School stuff.'

'And everyone's still fine with this?' I ask.

'Give it a rest, master criminal. We're here, aren't we?'

Blink says the soil can go on and Cassidy doesn't need to be told twice. He activates the hydraulic tipper on the first truck and, moving slowly, spreads brown soil over the ground.

Instructed by Blink, who easily resumes his supervisory role, Bill takes the second truck around to the western border of the land and activates the tipper. Denise does the same thing at the eastern edge. Soon, three loads of soil have been dumped and wait to be spread further.

The students have shovels and rakes in their hands. Cassidy starts up the bobcat. Alex and I grab a couple of barrows.

'It needs to be five or six inches deep,' says Blink. 'Don't spread it thinly to cover more area. Five or six inches is what is required.'

Once more he takes the sheet of paper from his trouser pocket, refers to it and slips it away. He repeats that process every few minutes, sometimes taking a pencil from behind his ear and spreading the paper across his knees to make notes.

He is driven by the work. Whereas the rest of us see only the tools in our hands and the dirt at our feet, Blink envisions what will become of it. I think he likes what he sees.

We work throughout the morning and the dimensions of the three mounds dwindle. By the time we sit for a welcome lunch it is clear that we have made good progress. Blink is bubbly and strolls the newly covered ground.

'Angus,' he says. 'Blood and bone, fertiliser. We'll need a bit of that to give it a kick along. And we've got to get the rest of the ground covered.'

'Once this soil runs out we have to wait until next week,' I tell him. 'Cassidy and the kids have to be at school tomorrow.'

I explain this in the full knowledge that the chances of Blink and I being here next week are becoming slimmer with every hour.

Blink puts a finger to his chin and turns away to face the area still to be covered. Again, he takes the paper from his pocket.

'No matter,' he says at last. 'There's plenty we can do in the meantime. We can put the fertiliser in. Plenty we can do.'

By about three o'clock, Cassidy says he has to start thinking about packing it in. 'It's a bitch of a road and I have to get this lot home.'

I agree and tell Blink.

'The ground will need a day or so to work out what's happened to it after we've bunged the fertiliser in,' he tells me. 'You and I can keep on with that. It'll keep us plenty busy over the next few days.'

'What have you got planned?' I ask him. 'What's on that sheet of paper I see you looking at all the time?'

The old man beams. 'Soon enough,' he says.

I suppose I could look at the mysterious paper at any time—when Blink's asleep, or when he's downstairs chatting to Gemma.

But I don't look at it. I don't want to pre-empt him or ruin his moment.

Also, I don't want to be confronted by what may be an act of sheer folly. If that's the case, I want to be spared that knowledge for as long as possible.

Meanwhile, Mark and Eloise have left the B & B.

'I cleaned their room,' says Gemma. 'They left a newspaper. It was open at the page with you and Blink.'

I look at the clock and know that every second that ticks by is my time running out.

chapter 30

Whenever I was in the Raymond Street garden with Blink, he made sure I knew I was there for work and not play.

He'd demonstrate the use of the little trowel to ease out the weeds without damaging the roots of the flowers or shrubs. He'd show exactly where secateur cuts needed to be made, the width and depth of seed furrows and the distance between the seeds to be sprinkled into them.

He'd show where the wooden stakes went and how to train the tomato vines. He squeezed out splinters and thorns and didn't feel a thing.

Years of putting his hands in the soil had turned his fingerprints into thin black tracks, starting and finishing somewhere and nowhere and anywhere.

He always scrubbed his hands as clean as he could because Isobel wouldn't serve dinner without checking them first, sometimes sending him back to the tap and basin.

I remember Blink once taking my hand and placing it in a shallow hole I had just dug. I felt the damp coolness of it.

'Feel that,' he said. 'Look at that.' He wiped my hand down his shirt.

Things are really starting to happen up at the land—I just wish Blink and I could stay to see them progress and reach their fruition.

We've been working so hard, especially Blink, to prepare Gemma's land for the garden. It will be a shame to call it quits, but I can find no option other than to notify the police.

Maybe it would have come to nothing anyway. Maybe this was always a waste of time.

As much as I know I should, though, I can't bring myself to tell Blink that it's over. Not yet. I fear what it might do to him because his zeal has astounded me.

We've spread and mixed in most of the fertiliser and Blink says he can't wait for the truckloads of soil to come and for the land to be completely covered.

Cassidy's soil has been all I hoped for and all Blink knew it would be. The fertiliser and other nutrients are at work within a splendid host and Blink says he can tell, even at this early stage, that the ground is drinking in the new goodness.

I should tell him that the new soil won't be coming. He deserves to know everything. But when he says there'll be no harm done in giving the land an extra day to its own devices, I decide to delay my bad news.

Anyway, a break will be good. We need to get away from the land. It won't be an escape, not like leaving Pleasant View, but a day off. That's all.

'What shall we do tomorrow, then?' I ask him as Gemma busies herself with dinner preparations. The aroma is of chicken roasting.

'I think a day off is a very good idea,' she says. 'As long as you're not under my feet all day. Go out and see the sights.'

'Sights?' I say.

'Yes, Angus. There's plenty to see and plenty to do in the west. You only have to look.'

I ask her about Strahan and she describes it as a town of many charms. 'People say it's beautiful but I sometimes think that's because there's no mine there and there's so little else around here that you can call beautiful,' she says. 'I suppose you could always go fishing there.'

Blink, who had been on the verge of sleep, is suddenly awake. 'Fishing? You would have loved our fishing mornings down at the orchard, Gemma,' he says.

'I remember them,' I say to myself, my mind crossing time to locate a scene in which there is a fishing spot, Uncle Phil is asleep and farting, and the air is filled with the sound of lines swishing and landing gently on the water.

But then uglier images begin to invade that scene and I try to shake them out.

'Angus, are you all right?' asks Gemma.

That night, Blink sleeps soundly.

There was a time when Macquarie Harbour was known only for cruelty. As a penal colony, it was the worst.

Strahan is on the harbour and its modern charm belies a dreadful past.

Today, the postcard images of cruise ferries and benign inland waterways as well as a healthy sea fishing industry are the more familiar face of Strahan. It has adapted well to tourism.

We have come to fish, although the freshwater fishing is known to be pretty ordinary. The best catches of trout, redfin and blackfish are found further east, in the lakes and streams of the midlands and high country.

The fishing really makes no difference to me. I don't care if we return to Queenstown with our esky filled or empty. It's the day off with Blink that matters most.

He sleeps part of the way from Queenstown and so doesn't feel the dips and turns of the demanding road. When finally we pull up beside the river, neither of us is in any hurry to assemble and bait the rods I hire from a tackle shop on the waterfront.

We find a good spot, sheltered from the wind with a view of the town and the other activities on the river.

A mother and her two children take up their position on a grassy bank just across from us. It's a cool day but the boy, the older of the two, has thrown off his boots and socks and is rolling his tracksuit pants above his knees. His white shirt is already splodged with dirt from a spill taken while lugging his rod and bait box along the water's edge. Unperturbed, he soon shows he is skilled in the functions of fishing—skewering fat worms and grubs on a silver hook, checking the sinkers and then, satisfied, casting out onto the water.

Throughout all these processes, he never stops asking his mother to watch him.

She is a pretty blonde and is also barefoot, her shoes and socks rather more neatly stored than her son's. Her jeans are rolled to just above her slender ankles. She has an easy way with the children and it is a pleasure to watch her divide herself evenly between them, as well as establishing her own authority and independence.

As I prepare our rods, the boy, who looks maybe nine or ten and has the whitest hair, reels in an untaken bait. When he recasts, he aims further left, telling his mother he can see a spot where insects are crowding above the water.

Meanwhile, the boy's sister is all action, wanting to do everything at once. She wears a purple shirt under an open jacket and I can see the shirt has "Surfers Paradise" on the front. Because she has managed to get her pants soaked within a few minutes of arriving on the river bank, she cavorts in her underpants. Her pants are hanging from a tree branch to dry. Like her brother, the girl doesn't feel the coolness of the day. She skips happily between him and her mother.

The water is as clear as a mirror and at times eerily calm. Boats moored to wooden bollards are reflected perfectly.

A tall man walks a small yapping dog. Fathers and sons in tin boats chug up the river. Their rods, erect and spindly, like aerials, are wedged into holders screwed on either side of whining outboards.

There are plenty of people around. A policeman strolls by, blowing the steam off his coffee, but his presence doesn't concern me. Blink and I are just another pair of tourists, two fishermen enjoying the lazy sag of a couple of Gemma's canvas chairs. We sip our thermos coffee and I can taste a hint of rum in it.

For the first time in several days, maybe weeks, I feel quite relaxed. Blink has a blanket over his knees and a peacefulness to his wrinkly face.

'Excuse me, sir,' says a small, high-pitched voice beside me. It is the white-haired boy and he points excitedly at Blink's rod, which is twitching.

I find it mesmerising, but neither Blink nor I make any move to reel in the catch.

'Tell you what, son,' I say to him, 'you bring it in and whatever it is, it's yours.'

chapter 31

I can never get it fixed in my mind. What came first? Was it the noise? I suppose it had to be the noise.

What I do remember is how I thought someone had thrown a rotten apple or pear at me, like they'd been hiding behind a tree, waiting to play a practical joke. We always had fruit fights in the orchard.

Or, I thought, maybe a bird had shat on me.

When I wiped my hand across my face, it came back red with speckles of white through it.

I called to Mick but for some reason I couldn't hear my voice, so I hit my ear a couple of times to see if that would clear the ringing. I shook my head. There was an unfamiliar taste in my mouth and a strange smell in my nostrils.

I tasted a grittiness and thought maybe it wasn't fruit or birdshit after all. Maybe I'd fallen face-first into the slippery ground, dazed myself and swallowed some dirt.

My hearing came back at last. I could see the smoke billowing from the chimney of the main house.

'Almost home, Uncle Mick,' I said, before spitting in an effort to clear my mouth.

Mick was staring at me. He was caught in the fence and his body was twisted.

He had one eye open and one shut, just like Blink sleeping. Then I noticed, as all my senses came back to me in a rush, that there was only one eye. The other was gone.

It was Mick's blood and bone that had splashed over me. I reeled, scratching at my face, using my shirt to wipe away what I could.

I spat again, now knowing what it was I had been tasting, and I retched.

The sound of Mick wheezing and whimpering brought me back. His fingers were twitching, plucking the barbed wire like guitar strings. The front of his pants was wet.

I fell to my knees and saw that Mick's rifle had landed stock down and come to rest against the wire. His sack was nearby and I could see the fluffy back end of a rabbit poking out.

The wheezing became a small whistle. Then it stopped altogether and Mick was absolutely silent and absolutely still.

I heard a bellowing and for an instant thought it was me. It had started low and built as it climbed, emerging from the throat and mouth ungodly and unhinged.

But it wasn't me. I was panting, not bellowing, and suddenly found it hard to move, like something had hold of me, squeezing the breath out of me.

It was Blink and the howl had come from him, long and terrible, until he ran out of breath.

Blink inhaled and roared again and when at last he stopped he held me tight into his chest, which was heaving.

He kept saying, 'Angus, Angus, Angus' over and over. I know now that Angus was both Mick and I at that terrible moment.

Blink wiped my face with a handkerchief and I became aware of the presence of others, I could hear their gasps and cries.

I saw Dot being held by my father and Uncle Rex, and I heard her yelling to Karen and Terry, 'Get back inside the house! Get back inside now!'

Blink had firm hold of me and my mother had to use all her patience and strength to take me from him. She touched every part of me, checking that I was all there.

Blink went to the fence and slowly untangled Mick's sleeve and his pants from the wire and, limb by limb, brought him to earth and lay him down.

'It happened twice to him, to your grandfather,' says Gemma, 'and both times he could do nothing to prevent it. It happened to Angus during the war and then to Mick.'

'I know, Gemma. That's why we're here,' I say.

Gemma tells me again that Blink talks to her about the war, about Angus and himself.

'He talks to me about the wire, almost as if it's human. Evil but human. And now I know why. How did—what was his name, Mick?—how did it happen?'

'I've just told you,' I say, annoyed. 'The gun went off as we went through the fence. It was an accident.'

'Yes, I know that,' she says. 'What I mean is, why were you there with Mick?'

Once again, I go back. I was there because Mick had always promised to take me out potting rabbits. Promised me for years.

He warned me about the cold nights and that we might not see anything but I wanted to go anyway. Finally, he took me.

'You were on your way back home when the accident happened?' asks Gemma.

'Only a few yards to go,' I say. 'We'd been out all night, no trouble. It was great. Just had to get through the fence and we were home for one of Dot's breakfasts.'

I stare into Gemma's eyes and find the understanding there. She holds my gaze.

'I fell over,' I tell her, my voice breaking. 'Going through the fence I slipped and the gun went off. I was just a kid.'

And Gemma knows for certain what I have never told anyone. She knows that I was holding the gun.

'Just for a minute,' I say. 'I just wanted to hold it for a minute. Bugged him all night about it.

'"Wait till it's daylight," Mick told me. And as soon as the sun came up, when we were on the way back, I bugged him again and he gave in.

'I took off with it, even though he told me to wait and slow down. He caught me as I was going through the fence.'

The family gatherings ended with Mick's death.

Soon after, Dot sold the place and she and the kids moved into town.

No one blamed me for the accident. No one shunned me or spoke unkindly of me, or to me. Typical of the Johns family, no one addressed it openly at all.

At first, I welcomed the silence. I was still so young, a boy barely into double figures, unable to really comprehend what had happened that morning coming through the fence.

With time, however, the silence became unbearable.

I tried to discuss it with my mother, thinking that her family background would make her more likely to want to talk honestly and openly, but she was as reticent as the others.

'Accidents happen. Especially with guns,' she said. 'Life goes on, son.'

My father wanted no part of it. He held things inside, which was the Johns way, hoping that eventually enough time would allow a kind of healing to take place.

I followed his lead and caged it up. I put Mick's death behind me and my life went on until, a few years later, I looked back and there was space.

'It seems to me that space has closed up,' says Gemma. 'How else to explain what you are doing down here, what you've been trying to do for Blink?'

'We didn't really notice it at first,' I say, 'but after a while there was no avoiding what was happening to Blink. He was losing us more and more after Mick's death. His mind just retreated. There wasn't enough room for all of us anymore.

'There were times when he knew us but they became rare and brief. As for me, one day I disappeared from his mind completely.

'It had been coming for a while. I mean, I was in short pants when he first called me Angus but it was a gradual thing. Some days he saw the real me, some days he saw Angus and he'd start rattling on about the war and all we'd been through together.

'But pretty soon after I killed Mick, I was Angus all the time. Just as I am to him now.'

'You didn't kill Mick. It was an accident,' says Gemma, with kindness. 'How did you react once Blink started calling you Angus all the time?'

'It was, it is, a privilege,' I say. 'When I was younger, I either didn't understand or simply took it as a nickname, a pet name, and it made me stand out, which every kid loves. And in a family that doesn't make a fuss of each other, or of anything for that matter, standing out was rare.

'As for Blink's war stories, I suppose I saw them as any child would, as storytelling, as adventures.'

'What did the rest of the family make of it all? They must have wondered what was going on,' says Gemma.

'Isobel cooked, cleaned and coped, as she has always done, and as for the others, well, Blink might talk to them if they were there but he hardly ever knew them.

'It's just that I always had that extra connection and I maintained it by following my grandmother's advice. When Blink's mind went and I was there, I went with him. I was Angus and he was always pleased to see me.'

It feels like I've been talking for hours.

Gemma speaks only occasionally. She knows the need to be unburdened and she is attentive and sympathetic.

I explain that Dot saw me in the street one day and crossed the road, avoiding any contact.

'I don't think it was an act of hatred or stubbornness,' I say. 'I think she simply didn't want to confront that kind of sadness again. She used to be so happy.'

I tell Gemma how, as Blink aged and descended even further, I learned more about Angus, the war, about Angus dying on the wire.

'I never learned the full details of Blink's debt. He'd never tell me. He just assumed I knew because to him I was Angus. But I became aware of my own debt. I saw what Mick's death had done to Blink and I knew my part in that and how much I owed him.'

'So, does Blink see you as a ghost?' asks Gemma.

'I don't really know,' I say. 'I just know he sees me as Angus and that it is utterly real to him.'

Upstairs, I check that Blink is asleep and cover him lightly with a blanket. I touch his shoulder. The movement of it stirs him and he wakes, looks at me, grins and says, 'Angus.' Then he nods off again.

chapter 32

Blink and Angus are in yet another French village, Lagnicourt. They're digging.

Blink is so worn by the monotony of it all that at first he doesn't feel or notice the blood seeping through his boot, which has been cut through by the spade.

When he does notice, he feels faint but manages to limp away towards a medical officer.

It is mid-April 1917 and the farmland around the village is trenched and pockmarked with deep holes from bombardments. The buildings in the village have taken a pounding.

When Blink returns to his company, his almost severed toe has been stitched and dressed. He has new boots and they rub.

The wound stings and he fears it might go septic but he doesn't say anything. He's seen much worse happen to blokes at the front.

The fighting is as fierce as Blink has experienced at any time during the war and the Germans overrun the village. Next morning, four Australian battalions take it back.

'I'll tell you something for nothing, Blink,' says Angus as the two men catch their breath and check their gear. 'When all this is over, I don't reckon they could get me back to France if they paid me.'

'They are paying us,' responds Blink, 'and you can't say you haven't seen the wonders of the French countryside.'

'I should have stayed at home,' says Angus.

'I've gone from one bloody great hole in the ground in Queenstown to a series of other bloody great holes twelve thousand miles away. There's bugger-all difference.

'Here or at home, there's no trees, no flowers, just this dug up, gouged-out, shelled and bombed ground. There's a fight every day, it rains like billy-o, it's freezin' in winter, the flies and the mud will drive you off your nut and you can die at any time. I was a mug to come here. I had all this at home.'

Blink laughs at his mate's exasperation.

'How'd we get out of that carry-on?' asks Blink, rolling a smoke. 'I mean, have a look at us all. What a bloody shambles.'

Angus turns left and right and sees soldiers beaten down by exhaustion, the weight of their experiences on every face.

In some places, groups of weary men slump together as if they have been dumped there from a height above the trenches. Their arms and legs entwine as they rest against each other, each bloke holding up another. They look to have neither the energy, nor desire, to move.

A boy soldier reaches out his hand to Blink. Blink kneels, passing him a just-lit cigarette. The soldier inhales but when he hands back the smoke there is a coating of blood gradually painting the paper.

'You keep it, mate,' says Blink. 'I've got plenty.'

The cigarette drops from the soldier's hand and his body shudders and stills. The smoke falls between the duckboards and rests on, then sinks into, the brown water.

'Silly when you think about it,' says Angus that evening. 'I've seen more of France than Tassie.'

'Same here,' agrees Blink. 'But when I get back I won't be in any hurry to travel anywhere or see anything other than home. If there's one thing that being a marching soldier teaches you, it's the joy of sitting down and staying still.'

Angus swallows a mouthful of his meal, grimacing as he does. 'Bloody hell, I reckon the Germans are supplying our food,' he says.

'If we were up at Windmill Hill, this time of year, this time of day, everything would be blindingly bright,' says Blink. 'The sun hits the river, sending out shafts of glare, but when you get used to it and take everything in, everywhere you turn has a sharpness to it. You wouldn't think anything could be so clear.

'I sit up there at the end of the day, whenever I can, and I just stand and turn slow circles.'

'Get any strange looks?' says Angus.

'Dunno,' says Blink. 'I've never noticed anybody else there.'

Angus says there is nothing like Windmill Hill in the west.

'Mind you, there are days when you can love the place. People hate the rain but, if you're up at the copper smelters, just the knowledge that it is raining is a help.

'And the feel of the rain hitting you, those first freezing drops after all the heat of the fire, that's really something to feel on your body.

'There's even a beauty to the hills, I reckon. They're being buggered up by the mine, there's no doubt about that, but when the light's right there's something about them. I don't know, it's almost brave.'

'I can stand at Windmill Hill and imagine I can see all the world,' says Blink.

'All the way to Queenstown?' says Angus.

'Yep, and further.'

'Well, my place is the last one on the left up Bain Lane.'

'Bain Lane? You're havin' me on.'

'Shut up and give us a sip of your tea.'

The village of Bullecourt had already been the scene of one battle.

Being back there wasn't easy for anyone, although Blink cursed himself for giving words to his thoughts that the war might be tougher for the Germans.

'What are you talking about, Johns?' said a private with galloping acne and a mouth full of broken teeth. 'Harder for them? How do you come up with that? Christ, we've had to cross oceans and rivers, tramp across the countryside, slog our way through mud, ice and water, bury our mates along the way in towns we can't even pronounce, take orders from the bloody Poms who don't know their arses from their elbows and whose only command tactic is to send us in first, live like rats with rats, and you reckon the bloody Hun has had it tough!'

Blink was silent. He hadn't said what he meant. What he meant was that the Germans were so close to home. It was just there, walking distance away. They could leave now and be there in a few days. Home was so close they must have been able to smell it. How difficult that must be.

'I'm glad we're a long way from home,' he said to himself.

Sergeant Stanley O'Connell, who was a tailor from Brisbane and who had belied the gentility of that profession with the urgency of his fighting, walked up to the soldiers.

'Get some sleep,' he said. 'We're going in early.'

'What do you think, Sergeant?' asked the private. 'Johns here seems to think we should feel sorry for the Hun.'

Blink went to object but O'Connell spoke up. 'Frankly, I've seen their dead and our dead and they all look the same to me. And I'll look the same if it's my turn tomorrow. So will you and so will they. I feel sorry for us all.'

'That's not exactly inspiring,' said the private.

The sergeant ignored him and addressed Blink. 'Private Johns, was it? Private, what do you do at home?'

'I'm a gardener, Sir.'

'No shortage of blood and bone on the Western Front,' said the sergeant. 'I reckon that when this war ends you'll be able to grow a botanical bloody garden stretching all the way across Europe. It'll look bloody lovely.

'What's more, if I had the uniforms of all the men who've gone in to make that blood and bone, I reckon I could sew a coat large enough to wrap the world inside it.'

Blink was in a rear trench. Looking up, he saw three small birds trying to ward off a larger one.

'Is that an eagle?' he asked Angus, next to him.

'Dunno. Might be. Maybe a falcon or a hawk.'

'Aren't they the same thing?'

'Dunno. Might be a kite.'

Blink kept his eyes on the sky. 'Whatever it is, those little ones are doing a grand job of keeping him at bay,' he said.

'Yeah,' said Angus. Everywhere you go there's a fight.'

Blink tried to sleep but never quite dropped off and, when it was just before three in the morning and the whisper spread to prepare for a push, he was relieved he no longer had to try.

Windmill Hill

Angus, on the other hand, was mightily frustrated. 'I want to know why it is that when I try to sleep I can't and when they come to tell me it's time for a fight all my eyes want to do is close.'

Forty-five minutes later, the order came and the attack began. It was the beginning of a long and dreadful May fortnight.

When it started, the number and density of the German entanglements were such that the men trying to get around and through them were easy targets. They didn't even need to be lit up by the flares. The Germans simply had to fire where they knew the wire to be and men fell.

Eventually, however, cuts were made in the wire, the German trenches fell to the advance and the Australians felt a surge of confidence.

The village, however, proved more difficult to capture. Over the next several days, the Australians took two steps forward and one step back, then one forward and two back. It was laborious and costly. The Germans resisted furiously.

Then Blink's war ended. And so did Angus's.

Blink was being dragged. Angus had him by the collar and they lurched across the ground back towards their own lines.

Blink was dazed and his shoulder wound pulsed with pain but he could hear Angus yelling, 'Come on, Blink. It'll be right, Blink.'

Angus couldn't be sure, though. There was blood sprayed over Blink's face and he had a glazed expression, one he'd seen on too many dead and dying men.

The blood on Blink's uniform had spread so that at first glance—and there was no time for anything more—it appeared he had been shot close to the heart.

Every now and then, Angus would check to see if he was dragging a corpse and it was during one of those moments that he noticed Blink was barefoot, that his boots and socks and puttees were gone. Angus could not figure out for the life of him how that could have happened.

Angus found cover behind a wall. An advertisement for a gramophone was torn and discoloured. He stared at it and tried to remember a song his mother used to hum in the evenings. The tune wouldn't come to him.

He hoisted Blink against the wall and saw that the wound was to Blink's shoulder, not below.

'Lucky bugger,' he said, smiling. 'It's a boat trip and home cooking for you.'

He ruffled Blink's black hair and dust and small stones flew in all directions. Blink closed his eyes and breathed deeply. It hurt him.

'I can walk,' said Blink. 'Where are our bloody lines?'

Angus pointed beyond a row of thick entanglements. 'Get through them and we're right,' he said.

It started to rain and the drops hit the ground and exploded, mimicking the bombs and shells.

'Where are your boots?' asked Angus.

Blink saw his bare, cut and filthy feet and was perplexed. He couldn't remember. The big toe he'd almost cut off at Lagnicourt was hanging by gristle.

'Couldn't have been a mine,' said Angus, 'otherwise those ugly feet you're looking at wouldn't be there at all.'

'Maybe my boots surrendered,' said Blink, trying to make light of a situation he couldn't fathom.

'Anyway, the supply sergeant will probably dock your pay for another pair of new boots. Probably go crook at you for being careless. I've heard him moan that blokes who get their heads shot off are a waste of perfectly good helmets.'

The sound of firing became louder and closer. Angus checked his rifle. 'Where's yours?' he asked Blink.

'I must have lost it when I went down,' said Blink. A jolt of pain seared through his shoulder and he felt faint but then collected himself. He vomited a vile green liquid and coughed.

'Charming,' said Angus. 'Come on, we've got to go.'

They ran towards the wire, bobbing and twisting in a deranged dance.

Loss of blood and the pain in his shoulder had weakened Blink, but not enough to divert him from the singular aim ahead of them. Get through the wire. Just get through the wire.

He couldn't really feel the ground beneath his feet, which was probably for the best because he was running over metal, glass and other sharp, jagged objects blown there by the bombing. Nor could he take the time to feel for the men he was running past and over. There were so many of them.

He expected to be among them soon as the firing increased in intensity and the Germans continued to counterattack.

He was so vulnerable with his bootless, sockless feet, his wound, the bone poking through, his lack of a helmet and the loss of his weapon. Yet he and Angus made it to the wire and rushed through a cutting. Blink began to believe that today might not be his last after all.

He ran, turning to see Angus on his knees firing and then getting up to run himself, all the time urging Blink forward.

A shell exploded close by and seconds later Blink was stuck fast, drenched with sweat and blood. As he caught his breath and thanked his lucky stars he was alive, a stickiness formed in the corners of his mouth. It hurt to move his head and he saw that his feet were bleeding and that some of the nails had been ripped clean out.

The pain in his shoulder worsened by the second, but above all of that, above the sound of warfare, the yelling of men, the clatter of guns, there was comfort in the knowledge that he was alive. He ignored the pain and turned to Angus.

'Mate, mate, mate,' he said, heaving the words. 'Couldn't go back and get my boots for me, could you?'

It took a second or two, maybe longer, for Blink to realise that Angus wasn't there, that the man beside him was another soldier.

Blink couldn't work out where he was. His head spun and he fought off unconsciousness. He tried to move his right arm but it snagged and it was then he knew. He was on the wire.

And once he knew that, he searched again for Angus and found him, also on the wire a few yards away, dangling there, slack and still. His rifle was snagged and his helmet was gone. No, there it was, upside down on the ground. Blood streamed from Angus's neck and throat, poured off the wire and formed a pool below him.

Other men were on the wire with them, men Blink didn't know or recognise. There was no mistaking Angus or his fate.

Again Blink tried to move but waves of pain surged through him. Grief filled him and overflowed. He rocked there, strung up like a puppet, overcome and entranced.

He howled—an outletting of misery and agony so great that men on both sides paused and looked to the men on the wire.

Blink lost consciousness then, his full body weight sinking back into the entanglement.

In a small room in Queenstown, with the morning sun just beginning to think about rising, Blink Johns rubs his eyes.

There is a pencil and notepaper on a small table between the beds and it is an effort to reach them, but he manages. He also takes another, much larger sheet of paper from a bedside drawer. Pulling his knees up beneath the bedclothes, he rests the papers there. The pencil shakes in his hands. Referring to one paper, he draws on the other with slow, deliberate strokes.

'It's coming along, Angus,' he murmurs.

chapter 33

Morrie Hinds had been posted to Queenstown not long into his police career. It was hardly a glamour station but he saw it as a place where he could build up a healthy nest egg in the two years he'd planned to be in the west.

Everything went to plan, so well in fact that when his two years were up he requested a couple more and the department was only too pleased to oblige.

Morrie saved and saved, his only major expenses being his weekly groceries. He lived rent-free at the station and there was nothing else in Queenstown on which to spend his money.

Assistant officers came and went but the longer Morrie stayed the more he felt at home.

When he met Patricia Jones—sister of publican Tom "Delilah" Jones—who'd come home to Queenstown to nurse her ailing parents, Morrie courted her and married her in a ceremony held in the back bar of the pub.

Morrie knows Queenstown can be a hard town but he also believes he has its respect. Morrie's losing his hair these days, but he refuses to opt for a comb-over, even though he once checked out the look in front of the bathroom mirror at home.

'Forget it,' said Patricia, 'it's going, love. Let it go with some dignity.'

He also has a paunch but it hasn't gotten away from him and, in fact, Patricia has admitted to her girlfriends, including Gemma, that she quite likes it.

'I like a bit of meat on a man,' she says at morning teas. 'Something to grab onto.'

The policeman has known Gemma Woodley longer than anyone else in Queenstown.

Morrie stayed at her B & B for a weekend before his permanent move to the west, thinking it sound police work to get a feel for a place that was going to be his home for a while.

Staying with Gemma eased his mind a little about Queenstown. In Gemma, he found normalcy and decency and he chided himself for falling for the bulldust from his colleagues in Hobart, who warned him about the Wild West and told horror stories about the place.

For the most part, he'd found the people hard-working and deserving of the small rewards they enjoyed and the diversions they pursued, messy as that might end up for him. Anyway, only occasionally did one or two go too far.

After almost twenty years in uniform and almost twenty years of local surveillance ranging from Delilah's pub on Saturday nights and church on Sunday after cleaning out the cell, to weekdays chatting and visiting and checking that all is as it should be, Morrie Hinds feels wise to his town.

He's always granted a similar wisdom to Gemma Woodley and she's been on his mind lately. Her behaviour the other morning, when he popped round with the pictures of the two missing men, wasn't like Gemma at all. Until this morning, it had him stumped and he'd tried to explain it to his wife earlier at the breakfast table.

'There was something different about her. Nothing too out of the ordinary, but I noticed it. As if Gemma was hiding something. Not like the Gemma I know.'

Now, seated behind his desk, looking at the pictures of the missing men, Morrie has his answer, thanks to that nice couple from Melbourne.

'Danson, Mark and Eloise,' he says, referring to his notes. 'That was good of them to call.'

Peering out the station window at a greying sky, Morrie Hinds cannot see much good in the day. He knows what he has to do but procrastinates, which is not in his nature. He makes a cup of tea and opens a packet of biscuits. Iced Vo Vo, his favourite.

Eventually, after an hour or so of further dithering, he swings out of his chair and locks the station door behind him. He checks his watch, adjusts the car's digital clock to his time, then flicks on the wipers as a misty rain begins to fall. He switches the wipers up a notch when the rain becomes heavier.

As he drives, he looks to the sky again and sees ominous grey turning to black. In the background, he hears thunder.

The rain is heavier still as he turns into Gemma's drive. The town's in for a soaking, he thinks.

He checks his watch again as he climbs out of the car.

It's just after noon. Gemma will have the kettle on.

chapter 34

It's good to be up at the land again, just the two of us
The work we've done so far would have been impossible without the help of Cassidy, Alex and the others and, as Blink and I walk to the graves, where fertiliser bags are stacked, it is equally impossible not to feel a real sense of pride and achievement.

Matching that, in my mind at least, is an undeniable sense of defeat. I have brought Blink to the land for the last time.

He wants to work and I haven't the heart or the courage to refuse him.

'Cuppa before we start, I think,' I say to him. He has perched on a couple of bags of fertiliser and is stretching his legs out in front.

He takes a healthy swig from the cup and says, 'We're in for some rain, Angus.'

I follow his pointing finger and see dark clouds moving towards us.

Blink cuts his fingernail along the thin plastic of one of the bags, a six or seven-inch slice, and shoves his hand inside. As I have seen him do countless times before with seeds and soil, he scoops a quantity of the stinking stuff and holds it under his nose. To my untrained senses, I see and smell only waste and decay. Blink sees and smells a key to life.

'Get a good whiff of that good stuff,' he says, holding out the lumpy muck.

'No thanks. I can smell it from here and have no desire to get any closer.'

'I love what happens, what's going to happen here,' he says. 'I love that you can take something as weak as this ground, cover it with good soil, fertilise it with stuff like this—muck and blood and bone—and make something of it.

'I've been a gardener all my life, Angus, and people have told me that flowers are the making of a garden. But it's the soil that is the real making of it. Without it, there is no garden.'

He takes another sniff, then replaces the fertiliser in the plastic bag.

'This is going to be something,' he says. With that, he reaches into a pocket and brings out a sheet of paper, which he opens out and holds before me.

'That,' he says, 'we're going to make that.'

It is a rough sketch, a blueprint of sorts.

'I have a bigger, more detailed plan back at Gemma's,' he says. 'I've been working on it for a while. I'll show you when we get back.'

The sketch is detailed enough for me to grasp his concept. Blink has drawn the field, our field, with two crosses marked in the centre to represent the graves. Extending out from that central point, he has indicated flowers to be planted in specific beds and in specific designs. There are places for roses, carnations, camellias, daphne, dahlias, hydrangeas and more. He has also made room for grassed areas which I assume to be walkways. Within each of these is written the letter B.

'B for bench,' he says, when I ask.

'Will all these things grow here?' I ask him. 'Even I can tell this part of the world is no friend to flowers.'

'They were here once,' he says, 'or at least they could have been here.

'If something's missing for long enough, people will just forget about it. Maybe that happened here.'

He says there has to have been a time when there was no mine, no furnace, no logging and no foulness in the air sprinkling poison on and into the ground.

He says that this was a place of forests, lush grass and strong soil and if the land was able to support these at one time, then a few flowers shouldn't pose too much of a problem now.

'But there has been a mine,' I interject, 'there have been furnaces and all those other damaging things. You need only look around at these hills to see what happened here. Who's to say what can grow anymore?'

'I say,' says Blink, and I believe him.

He puts his arm around me and says, 'Angus, it's all for you.'

He stamps his boots a couple of times as if trying to thump out pins and needles. Then he holds the wheelbarrow steady and I open and empty fertiliser bags until the barrow is full.

I don't care that the work is futile.

When Blink falls, everything falls with him.

The clouds turn black, the rain builds and within minutes is tumbling down on us. It falls so heavily that the ground quickly turns to mush. Thunder booms.

I hear a faint cry behind me and turn to see Blink on the ground, his feet scrambling for grip in the mud.

He must have hit his head on the wheelbarrow as he was falling because there is a deep cut on his cheek and another above his eye. The rain rinses the blood away but new blood flows afresh and it is dark red.

Water runs down my back and front, into my boots, soaking my feet. It fills the barrow, dilutes the fertiliser and turns it into an ugly, stinking soup.

Blink reaches for the handle of the barrow for some leverage but, as he tries to pull himself to his feet, he succeeds only in sinking the metal stands into the mud. The barrow tips onto its side and, off-balance, Blink tips with it, slipping and falling once more.

I rush to him and he peers at me through the rain and the blood washing into his eye and down his face. His expression is one of total confusion. His boots won't grip and neither will his knees or elbows. Every move he makes sinks him further into the mud.

I grab him by the armpits and he yells, frightening me, 'There! Over there! Get behind there!'

He is pointing to the upturned wheelbarrow and I drag him to it, his feet kicking.

'Stay here,' he says, 'we'll stay here.'

The unrelenting storm drenches the land and washes it away.

I hold Blink, cradling his head, and we shiver. I tell him I can help him to the car but he doesn't understand.

'Too far,' he says, 'too much in the open, too much danger. We'll stay here until we're relieved. They've got to be coming soon. Just keep your head down.'

He babbles. He shakes every time the thunder claps and he drives his head deeper into my chest. Occasionally, he sneaks a peek over the rim of the wheelbarrow. 'Not yet,' he says.

I try to stem the flow of blood from the two cuts. The one on his cheek has already begun to bruise.

I am crying as I watch this man return to feebleness, when so recently he has been so strong.

It is hours before the storm breaks. Water tumbles from my clothes as I lift Blink to his feet and survey the scene.

The new soil that had been laid is gone. There are clumps, like fresh cowpats, dotted about, but mostly the land is now a mass of streams and small lakes sprung by the storm. The chocolate earth has melted.

Water drips from the two gravestones and I am struck by the appropriateness of their presence.

Carefully, I hold Blink as we trudge down to the car. I ease him inside. He watches me walk around the front of the car and he's still staring when I take my spot in the driver's seat.

'You're not Angus,' he says. 'Where's Angus?'

chapter 35

Gemma helps me to bring Blink inside.

He seems not to recognise her or his surroundings. He is stooped and shuffling and cold as we guide him into the lounge and stand him by the fire.

He makes no protest, shows no emotion at all. We strip off his wet clothes and Gemma wraps a towel around his waist while I go upstairs to dry off, change and bring fresh clothes for Blink.

A few minutes later, I'm sipping a whisky and beginning to explain to Gemma all that has happened. She dries Blink's hair.

It's then that I recall the police car in the driveway and it's then I see a policeman in the room, also cradling a drink.

'I've rung Dr Hayes,' says Gemma. 'He'll be right along.'

By that evening, Blink has been admitted to hospital. His breathing is fluidy and he won't stop shivering, even under the thick hospital blankets.

Morrie Hinds is understanding. Gemma has filled him in on Blink and me and, though he considers the situation serious and needing to be rectified, he no longer regards it as criminal.

There are routines that must be observed, of course: notifications that two missing men have been found, paperwork to be completed and signed, a call to Launceston Police to confirm a time for our arrival home. He drives me to the station.

Inside, I ask the policeman whether I can make my one phone call.

'That's only in the movies,' he says, passing across the telephone. 'Call as many people as you like. They'll all need to know. Then we'll go and check on Blink.'

I thank him, adding, 'You sound as if you know him.'

'Gemma has a way with words,' he says. 'He sounds like a decent man and I don't think you're exactly Public Enemy No.1.'

It had been Isobel's decision to place Blink in a nursing home.

She hated having to do it, seeing the failure as being in herself rather than in her husband's faculties and capabilities. Yet, as much as she hated it, she knew it was the right thing to do. She could no longer provide the type of care he needed. What shocked the rest of the family was her decision not to go with him. She chose to remain at Raymond Street.

'Pleasant View is a lovely place,' she'd told us. 'It's ideal for those who need care, like Blink. But I have a way to go before that day.

'And Blink doesn't really know me anymore. He sees me in the house and sometimes I feel as if there's some recognition, but it never lasts long.

'If I could care for him, I would. You know I would. But I can't and he deserves better than that.'

She visited him often, aware each time that he had no notion of who she was, and it hurt her when Blink would talk to her about Isobel, never realising that was who *she* was.

He would talk about Angus, always about Angus.

After a few hours, she would kiss him goodbye and wait for the taxi to return her to Raymond Street, which eventually felt so huge without him that she sold it. It broke her heart.

In her new tidy unit, she would drop off to sleep and dream of Blink when he was strong and his own man, dream of him in connection with the sweet scent of an orchard, or trying to keep his balance on the deck of a boat, or working in the Raymond Street garden.

Or when he was a small boy and she was a small girl who has just fallen into a fishpond and is laughing so hard and loud that Isobel is wakened from her dream.

I've forgotten how quiet Isobel's voice has become and there is a weariness in her questions and responses as I try to explain what I have done and why.

'He's an old, old man,' she says, so quietly I have to have her repeat it. 'He's an old man. He was in a home. He was there for a reason.'

A few simple words. They sum up all I have done wrong.

All my talk of gardens, of Angus, Queenstown, making amends, all the explanations I offer and try to convince myself are plausible, ring hollow as I speak to my grandmother and listen to her quiet voice.

She understands my good intentions. What she cannot fathom is how I ever believed they could end well.

'But you should have seen him,' I tell her. 'It was like he'd come back to life and was his old self. He had a purpose and he knew it.'

'Does he know who you are?' she asks.

'No.'

'Does he know where he is?'

'No.'

'Does he have a purpose now?'

'No.'

'Then nothing has changed,' she says.

I tell her I'll be bringing Blink home soon and will stay in contact. She asks me how I am coping and again I apologise for putting such a strain on her.

'I just didn't think it through. I didn't think of anyone else,' I say.

She softens and I love her for it. She says people make mistakes and as long as Blink and I come home safely, things will sort themselves out.

We say our goodbyes and I am about to hang up when Isobel's voice is back on the line. 'Would it have been a good garden?' she asks.

I still have Blink's draft. I open it out to reveal his rough drawing of the garden. The paper is crumpled from folding and unfolding and is now smudged in places. His handwriting is spidery, like a child's.

Blink knew the difficulties of trying to garden here and he also knew—and this paper confirms it—that such difficulties might be overcome. I hold the paper before me and realise it stands for what is possible.

There are no gardens here because, like Blink says, if something is left for too long, people will forget. There are no gardens here because people have given up growing them, not because they cannot be grown.

'Are you still there?' asks Isobel.

'It would have been a wonderful garden,' I say.

I crumple the paper and toss it into Morrie's bin.

The Queenstown District Hospital is a no-frills facility, a red-brick, single level group of buildings built in the 1960s.

One building is used for maternity and postnatal care and the sound of babies squeals through the hospital day and night. A second building is a nursing home for Queenstown's elderly. The third, and the one in which Blink is housed, has five six-bed wards. There is a small theatre for emergencies, most of which have their origins at the mine. Usually, patients are transported to Hobart or Burnie for other operations.

Blink doesn't need surgery. His need is rest.

I ask myself what will happen to him now. Is he about to be consigned to the type of unaware and weakened state that had been his lot at Pleasant View?

Or will he regain the kind of enthusiasm, even youth, that he's displayed during these weeks in the west, with Gemma and me up at the land?

He breathes heavily, asleep with one eye shut and one eye open. There is still the sound of fluid bubbling in his lungs, although the pneumonia which had been feared has not come to anything.

I stroke his rough hand. Around his wrist is a plastic band bearing his name and his birthdate. I see just how old he is and again my selfishness is brought home to me.

Furthermore, I feel a new fear, one of disappearing.

'You're not Angus,' he had said. 'Where's Angus?'

The recollection of those words cuts through like a scalpel. For if I am no longer Angus, who has been so clear in my grandfather's mind since I was a child and who he has recognised in me, and as me, then who am I to become to him?

Am I to be just another stranger in his life? If so, has Angus been killed again?

There is one final question and it is the one that most fuels my fear.

In seeking to make amends, for Blink and for me, have I succeeded only in increasing our debts to a magnitude that can never be repaid?

Blink heaves on. His sheets and blankets are tossed about.

I hold his hand more firmly and try to will my apology into him and, at the same time, search for any response at all that might indicate his forgiveness.

chapter 36

When I call them from Gemma's, the reaction of the others in the family is hardly unexpected and swings between nonchalance and near-hysteria.

The latter is provided by my mother, who berates me for letting the family down and putting Blink at risk, not to mention—and she mentions it a couple of times—the considerable embarrassment I've caused.

I don't interrupt. I let her bluster away until her voice and her emotions come down from the clouds and settle at a more stable level from where she can tell me she loves me and is there for me if, and when, I need her.

She has every right to be furious and upset. They all do, which makes my father's good humour such a welcome relief.

'I knew you had the old bugger,' he says. 'I knew you were up to something that day you brought him out to my place.

'I figured you'd be okay but it's caused a bit of a stir around Longford.'

'In what way?' I ask him.

'Oh, the pictures in the paper of you and Blink. People out here, once they found out, seemed to like the fact that I was the father and the son of a couple of runaway celebrities.

'I've never been so popular. Got plenty of work on as a result. Cash too. Couldn't take him away again next year, could you?'

I am grateful for his casual acceptance and wish it could last. I tell him about Blink's condition, that his father is once more a broken man.

'Mate,' he says, about to surprise me again, 'Blink's never known he was broken. Blink's never known anything was wrong. We all knew because it was happening in front of us. But not him.

'Drop out my way when you get back and I'll buy you a beer. Got a trifecta up the other day and it paid pretty well. Who else do you have to ring?'

'Uncle Rex. Stevie. And Aunty Dot,' I reply. 'Isobel offered to do it, but I think I should.'

'Dot, eh. Well, you can have that on your own.'

I have spoken to Dot maybe half a dozen times since the day Mick died, a generation ago, the day my debt to Blink Johns really began.

'Hello, Aunty Dot, it's me, Angus.'

'Who?'

'I'm sorry, Aunty Dot,' I say, cursing my error and correcting my name for her, though it sounds alien to me.

'It's a bit late to be sorry,' she says. 'What have you done with my father?'

'He's in hospital in Queenstown.'

I hear her gasp.

'He's all right, he's had a bit of a turn but he'll be home in a couple of days. I just wanted to tell you what's happened.'

She bawls into the phone and I have to hold it away from my ear. When I put my ear back to the phone, there is a sobbing at the end of the line.

'Aunty Dot,' I say, not really knowing where to go with the conversation, until she makes it clear that I'm not going anywhere. Dot unleashes years of anguish.

I can do nothing but listen and accept my part in her pain as she reels off that it is my fault Mick is dead, that it is my fault that Blink's downhill spiral gathered such pace from that day, that it is my fault that all the good went bad.

She traces everything back to that moment coming through the fence just a few steps from home. She vents all her grief and frustration, her voice rising in anger, falling in sorrow, cracking in disbelief.

'And after all that, after all you've done, you take Blink away and drive us all mad with worry and make him sicker than he already was. Are you happy now? Are you finished now? What else do you want from us?'

'Aunty Dot. I just wanted to help him. I wanted to help us all.'

'I think you've helped everyone enough over the years,' she says. 'I think you can stop now. Just bring my father home.'

There is silence but neither of us has hung up. There is more to come.

'What's that name he calls you?' she asks.

'He calls me Angus, although that might have changed.'

'Does he know who you really are?'

'No. Not for a long time. And I'm not sure he even knows me as Angus anymore.'

'Good,' she says. 'Then you've lost someone too.'

I have no means of closing the chasm between us. I tell her Blink will be back soon and that I will contact her.

'Don't bother,' she says, 'Mum will keep me up to date. You just bring him home and then leave him alone.'

'Goodbye, Aunty Dot. I'm so sorry.'

The connection ends abruptly.

A week after entering hospital, Blink is back in the front seat of the car. Every now and again he gives a thick cough.

'I used to get the 'flu all the time in France,' he says, unexpectedly. 'I was always coughing up muck, always being sent to the doctors and being put in a bed for a couple of days.'

'Is that right?' I say, wondering if Blink knows who he's talking to, or whether's he's just talking.

'It wasn't just me either. Beds were full of blokes with the 'flu. People back home probably didn't know that, probably thought hospitals were just for the wounded. There were plenty of wounded, don't worry, but the army was just as concerned with blokes coughing up phlegm as coughing up blood.'

I turn the car into Gemma's drive. He chats on.

'During those couple of winters, I've never felt cold like it. Miserable bloody place, dug in day and night. Sometimes I even looked forward to attacks because at least they took my mind off the cold. And if a bloke was wounded, it meant he got a hospital bed and maybe a trip home. Get yourself killed and at least you didn't have to freeze anymore.'

New guests have booked in during the past few days and only one of the four bedrooms is vacant. Gemma has spent the morning cooking and cleaning and helping her guests to settle in. Tomorrow, she can put new people into Blink's and my room.

'The army couldn't have afforded 'flu to spread through the lines,' says Blink, still at it, 'and back there in that place it would have spread fast. That's why, once you were heard hacking away and spitting up globs, they'd whip you out of the lines quick-smart.

'You have to be healthy to be a soldier. You have to be fighting fit and in the prime of your life in order to be in top shape to go out and get killed. Silly business, if you ask me.'

He talks all the way into the house and is seated at the kitchen table when he finally stops. Not once has he called me Angus or asked my name. He shows no sign of knowing Gemma and while I know she understands, there is still hurt at his innocent rejection of her.

'We'll leave early tomorrow,' I tell her. 'I suppose I should settle my account.'

'Later,' says Gemma. 'First we'll have a bang-up farewell dinner, a drop of the good stuff and we'll concern ourselves with formalities when the time comes.'

'We'll be on the road before breakfast,' I say.

'I'll be up,' she says.

I hold Blink's head and swing his legs onto the bed.

He is light, as if there is nothing of him. He feels the way he did when we first came to Queenstown. I lean him back on his pillow and when he coughs I reach for a glass. He spits.

'I knew a nurse once,' he says, wearily, 'I knew a nurse whose job it was to come round the wards in the morning and check the phlegm jars. Check them for blood, hard chunks, colour, all sorts of things, even Germans for all I know.

'She'd hold up the jars, smell them, shake them. What a bloody job. The doctors had to do it too, but I figure they were men and could stand that type of thing.

'Not a thing for a woman. Geez, the things those nurses saw and had to do. Phlegm, bone, blood, rot, stench, dysentery. You couldn't help but love those nurses. They had more guts than us.

'It doesn't take any thought at all to go out and get shot. But I reckon it takes real gumption to want to look after those men who cop it hard and messy. Real gumption, I reckon.

'Men fell in love with nurses all the time and you couldn't blame them. Some were bloody gorgeous. Christ, there were some ugly ones but.'

'What about you?' I ask him. 'Did you fall for a nurse?'

'Every time I went into hospital,' he says, smirking. 'Didn't do me any good. It's not the most romantic thing to try and squire a nurse while she's got hold of your phlegm jar, or worse, your balls. And anyway, I had someone at home waiting for me.'

'Who was that?' I say. He looks at me blankly.

I stroke his hair and, all talked out, he falls easily to sleep and I stay and watch him for a few more minutes.

He looks old, but peaceful, and I am relieved that the trauma he's endured has not robbed him completely of the memories he holds dear.

I am selfish about him not knowing me, however, whether as Angus or myself, and it forces me to ponder whether the loss of this influential man in Blink's life is a good or sorry outcome.

'Usually, I don't mind it when my visitors leave,' says Gemma the next morning. 'I quite like the idea of not having anyone to miss and only new people to welcome. I've become used to that.'

She studies the sky. It is clear to the mountains, and the drive up the coast to Burnie and then on to Cassidy's place should be relatively easy.

'This time, though,' she continues, 'this time I do have someone to miss.'

I hold her hands. She moves forward to hug me and she squeezes hard and with real affection.

'I think if we achieved nothing else, we did give this old house another story to add to its collection,' I say, releasing her. She moves across to where Blink is standing.

'Goodbye, Blink Johns, it's been a pleasure to know you,' she says, wrapping him in her arms and catching him off-guard. His feet shuffle on the gravel as he fights for balance.

'Goodbye, missus,' he says. 'Aren't you coming with us?'

'No, Blink,' she says. Her voice is a sad whisper. 'This is my home. Don't you remember?'

He doesn't and she lets him go. I recheck the boot to ensure I've packed everything but I don't really have my mind on the job. I have to keep going back to the start until I decide that what is packed is packed and what is left behind stays behind.

Strapped in, Blink stares ahead. I take out my wallet.

'Here you are, Mrs Woodley, time to balance the books.'

She refuses to take the money.

'Gemma, please,' I say, pushing it into her hand and closing her fingers over it, 'this is one debt I can pay.'

Another hug, another kiss on the cheek, a last look, a last smile, a last wave.

Queenstown fades, growing smaller and smaller in my rear-view mirror until, just like that, it is gone.

It's not long before we are nearing the turn-off leading up to Gemma's land.

'Let me see up that road,' says Blink.

Puffing and panting, not helped by the slippery going and his still weak condition, Blink makes it to the gravestones, where he reads the inscriptions and puzzles over the few bags of fertiliser still there as we'd left them.

'Someone's got a plan for this land,' he says, patting one of the bags. 'They've had a good go already.'

'Not the best land for working,' I say.

'Maybe not at the moment,' he says. 'The land needs to work on itself for a while before it starts to work on anything else and, to me, it looks like that might be happening. Big job, though.'

'Too bloody big,' I say. 'What could grow here? Have a look at the place.'

'Anything, everything,' says Blink. 'Use enough topsoil, enough of this stuff'—he pats the fertiliser—'use enough nous and you could do something with a spot like this.'

I am washed over with despair.

'Roses there,' he says, pointing. 'Hydrangeas, carnations over there. Grass is coming through in patches so you could do a bit with that. It's tough country but it'd come up.'

'Blink, we have to go,' I interrupt. 'We have to drop the car off at Cassidy's. Do you remember Cassidy and Alex?'

He coughs and his eyes water as he hacks away. Recovering, he carries on. 'People say flowers are delicate and fragile and, fair enough, they look it. There are some that are just too fussy and too much trouble. But there are plenty of hardy, tough flowers that have all the colour and all the beauty and oodles of strength. They'd grow here. Big job, but they'd grow here.'

Back on the main road, we pass a sign which arrows Queenstown behind us and Burnie ahead.

'The best bloke I ever knew came from Queenstown,' says Blink about two hours later.

'Who was he?' I ask, my heart lifting. 'Another gardener?'

'He was a miner. Angus Bain. Short, tough, freckly, ruddy. Had the clap once, poor bugger. Geez, did he ever look after me when we were away. He got knocked in France.'

I let him reminisce, ecstatic that Angus is still there in Blink's mind, if not in me.

'Do you know that he saved my scrawny arse twice? Twice. And on the second time, that's when he copped it.'

Cassidy and Alex are on their balcony, pictures of high fashion in their dressing-gowns and slippers. It's still early.

The kids run to meet us and Alex heads inside to put the kettle on.

'You'll like these people,' I say to Blink. 'They're good people.'

'What's your name again?' he says to me. 'I can't remember your name. What is it?'

Windmill Hill

I switch off the ignition and as the kids push their noses and mouths against the driver's side window, I turn to Blink and say, 'My name's Angus, too.'

'Get out! Really? Well, I'll be blowed.'

chapter 37

I am shocked to find a news crew at Launceston Police Station.

We're barely out of the car when a young, heavily made-up reporter thrusts a microphone under Blink's nose and asks him, vigorously, 'How do you feel, Mr Johns?'

Blink grabs my arm and spins me around to face into the city. He points beyond the buildings and up towards Windmill Hill. I can see the transmission tower.

'Can you take me?' he asks. 'Take me up there.'

The reporter is confused, then annoyed, and makes the throat-cutting motion to indicate filming should stop.

As well as the media, there is a family welcoming committee and I hug them all, assuring them we are both safe and reasonably well, all things considered.

I have to report in at the station and a polite constable is manning the desk. He confirms Blink's and my identities and says Morrie has rung from Queenstown to check whether we've turned up or done another runner. No charges are laid.

'Morrie says to say g'day to you and the old fellow,' says the constable.

My mother holds Isobel's hand and my father stands to one side. Rex is here, but not Dot.

'She's already up at Pleasant View,' says my father.

There is a white van parked outside and the words "Pleasant View Home for the Aged" adorn its bonnet and back door.

'Can't I take him back?' I ask the constable.

'I'm sorry, but no,' he says. 'We need to see Mr Johns into the care of the nursing home again. You are welcome to follow him to Pleasant View, but he must go in the van.'

I hate the thought of it, the finality, but also know I have no grounds to protest and should not have the gall to try.

Isobel and my mother fuss over Blink, tidying his hair and tucking his shirt into his pants. He submits himself to this, showing no sign of recognition.

I sign some papers I am too tired to read, but which the constable assures me are routine. A few minutes later, a man in a white coat takes Blink by the arm and leads him towards the van. A door slides open and the driver folds out two metal steps.

'He wants to go to Windmill Hill,' I say. 'Can you go via Windmill Hill? It will only take a moment.'

The man shakes his head. 'It's a bit out of our way, Sir. We've got to collect another old lady yet and she's on the other side of the river.'

Blink treads slowly up the little steps and I feel myself about to fall. Someone takes my elbow and I turn to see it is my mother. Blink is in the van and the steps are retracted.

The door is still open and I lean in to Blink and say, 'I'm sorry.'

Once again, the driver tells me they have to leave. His colleague is seated beside Blink, who peers out at me.

The town clock chimes. The ghost of Stocky Johns trying to get out.

I rap on the driver's window and he rolls his eyes.

'Please, take him to Windmill Hill. He's been through so much. It won't take long.'

'I'll try,' says the driver. 'Now, if you don't mind, Sir.'

He starts the engine, pulls away and I am empty.

I bid a hasty farewell to my family and a few minutes later I am at Windmill Hill, waiting, turning circles, trying to see what Blink sees when he comes here. When he came here.

I wait throughout the afternoon, until the sun begins to set and long shadows pierce the city below.

The van never comes.

The nurse is plump and trying to cram far too much into too small a uniform.

Her cap is pinned at what might be called a jaunty angle, but there is nothing else jaunty about her. In charge of the reception desk at Pleasant View Home for the Aged ever since the stricter regulations have come into being, her days off never seem to coincide with the days I visit. She rules her roost and is always particularly dictatorial with me.

The ease with which I had removed Blink from Pleasant View has forced the nursing home to strengthen its security procedures.

New visiting rules have been adopted, calls are monitored, registers signed and labels worn at all time. All my doing.

The staff pay particular attention to me and their constant close presence frustrates me, a situation I try to ease by reminding myself how fortunate I am to still be able to see Blink at all.

I try to lessen the threat they see me to be. I use taxis. I leave my wallet and keys at reception. I smile and say hello. Yet each week, an orderly is only ever a few steps away, indiscreet, as I sit by Blink's bed or push him around the grounds in a wheelchair. Occasionally, my frustrations boil over.

'There's no point arguing the toss with me, Mr Johns, there's nothing I can do,' says the fat cow at reception. 'You made your bed. Now you must lie in it.'

I try to make my point as I have done every week of every month since our return from the west. 'Look, you know I come by taxi, so even if I did want to take him away I couldn't, because I have no transport. And I don't want to take him away. I have no intention of taking him away.

'All I'm asking for is some privacy. Just him and me. Surely, that's not too much to ask.'

'It is too much to ask, Mr Johns,' she says, 'and furthermore, you know that to be true. I wish you would stop this carry-on every time you come here. There are rules and they are there for a reason. I think you know the reason, Mr Johns.'

By now, our west coast escapade has diminished in notoriety.

Apart from the news footage that first evening, there was one newspaper article reporting our safe return and then a subsequent feature article in a weekend edition, for which I was interviewed and sought to present fuller details of what I had done and why.

Something must have been lost in the translation. Edited back to bare bones reportage, the article served only to make the whole affair seem more spurious.

Worse though, time has seen Blink diminish. His health is becoming noticeably more precarious.

chapter 38

Gemma Woodley has good reason to smile. Everywhere she casts her eyes she can see people enjoying each other's company and the grand occasion. She is glad of it because the months since Blink and Angus left have been hard on her. She knew she would miss them but just how much has surprised her.

The whole town seems to have turned out for the big day. There is plenty for them to see and do.

As Gemma strolls, she can see the oval and its surrounds are bustling. Families are wandering through the tents and stalls and the kids are streaming towards Sideshow Alley, frightened they'll miss something.

Their faces are smeared with the remains of show food—sugary doughnuts, fairy floss in thick curls of pink, blue and green, and Dagwood dogs covered in batter and dipped in tomato sauce.

'Hello, Gemma, nice to see you here. You're looking good.' It's Morrie Hinds, in uniform and on duty. 'I'm just on my way to the bar to check on things. Join me?'

'It's a little early for me,' says Gemma, 'but I'll walk you there. There's someone I want to see over that way.'

The pair of them head towards the hall. Inside, the bar is already doing a memorable trade.

Gemma promises to catch up with Morrie later and, as he enters the hall, she moves towards the orchestra setting up. Cassidy and Alex are there helping a group of students with their chairs and music stands for the schools concert competition.

'I didn't know you were musical,' says Gemma.

Cassidy looks up from tightening the metal legs on a stand and smiles as he sees her familiar and friendly face.

'I'm not,' he says, 'not in the slightest. I don't know whether I'm tone deaf but it always sounds to me as if school orchestras are out of tune.

'Or maybe everyone is in tune but not with each other. Either way, they sound bloody awful, without exception. I don't know. I'm more used to footy club songs.'

Gemma laughs as she moves forward to give Cassidy a hug. She does the same with Alex.

'Anyway,' Cassidy says, 'I thought I'd better come down and check on you. It's been a while. And it's good to see you.'

Gemma is about to speak, but is distracted by a droning she first thinks might be coming from a saxophone being tuned or a trombone finding its range. The drone increases in volume until, over the hills to the east of town, the culprit can be seen as well as heard. The shape and whir of a helicopter become clearer as it approaches and then lands in a roped-off area away from the oval.

Even before the rotors have stopped spinning, a line of show patrons has begun to form and their eagerness is obvious as they clutch, check and recheck the tickets in their hands.

'Are you ready for this?' Cassidy asks Gemma.

One in the front and three in the back, four passengers at a time can squeeze themselves into the confines of the chopper for the fifteen-minute joyflight over Queenstown.

On good days, and this is a good and bright day with the chopper untroubled by crosswinds or turbulence, a flight of even the shortest duration allows glorious views of the west.

The hills around Queenstown, with their unusual and striking colours, stand out, but so too does the evidence that the hills are healing.

More time is needed for nature to do its work, but there are pronounced pockets of new vegetation coming through and encouraging splashes of green where for years there has been only barrenness.

Cassidy, Alex and Gemma, though she is nervous at the prospect, are due to go up in the mid-afternoon. The helicopter is a first for the Queenstown Show and it's proving a winner.

As people leave the chopper after their flights, Gemma can see the excitement on their faces. But there is something more, more than just the novelty of a flight, and she can see it as people hurry away to find their friends and families. Gemma has heard them and Cassidy has heard them.

All the talk is of the garden.

chapter 39

It is not the easiest thing to do in a space as cramped as a helicopter, but the three of them, Gemma, Cassidy and Alex manage to embrace.

As the pilot swoops over and between the hills, he too can barely contain his enthusiasm. 'Who'd a thunk it?' he says. 'It's just there, out of the blue. I've flown over it Gawd knows how many times today and I still can't come to grips with it. It just appears, like those things in England, in the crops.'

'Crop circles,' says Alex, having to speak above the rotors and the engine.

'Yeah, that's them,' says the pilot. 'I heard somewhere that some people reckon the crop circles are a message from outer space. No one knows how they got there or what they mean.'

There is no such confusion for his passengers. As the chopper turns, they look below and see the highway and the coloured hills, the town and Mount Lyell. In its own unconventional way, it is undoubtedly magnificent territory.

Gemma picks out the dirt road off the highway and, as they approach, flashes of new colour are tantalising—hinting at something out of the ordinary. When the view opens completely it is breathtaking and Gemma, overcome by it, holds her hands over her mouth and nose. Her eyes fill and there is a pain in her throat, but she swallows it down and blinks away any threatening tears, determined that nothing will obstruct her vision.

On the ground, during all the weeks and months of work leading up to this moment, she could only hope and imagine and fear what the outcome might be. Now, from hundreds of feet above the land, she marvels at Blink's genius and chides herself for ever doubting it. How she wishes the old man were here now.

'Don't tell Angus. I want to surprise him,' Blink had said to Gemma during one of their regular get-togethers downstairs while Angus slept above them.

'This is what I have planned. I've done a couple of drafts but this is the finished product. It's the land as it will be.' Blink unrolled a large sheet of paper and Gemma marvelled at the detail on it. 'Angus hasn't seen this,' he said. 'I've only shown him the rough plan. But this one's the cat's whiskers. Took me a while, but there it is.'

'Blink,' said Gemma, 'it's incredible. Is it possible?'

Cleaning the room a few days after Blink and Angus had gone, Gemma found the detailed plan folded under Blink's mattress. Since then, she had kept that one room vacant, turning people and their money away just in case Blink and Angus might turn up on her doorstep and need a place to stay.

Though they had known each other for only a relatively short time, it had been long enough for Gemma to feel a kinship with Blink and Angus. She had opened up to them and they to her. She had heard and told intimacies.

She missed them more each day, convincing herself that letting people into their room was as good as admitting they were gone for good.

'Look at it, look at it,' shouts Cassidy, rousing Gemma back to the moment. He leans across to her, ignoring the safety harness as it digs into his hip, and again wraps his arms around her.

They both know how fortunate they have been these past few months. The good luck that ran out for Blink remained for them.

School holidays, weekends and any spare time they had was devoted to the garden and following Blink's plan.

The storm that had forced Blink and Angus's departure was not the forerunner to other similar storms. There was rain, because in the west there is always rain, but there were not the deluges that can transform good ground to useless mush. It had been a benign season and, while the days were cold, the sun had shown stamina and stayed out, helping to nurture the ground and assist its goodness to strengthen and expand.

The soil wasn't a problem. There was plenty and it was good. Neither was any cajoling required to bring the students back to the west to bend their backs, lay and turn the soil, dig in the fertiliser, plant the seeds and cuttings.

Alex didn't have to be asked twice. Blink had impacted on her, as he had on the others. Surprisingly only Cassidy had initial reservations and it had been up to Alex to sway him.

'Commonsense is fine most of the time,' she'd said, 'but sometimes you've got to try things that seem to go against it.'

The next morning, up in the little shed, Cassidy watched the sun come up as he milked Frolic. He saw the paddocks from which the first loads of soil had been dug and he saw that his ground had already begun to regenerate. It was still early when he called Gemma.

'We're not gardeners, Gemma,' he said.

'No, we're not,' she replied, 'but we don't need to be. It's all here, Cassidy, written down and sketched. You should see it. Blink knows what he's doing. Don't you see, he always did. We just need to follow his lead.'

Cassidy stares as the helicopter makes broad sweeps and takes different approaches to reveal all aspects of the garden below.

The garden is a windmill, a windmill of flowers, and the dance of light and shadow from the clouds moving overhead gives the appearance of the windmill's blades slowly turning. Sprays of gypsophila planted either side of each of the four blades enhance the illusion. The blades themselves are roses, thick and deep red. They spear from the windmill's hub.

'I've chosen Chateau de Clos Vougeot roses for the blades,' Blink told Gemma. He'd pronounced it "Chatto der Klo Voojo".

'They've got good shape, good colour, good scent. They're strong. There's a climber now, but the original keeps low and sprawls. And they're French. That's important.'

Blink had said it was a determined rose and there could be no other for his blades.

Meanwhile, the hub of the windmill features a circle of other roses, Fruhlingsduft and Fruhlingsgold, the latter more vigorous and darker than its counterpart, which has larger and more impressive blooms.

The effect of their pairing is an interplay of white and gold, reaching out and clutching for prominence. They are planted to encircle the two gravestones, but are separated from them by a grassed inner ring.

As Cassidy surveys the scene, he sees how the contrast of the grey stones, the light green grass, the yellow and white roses and the fierce red moving blades, is remarkable.

The mill tower, which widens below the blades and forms the main support structure, boasts an array of flowers and shrubs positioned to offer dimension. Height, form and perspective are granted thanks to the order of petunias, dahlias and chrysanthemums. Blink had written the order for each to be planted and Gemma and Cassidy obeyed to the letter.

Between the windmill blades, grass has been planted to form wedges of relief from the bold roses. At the centre of each wedge is a wooden bench and each bench is backed by a small bed of hydrangeas.

As fine as the other views of the west are from the chopper, nothing compares with the view of the garden. Gemma had seen the garden from the ground and knew it to be a landmark. Now, from the air, she knows it to be a masterpiece. As they peer down, they can see cars leaving the showgrounds. Traffic is streaming north on the main road.

Throughout the day, people drive and take the turn-off, then leave their cars and head up the slope to the plateau. Gemma, Cassidy and Alex, once back on the ground, join the exodus.

'Wherever you stand in the garden, there is something new to see,' says Gemma, 'but it all comes together.'

The wisps of baby's breath softly infiltrate the dark roses and yet also stand out for themselves. Rows of small shrubs with tiny, bright flowers make their mark, contributing to the overall image while commanding their own singular place.

There are contrasts of light and shade, petal and stamen, strength and fragility. There is power and purpose, just as in a real windmill.

Ironies abound. A ramble of roses, which one person might celebrate for their beauty alone, Blink had envisioned as an entanglement, as wire to trap and hold fast.

'Some people see roses just for their colour and scent and that's fair enough,' he'd said to Gemma, 'I see them for those things but they have other meanings too.'

Gemma and Cassidy can hear the questions as they wander the windmill garden—Who did this? How did it get here?—until finally, people come to the most intriguing and important questions of all.

Why has this been done? Who is it for?

These questions turn around and around in people's minds.

chapter 40

The sickly sweet swirl of violins flows through the nursing home, never too loud, but inescapable, a mosquito in every ear.

Competing with the music that oozes through the speakers, in a corner of the entertainment room a skinny and leathery old woman in a mauve dressing-gown and bowler hat pounds on a piano, reliving a past during which she has taken music lessons, but apparently never quite enough of them.

She thumps out the tunes as if beating a rug hung on a clothesline, removing from the songs any subtlety or mood.

Everything she plays comes with a marching beat, with some notes going AWOL and others appearing where they are not welcome. Yet always there is just enough of the original tune remaining to be recognisable and thus inspire the voices of the other elderly people gathered around the piano.

They soar and dive around, above and below the melodies, occasionally finding them, singing "I'll Be Loving You Always", "Begin The Beguine", "The Man Who Broke The Bank At Monte Carlo" and "Roll Out The Barrel".

Sometimes, solo turns are urged. A man sings "I've Got To Be Me" as if he wants to be someone else. A woman trills "Three Little Maids From School".

All together, this wrinkled choir bobs and bounces and laughs as its members sing, ending each number with a rousing burst of their own applause.

From somewhere else, the sound of cheesy, modern country music filters through the doors and windows.

Music is everywhere, fighting for space and combining into a stew of sounds.

The entertainment room has the piano, a pool table, an indoor bowls mat and other tables for cards, draughts and chess. The room is always busy and loud and the residents who aren't deaf or heading that way try to shut out all but the sound of their own pursuits.

A short walk or wheelchair roll down the hall is the TV room. Here you have to be quiet so that old ears can concentrate on the programs, the personalities, the newsreaders, weather reports and sports results.

No newspapers or magazines are allowed in the TV room, lest the sound of pages turning be enough to cause a viewer to miss some vital information. There's a reading room two doors down. The TV room has a number of chairs and two worn settees covered with crocheted rugs made in handicraft class.

All the seats are taken when the old man shuffles in. He has just had his bath and feels toasty warm in his new slippers, flannelette pyjamas and dressing-gown, which his son bought for him the last time they'd gone out for the day.

The old man remembers the town clock chiming and being in the car but not much else about that day.

He always watches the news and an orderly fetches him a chair from outside. He sits and waits for the music which signals the start of the bulletin.

The news is news. The prime minister is his usual self, all po-faced and humourless, announcing how cutting back... the old man doesn't quite catch what it is that is being cut back but it can't be good because the pictures to go with the report feature elderly people like himself.

Next is a story about the future of one of the mines, followed by news of a small boy helping to deliver his baby brother after his mother collapsed and the ambulance didn't arrive on time. International news follows, then the finance.

The sports report—gearing up for the cricket season, local racing—gives way to the weather.

He peers down at the notepad he always carries with him and on which he writes messages for others and those things he thinks he needs to remember. This broadcast has left his notepad blank. He gets up to leave.

But then, after the weather and the return from commercials, as the newsreaders are about to wish everyone goodnight but always manage to fit in that one quirky little story to close out the bulletin with a smile, the old man pauses.

Usually, he doesn't bother hanging around the TV room once the weather report has finished because he needs to be in the entertainment room where he has the pool table booked for 6.30.

He needs a minute or so to get there. A minute late and someone else will claim the table. He's often wondered whether the bastards would jump into his grave as quickly.

This time, however, he is stopped in his tracks.

On the television screen, he sees what beyond doubt is Queenstown. It's an aerial view, panning across the town and showing the mine, the footy oval and the hills.

Resting his hands on the back of his seat, he stares as the camera zooms down and in. And what the camera captures next almost stops his heart.

It is a windmill of flowers.

'Isn't that lovely?' says a woman, breaking into the newsreader's commentary about the garden, causing Angus to miss the first part of a short interview with a woman.

His knees begin to buckle. Gathering himself, he resumes his seat, takes the notepad and pen from his dressing-gown pocket and writes in large letters that take up a whole page: "BLINK".

He doesn't move as people file out of the TV room after the news. He sits and thinks and, though he says nothing, he smiles.

Then he laughs, a husky, whispered wheeze that is really no noise at all but is still enough for two people who have remained in the room to turn to him, put their fingers to their lips and go, 'Ssssh!'

Angus Bain laughs anyway. He laughs because he can't, and won't, stop.

And finally, several minutes later, when he returns to the silence he has known for most of his life, he writes some more, a spidery scripted letter to his son and daughter.

A nurse enters the TV room and says, 'Mr Bain, your friends at the pool table have given up waiting for you. Mr Harold has taken your place.'

Angus nods to her, giving her such a smile that it slices through the professional distance she likes to maintain and bayonets her heart.

These past few months have seen Blink's life return to a routine of pills, soft, lukewarm meals and monotony.

When he started to bring up green phlegm, the staff kept a closer eye on him, commenting among themselves that it was probably the beginning of the end.

I can see it too. His lungs are filling up, his mind is long gone and now his body is joining it.

Blink is dying.

'How's that, Mr Johns?' asks Max, adjusting Blink's pillows.

Blink digs around with the back of his head until he finds a comfortable position.

Satisfied the old man is fine, Max goes to attend the patient in the next bed.

Blink's in a four-bed ward and each bed has the luxury of its own TV.

The hospital section is the part of Pleasant View where age, decline and conclusion are most obvious. I see how obvious during one of my visits.

'You can't come, Dad,' says the woman to the man in the opposite bed. 'We'd love to take you but you're in the hospital and we can't take you. You're not well enough.'

She is still quite young, in her early thirties maybe, still pretty and sad and dressed for something special.

'I can come,' says her father. 'Where're my slippers? My good suit's in the wardrobe at home. Get it for me, darling. I'll be with you in a jiffy and we'll all go together. Now where's your mother? She's always so slow.'

The woman, with her shiny brown hair falling over her face, says again, 'No, Dad. Mum's not here anymore. Remember? It'll be too much for you. You have to stay. I'll be back tomorrow to tell you all about it.'

Before she finishes, and she speaks forlornly down into her chest as if unable to bear the thought of looking her fading father in the eye, the old man is out of bed and unsteady.

'Slippers, slippers, slippers, slippers, slippers,' he says.

A nurse appears and kindly admonishes him, putting him back to bed where he promptly falls asleep. She places a consoling hand on the woman's shoulder. 'Don't fret,' she says.

'He won't remember anything in the morning. Not a thing. He never does.'

'What can I do?' asks the daughter. 'He so wants to come, but it's too much. He wouldn't cope. He wouldn't be strong enough.'

The nurse lifts the bedsheet further up the old man's chest and he snorts at the disturbance.

'Tell him he went,' says the nurse.

'Pardon?'

'Tell him he went. Tell him he was the life of the party. Tell him he went.'

'But that seems so cruel,' says the woman.

I have continued coming to see Blink, but he doesn't know me and hasn't shown any sign of doing so for months.

Until one day he calls me Angus.

I don't know whether it's an aberration and he will return to a state of unknowing within a few seconds of my leaving or whether, as his body surrenders to age and illness, his mind is making one last gasp effort at sense and recognition.

I have been waiting for this. I have heard that the sick and dying can suddenly appear to make an incredible recovery just before the end.

They feel well, can be moved and can move themselves. They can be sent home to loved ones for a few days during which they eat full meals, toss back a beer, enjoy a smoke and welcome the queue of friends and relatives who come calling. They can get out in the garden or enjoy a trip in the car.

They become so well, so ridiculously and miraculously well, that friends and family think, *perhaps the old devil's still got a few years left in him.*

I am told that it is uncanny how many times these recoveries coincide with an impending occasion—a wedding, a birth, a football premiership, a visit after many years by a friend or family member.

Then a week or a month or so later, after the big event and at the funeral, people mingle and say to each other, 'He looked so well the last time I saw him.'

This brief recovery is like a wick that has found an extra length of itself, still unburned. It's like a finish to unfinished business.

And what is memorable about it, I believe, is not that a dying person dies but that there is this final burst of life.

It is what you remember most vividly and it is what you most mourn because you have seen someone back at their best and shining.

Blink has called me Angus again and when he does I see him as a firework, a sparkler like the ones children hold and wave at parties. Gradually they fade, except for a moment near the very end when they take on a sudden brightness that burns hottest and lasts longest in the memory.

chapter 41

Angus recalls times when he would roar at the world above from his place in the darkness below.

The lights from other miners' lamps might catch him in these times of torment, but no one ever heard a sound from him.

It took just a few years after the war for Angus to feel that he had been away from Queenstown for so long that it had seemed to have distanced itself from him even further than the twelve thousand miles between Tasmania and England.

A very real connection remained, however, through the habits of mining, which bridge any distance and never more so than when men emerge from the end of a long shift wanting to fill the air with the sound of themselves, shrugging off the dirty and torturous anonymity of their work.

Angus remembers how they spoke and sang and laughed and whistled, all competing to be heard above each other after having said so little as they laboured underground, where there is no day or night and where they must concentrate only on the rock and hear only the noise of spades, picks and machinery.

Away from the mines, they tramped the roads and footpaths and crashed around their homes and the pubs in their big boots until the time came to return to the mines and be lost again.

Before the war, Angus had taken such ways for granted. This was how things were and had always been for miners. The war had changed that, with uncompromising force and immediacy. The war revealed how change was constant and everywhere, whether it came suddenly or was slow-burning.

Angus thought that if the war taught him anything, it was this: in life, the very next second is always a mystery.

Seeing the windmill garden on the television has again reminded him of how rapidly things can change.

Years of assumption have been blown to dust.

Blink is alive.

Blink is alive.

Angus Bain had lived a long and good life.

His war had ended on the wire and, when he cast his mind back, he could remember running and yelling at Blink and then being tossed high in the air. He could feel the jaggedness of the entanglement through his uniform and into his skin.

There was the taste of blood in his mouth and he could see it pouring over his hands when he reached for his neck and throat, where his pain was centred.

He remembered hearing a howl, long and pure and awful, but it did not come from his own mouth and he knew it had nothing to do with any physical pain. Rather, it was a howl of loss the depth of which was beyond physical. The sound of it had remained with him all his life.

He remembered trying to find Blink and seeing him there on the wire, prone and bloodied. He had tried to speak but there was no sound, just a gush of blood from his mouth.

Angus didn't know how he had come to be taken from the wire, but when he woke he was in hospital and could hear the sound of groaning, though again it was not his own.

The first things he saw clearly were his thick toes poking out from beneath a white sheet and blanket.

Across from him was a soldier with bandages stained a nasty yellow over his eyes. Whoever this bloke was, the extent of his injuries could not dampen his spirits and he chatted chirpily with the nurses who came to change his bandages and swab his blinded eyes.

Angus had no real sense of time or place or of his own injuries.

His arms and legs were neither strung up nor plastered nor, thank God, putrefying in a bucket after having been amputated.

He had bandages around his arms and he could feel other bandages around his left knee and his right foot. He felt another one, this one much thicker, around his neck.

It hurt to breathe, but he was aware of his fortune.

'Lucky me,' he thought, 'just a few scratches, that's all. Could have been worse.'

The thought of luck brought Blink into his mind and Angus was almost overwhelmed by grief. A lump formed in his throat and the pain it brought wracked him.

He turned his head to see if there was any water he could sip to calm himself and soothe his blazing throat, but when he moved the pain ripped through him in a way he could not believe possible. He lost consciousness.

When he woke again, it was to an agony that demanded expression, a cry such as he could hear from other wounded men in their beds.

He opened his mouth but no sound came, only more fire. Once it subsided, and it took him to the edge of consciousness again before it did, Angus resolved to keep his stupid bloody head quite still until he knew exactly what was going on.

'You all right, mate?' said a small voice from the bed to the left. 'You still look a bit off-colour. You've been in and out of it for a couple of days.'

Angus, ignoring his own advice mere seconds after he'd given it, turned his stupid bloody head and immediately regretted it.

'Sorry, mate,' said the voice. 'Best not move your noggin. You've got a bandage around your throat the size of a winter scarf. What did you do, cut your bloody head off?'

Without moving his head this time, Angus tried to speak. It was futile. He gestured towards his mouth.

'That's all right, mate,' said his neighbour. 'Just wave at me to shut up if I get on your nerves. I like a good chat. Missed a good chat at the front. Too serious up there. Still, we're okay now, aren't we? Sorry again, don't answer that. Take it easy. We're okay now. Few more weeks of this and we'll be ready to head home, I reckon.'

Angus took turns listening and ignoring. He didn't mind not having to respond and his pain was tolerable as long as he kept his head still. The bed was comfortable and warm and he could sleep when he wanted, which was often.

Though he had yet to discover the full range of his injuries, Angus did not share the confidence of his chatty neighbour.

He expected to be back at the front and fighting as soon as he was declared fit and able.

He had no doubt that he was healing. Apart from his voice, which for the time being refused to come back, he was feeling physically stronger by the day and knew that all he needed was to be patient and he'd be right as rain.

The prospect of returning to the lines chilled him, although he knew he had been so much luckier than Blink—barefoot, dangling, bleeding Blink, flung across the wire and dead as a doornail.

Angus woke and stared into the face of a doctor, whose serious expression softened as he saw Angus's eyes open.

'Welcome back, Private Bain,' he said. 'You're a very fortunate fellow. Very fortunate indeed.'

That afternoon, when a nurse came to change his bandages, Angus was able to see his ravaged neck for the first time. He held a mirror uncertainly, slowly scanning the mess of tissue, stitching and gnarled skin that stretched almost from ear to ear.

In places, seeping through and clinging to the sutures, was a foul, greenish fluid that turned Angus's stomach.

Staring at the stitches again, he reckoned the bloke in the next bed was right and that his entire head must have come off and had to be sewn back on.

'This is what we think happened,' said the doctor, examining Angus's neck as a nurse swabbed away the pus and dropped the discoloured pads into a bucket. 'It was a shell, obviously. You've got no bullet wounds so it must have been the force of a shell exploding which threw you into the wire.

'You've done serious damage to your neck and throat and other tissue. There's considerable nerve damage, minor and major muscle tears, not to mention the general lacerations.

'You were still quite a mess when we got you. You lost a lot of blood and the only reason I can fathom why you didn't choke on it was the way you must have ended up on the wire.

'Obviously, the medical personnel got to you in time and kept you together somehow and now you're here. Some sewing and swabbing and some decent food and rest should see you right.

'You can thank your lucky stars, Private, and your good constitution. I've seen plenty of men during this war die with lesser wounds than you've sustained.'

Angus made a gesture with his hands, a writing motion, pencil on paper. The doctor understood and took a neat, leather-bound notebook from his coat pocket. His pencil was chewed at the top. He passed both to Angus, who wrote three questions: "Where am I? The war? Return to front?"

The doctor took back his book and pencil, then took hold of Angus's hand. Angus thought he was about to have his pulse taken but, in fact, it was a gesture of comfort as the doctor proceeded to provide the answers to his questions.

'Private Bain, you are in London. The war is still going but has turned our way. No, you will not return to the front. Your war is over.'

Angus tried to take it all in. He also needed to know more. He pointed to his throat.

'You were a very lucky man, Private Bain, as I say,' said the doctor. 'But I hope you weren't planning on a career in the opera.'

Angus's eyes widened and the doctor apologised for his flippancy.

'I'm sorry. That wasn't appropriate. The war seems to have cost me most of my bedside manner. Private Bain, all that needs to be said is that the damage to your throat, your vocal cords especially, is irreparable.

'Do you understand what I'm saying?'

Angus did.

'It's not such a bad scenario when you consider what might have happened. As long as we can keep the infection under control, you'll be right.'

Again Angus thought of Blink and tugged at the doctor's sleeve as he was getting up to continue his rounds.

Out came the notebook and pencil and Angus wrote "Private B Johns. Tasmania?".

'The name isn't familiar to me,' said the doctor, 'but I can check the records for you.'

It was another day before the doctor came back to Angus's bed and again took his hand.

'I'm sorry, the only Private Johns we've had died of his wounds. Same battle as you.'

The wounds took time to repair. There were infections and other difficulties. Angus became sullen and withdrawn.

His food had to be puréed or jellied and was not much better than the stuff he'd been eating at the front. It was murder to swallow.

Eventually, however, the day came when he did leave the hospital and, dressed in a new uniform, paid up, with his coat pocket filled with tubes of ointment and wearing a scarf to conceal the scars which railway-tracked around his neck, he saw the city of London.

He had written to his parents in Queenstown to say he had been discharged and expected to be home soon.

Things changed, though. As the war wound down and talk was at last of peace, Angus stayed with the army hospital, helping out with whatever jobs needed to be done. He cleaned, cooked, did carpentry and other repair jobs, all silently, always wearing a scarf.

When the war did end, he wrote home to say he would be staying in England for a while.

Despite recalling a conversation with Blink about going home and staying put after the war, he now felt differently.

Angus wasn't ready for home. He promised his parents he'd stay in touch, explaining he would pick up work as there was plenty to be done. He wouldn't go hungry or poor.

For the next year, Angus roamed England. He shepherded over the green fells and through the stone-lined roads of Cumbria. He laboured on road gangs in the south, thatched roofs in Wales, even did a week's fishing on a boat out of Ullapool and was so sick he vowed never to go to sea again.

People were happy to employ him and disappointed to see him go because he was strong and never shirked. Once they got over his silence and knew why it was there, people were understanding.

All the jobs he took were either solitary or close enough to it, which was as he preferred. He wanted to be by himself and he didn't encourage conversation or companionship.

Though once determined never to enter another mine, his arrival in Yorkshire gave him a sense of belonging. He went down into the darkness.

Only occasionally did his memories build to a breaking point and force him to lay down his pick, lean into the mine wall, toss his head back and silently roar.

Angus never did return to Queenstown. In fact, it was his parents who returned to England. The Bains rented a tiny house on a wet and cold street, not unlike the tiny house on the wet and cold street they'd left behind in Queenstown.

Angus didn't live with them but he was close and the family ate dinner together every Sunday, even though there was no denying the years apart and the experiences of the war had made them all but strangers and had erected a barrier none knew how, or tried, to climb.

Harold and Maggie Bain died within a month of each other in the winter of 1927. After that Angus hardly socialised at all. It made him uncomfortable. He kept to himself and people left him alone.

Then, on a chilly evening, he dropped into a tea room for something to warm his bones and wrote on the notebook he always carried: "Sweet tea".

Lizzie Falls took the note and gave Angus the smile of an angel. For the next few weeks, he was a regular at the tea room until one evening he summoned up the courage to write to Lizzie and ask her out.

It took him all night to compose the note, to explain himself and the way he was. Lizzie read it and simply said, 'Men talk too much anyway.'

Their courtship began and from then on Angus couldn't wait to get up, get out of the mine and rush down to the tea room to collect Lizzie and walk her home.

Theirs was a simple story, an unaffected romance. Angus and Lizzie courted, engaged and married. A year later they welcomed their son, Adam, and felt blessed by him after doctors said Lizzie would bear no more children. In defiance, three years later Annie was born.

Angus and Lizzie Bain raised their children to become good adults and they were married for almost fifty years before Lizzie passed away.

In all that time, Angus had not uttered a single word to her and yet he knew she had always known exactly what he was feeling and thinking, and how much he felt for her and their children.

Even if Angus could speak, no words could express the happiness Lizzie gave him.

On their second evening together, on the way back to her parents' house after leaving the pub where they had eaten dinner, they huddled under an awning while a shower of rain passed over. They held hands. Lizzie unravelled the scarf Angus had tied around his neck and, while he was self-conscious about the scars, she was not. She kissed his neck.

As the rain pat-pat-patted on the awning, Angus Bain came back into the light of the world.

The day Lizzie died, he kissed her neck and she said, the very last thing she would say to him, 'Yes, my love. I remember.'

chapter 42

A middle-aged woman confirms the booking and signs the register.

She speaks with an accent Gemma has heard on the telly occasionally. It's working-class but still exotic to Gemma's ears.

Gemma turns the register after the woman has finished signing and tells this Mrs A. Parkin that she hopes she will enjoy her stay in Queenstown. The woman thanks her, smiles sweetly and turns as she hears her brother and father entering the big house.

'Let me,' says Gemma. She rushes around the desk to hold the door open for the two men. 'I'm Gemma, Gemma Woodley. Just call if you need anything and I suspect the first thing you need is a good, strong cuppa after your long journey.'

Adam Bain agrees. 'Yes, that would be lovely,' he says with the same accent as his sister. 'It was a long flight from England but I think the drive from Launceston to Queenstown felt even longer, especially that last hike down the coast.'

With that, Adam officially introduces himself. 'I'm Adam, Adam Bain,' he says, 'and this is my father, Angus Bain. He was born here in Queenstown.'

'Hello, Mr Bain,' says Gemma, steadying herself, feeling as if her jaw might be clattering around at her feet, having dropped at the sound of the old man's name. 'It is an extraordinary pleasure to meet you.'

Gathering her wits about her, she says, 'You've come to see your garden.'

'My father cannot speak,' says Annie. 'He was wounded in World War I.'

'Yes,' says Adam, 'like I said, our father was born in Queenstown and this is the first time he has been back since the war. It's all been a bit hard on him, I think.'

Gemma studies Angus and sees that what Adam is saying is true. The travelling has taken a toll on Angus, although it is another kind of wear and tear she feels is troubling him more.

Gemma sees Angus is struggling for equilibrium, as if being back here in Queenstown, and the emotions stirred up as a consequence, have tipped him off-balance.

'You said "your garden"?' says Annie to Gemma.

'Excuse me?'

'You said "your garden" to my father. That's why we've brought him back or, to be more accurate, why he's brought us. He saw the windmill garden on TV back in England and he hasn't really been the same since. I'm not sure Adam and

I really understand what it all means. It's difficult when you communicate in small notes.'

Gemma is listening, but can't take her eyes off Angus. 'I feel like I know you,' she says to him. 'I feel like I've known you for a very long time.'

'How could that be?' asks Adam. 'Did you know my father when he was young? Or his parents? You must have been very young.'

'No,' replies Gemma. 'I've never met your father. I just happen to know an awful lot about him.'

'It's all been such a rush,' says Annie. 'A few days ago he was in a nursing home in England. The next thing we know I'm booking planes and accommodation across the world.'

'Come in,' says Gemma, 'we'll get you settled and then we'll have a sit down in the lounge. I won't worry about the tea just yet. Perhaps a drop of the good stuff?'

An open fire is crackling as Gemma pours four stiff whiskies and serves them in the lounge. Her new guests barely have the energy to drink them and soon retire to their rooms upstairs.

She checks the register again and confirms the family is staying for a full week.

She calls Cassidy.

'Come and see the garden,' says Cassidy. 'It's about time. It's the right time.'

I want to see the garden, but I don't want to do it without Blink. That's what has stopped me from making the trip west since the garden was revealed. It doesn't seem right to see it without him.

I phone my parents and Stevie. My father uses the pub phone to ring his brother and sister, perhaps for the first time ever, and Isobel. For the first time in years, the family is coming together, although it is no easy task convincing the management at Pleasant View Home for the Aged to release Blink. The management has Isobel signing waivers and declarations and listening to various warnings about responsibility and time and medication and sundry other matters.

It is a masterpiece of bureaucratic rigmarole but everybody understands why.

The nursing home staff are particularly worried about Blink's ability to withstand such an arduous journey.

The overnight stay with Cassidy and Alex swings the situation and Blink is granted a release, although many a brow in Pleasant View Home for the Aged furrows when I am among the family party that comes to collect him.

I make sure to smile at everyone.

Alex North sets the dining table for the evening meal and Cassidy knocks the tops off a couple of beers.

The kids are in the living room watching cartoons and every now and then the sound of pianos falling, explosions, boings and whistles comes through to us.

My mother sits next to Stevie and Isobel, who has Blink's hand. Then there is my father, as well as Cassidy and Alex. Rex and Dot are staying in town. I wish Phil was here.

Blink is oblivious and strains with his breathing. He calls me Angus, which thrills me, and he even seems to know Alex, but the rest are strangers. He doesn't seem to mind.

'You can help me milk Frolic in the morning, Blink,' says Cassidy after the meal. 'Bright and early, then we'll hit the road after breakfast.'

'Frolic,' says Blink.

After dinner, Blink is helped to a chair out on Cassidy's balcony.

'I'd love a fag,' he says. 'Angus, could you get me one?'

'You're not supposed to smoke, Blink. Your lungs were never the best and now they're getting worse. Do you think a smoke is a good idea?'

'Not the end of the world,' he says.

My father is soon asleep in front of the television. The children are still there and it's past their bedtime. I take a packet of smokes from my father's top pocket and a book of matches from a glass bowl on the mantelpiece.

I light the cigarette and place it in Blink's mouth. He makes a V of his index and middle finger and wedges the cigarette between them, before resorting to old habits by transferring the smoke to his other hand and concealing it, holding it palm inwards and between his thumb and index finger.

He draws back and I think he might inhale the lot in one large breath.

'Beautiful,' he says, blowing out the smoke and trying to suppress a cough. 'I was in hospital once, I remember, and you could have as many smokes as you liked. I met you in hospital, Angus. I was coughing up yellow and green muck from my lungs and you were leaking green and yellow muck out the end of your dick.'

He laughs, coughs and drops the fag at his feet, grinding it into the balcony boards. He looks at me. 'Are you a ghost, Angus?' he asks. 'Are you a ghost? Because how else can you be here?'

I telephone Gemma and tell her when to expect us. It is wonderful to hear her voice.

'The garden is even more personal now,' she says. 'And more beautiful because of it.'

It seems an odd thing to say.

chapter 43

It rains overnight and the drive to Queenstown is demanding, but by the time we reach the turn-off, the sun is peeping through and the prospect is of a fine day. Crisp, but not cruel.

I drive up the little road I know so well and thought I might never see again.

Gemma is waiting and almost smothers me with her embrace. Blink, Cassidy and Alex suffer the same lovely fate.

We go through the introductions with the rest of the family once the other cars have pulled up. Gemma is her usual buoyant self with everyone except Dot, whom she holds close to her.

'Come and see your father's garden,' Gemma says to her.

As we walk up the slope to the plateau, she passes me a rolled up sheet of paper.

'The evidence,' she says, and as I unroll it I see Blink's detailed diagram of the garden. It stuns me. I have seen the garden on television and the pictures in the newspaper and I think I am ready to see it for real. I am not.

I stand at the graves and fight to absorb what is around me, the colour, the scent, the sheer magnitude of it.

'Whadya reckon?' asks Cassidy and all I can do is hug him, crash-tackling him with my gratitude before repeating the same with Gemma.

'How did you possibly get this done?'

My father and mother, though usually awkward in each other's company these days, are holding hands. My father wipes his sleeve under his nose and he coughs every few seconds. My mother shakes her head from side to side.

'The flies will get in,' my father says to her. She shuts her mouth but it just falls open again.

Isobel is with Alex.

'Blink likes you, I can tell,' says Isobel. 'He always had an eye for a pretty face.'

'He is a dear,' says Alex.

'You should have seen his garden at Raymond Street,' says Isobel, hooking her arm around Alex's. 'He has a gift, he always had a gift. He did everything to plan but somehow it never ever looked planned or clinical or calculated in any way. He just had a gift.'

Blink, meanwhile, surveys everything. Leaving Gemma and Cassidy, he wanders away from the graves and I go to join him, to be there if he needs me.

'That came up a treat,' he says, pointing to a whisper of baby's breath. 'Those hydrangeas might need a little something, though. The roses are good. I thought they would be.'

'Jesus, Blink,' I say. 'It's bloody incredible.'

'No, Angus, it's a garden,' he says. 'It's what the earth can do. Just needs a kick along every now and again.'

'Are you okay?' I ask him.

'Yes,' he says. 'If I fall over, you'll pick me up.'

'Well, I'll be blowed, look at that,' he says, looking up. There are birds.

I leave Blink and return to the centre of the garden, to the hub of all this beauty.

Blink criss-crosses from one area to the other, bending and touching. He doesn't fall and the rest of us, Gemma, Alex, Cassidy, my parents, Rex, Dot and Stevie, watch him not fall.

He doesn't need us. He seems new. He is sparkling.

'Fetch your grandfather,' says Gemma, and the force of her hand on my back is not to be denied.

I go to him—he is kneeling among the roses of the windmill blades—and as we make our way back I see that three new people have arrived. I don't recognise them.

Gemma walks to greet them and while I wait for Blink to finish another examination, I glance across to the graves where the new arrivals are standing with my family. I see Rex grab Isobel.

'Come on,' I say. 'Something's up.' Blink takes my arm. He has a real spring in his step, but slows the closer we come to the trio of people Gemma is now leading towards us.

There is an old man in the centre of the party and he breaks free of their arms and moves towards Blink and me.

'Angus,' says Blink.

'Yes, Blink, I'm here,' I say, but Blink is looking at the man.

'Angus,' he says again, gripping hard on my arm and then releasing it. He walks ahead of me.

Gemma comes to me and again the force of her hand, this time urging me to stop, is as irresistible as before. 'Just wait,' she says.

The man and woman who have arrived with the old man have also stopped in their tracks.

Between us, in the centre of a triangle formed by Gemma and me, the members of my family and this other couple, the two old men stand face to face. They shake hands and the old man gives Blink a piece of notepaper and Blink reads it.

I will never learn what it says and that is only right.

Then Blink says something the rest of us cannot hear and that too is only right.

Blink puts his fingers softly onto the other man's neck. The other man touches Blink's left shoulder.

And I know who he is.

At last, we all come together again, back at the graves.

'I'm Adam Bain, Mr Johns,' says Adam to Blink, 'and this is my sister Annie. It is a pleasure to meet you.'

'You're taller than your old man,' says Blink, 'copped the red hair and freckles, though.'

Annie's bottom lip is quivering.

'And you must have inherited your mother's looks,' Blink says to her. 'You can thank your lucky stars about that, my girl.'

Blink faces the rest of us and he takes Angus by the arm.

'You've met Gemma,' he says assuredly. 'This is my wife, Isobel, and my grandson Stevie.

'This is my daughter-in-law, Barb.

'This is my eldest son, Rex. Phil's not here, he's gone now. This is my daughter, Dot. It's all right, Dot. Everything is all right, love.

'This is my friend Cassidy and my friend Alex and, if they'd brought Frolic, you could have patted her.'

Blink and Angus then turn to my father.

'This is my other son, Tommy,' says Blink, 'but I like to call him Whiskers.' He strokes my father's face.

Then it's my turn and Blink looks at me and then at Angus and his expression changes. He is baffled, then bemused and I fear he might topple over and I might go with him.

Blink's face lightens and he is strong again. 'This is Whiskers' boy,' he says. 'His name is...yes, his name is Paul.'

And it is only then that the two old soldiers fall into each other, sinking into the past and realigning it through the touch of a wounded shoulder and a wounded neck.

Michael Jacobson

And it is only then that all the years of doubt are removed, all the years of guilt are absolved, all the years of error are corrected, all the years of loss are found, and all the years of debt are repaid.

chapter 44

The next few days are extraordinary. So much becomes clear.

Gemma has everything organised. We're all together. We're all talking, asking questions, providing answers, filling the gaps in our memories or placing stories there for the first time.

There's always tea brewing and sometimes something stronger to really loosen the tongues. The best stories come then.

When it is finally time to leave, I feel it is a perfect ending. Except that it isn't quite the ending, because now, weeks later, I'm back in Queenstown, this time by myself.

Typically, I'm here at Gemma's persuasion.

'Come on,' she'd said, 'it's too good a story to keep to yourself. And where better to write it down?'

It rains nearly every day. Not that I needed to go out. I know what's there. And being holed up inside Gemma's huge house again, with its fire and familiarity and home cooking, isn't hard to take.

I've come here to try and bring all that has happened to some kind of coherence.

As well as those wonderful few days with everyone after Blink and Angus were reunited, I have had the benefit of long conversations with Adam and Annie, since they and Angus returned to England. The calls have cost me a fortune, but they have revealed so much more about their father, including details even they have only just learned. They've sent me papers, anything they think that might be of value.

'Use it all if you need to,' said Annie.

I've trawled my own memories and my hand and wrist have ached from transcribing them, as well as the tapes and notes from my talks with the others in the family. I have read and reread the old letters and diaries.

As for Blink, every time I have talked to him I wondered if this was the moment he'd lose me again and if that last sparkle of dignified life would fade. It didn't.

I have come to know everything and it is both thrilling and tinged with sadness, because now there is nothing left for me to know.

So I'm back in Queenstown.

Gemma said I should do this. I tell her I'm not a writer but she says it doesn't matter.

She says the story will guide me.

I'm looking back, remembering everything.

chapter 45

The call everyone dreads comes in the middle of the night and shocks you from sleep.

It's the call you know cannot be good news, nor is it when the call is for me.

I cut short my business trip and then I'm on a plane, an evening flight, the earliest I can get, and I am terrified as usual by the prospect of flying, yet at the same time anxious that, no matter how fast we fly, I may still be too late.

I lean forward, as if it might help, and the man in the next seat shoots me a glance that asks me what I'm doing.

Numb and frazzled, I eat the stiff and tasteless airline sandwich and drink the weak coffee.

As it turns out, I do arrive in time to be met at the airport by my brother Stevie, who drives straight to the hospital. As we enter Blink's ward, it's close to midnight.

My grandmother Isobel holds the old man's limp hand, but on seeing me she rises, kisses me, then returns to him.

My father watches from the discomfort of a vinyl-covered chair, grown soft and misshapen from years of other people's backsides and similar bedside vigils. Rex and Dot are by the window.

The intern—are they still called that?—has a swagger when he comes in, a confidence which Isobel pierces with her question.

'Is that it?' she asks, then again, referring to the noise coming from her husband.

From my position, I take in the young man's haircut, his trousers and shoes, which are trendy and somehow ill-fitting against the well-pressed tradition of his white neck-to-knee doctor's coat, with the curl of stethoscope looping out of a pocket.

He checks the drip and writes down whatever it is he finds of importance in the bright green readouts flashing on the machine at the side of Blink's bed.

The noise grows even uglier, inhuman, and again Isobel asks, 'Is that it?'

It had begun as a quiet drumroll, then changed to a *click-clack, click-clacking*, reminding me of the sound when Stevie and I were kids and we pegged Dad's playing cards to our spokes and raced our bikes down the street.

Now the noise is a bubbling, like soup on the boil, and Isobel moves forward in her chair and asks again, 'Doctor, is that it? Is that the death rattle?'

The death rattle. It seems such an old-fashioned term.

'Excuse me,' he says, rattled in his own way. 'I'd better fetch the sister.'

Blink is gone before she arrives a few minutes later.

'I'm sorry,' she says, holding Blink's wrist, 'someone should have been here.'

A fluorescent light on its last legs flickers in the hallway. The padding of a nurse's soft-soled shoes grows, peaks as she passes, then fades.

A car with squeaky brakes pulls up outside and three doors open and shut with six distinct sounds.

A volley of gunfire comes from a neighbouring ward as another patient and his visitor watch a western or a war movie on a small television.

A Seiko clock ticks. A machine beeps. A telephone rings.

'It's all right,' says Isobel. 'We were here.'

'I'll give you some privacy,' says the sister. 'I'm afraid there'll be some formalities to attend to, when you feel you're ready. I'll leave you now.'

Isobel's brittle composure finally shatters and I go to her and hold her as big sobs wrench her small body. She feels sharp to me, her bones worn down to points by the ordeal of the past few months as the illness quickened and steeled its resolve to go all the way and take Blink from her.

She pushes her head into the space between my neck and my shoulder, seeking that place where people seem to find most solace.

Looking over her grey, dry hair, I can see my grandfather. He is still, with one eye and his mouth open, and I think of the manner of his dying.

A few seconds after the intern leaves the ward, and as we are waiting for the sister, Blink's breathing becomes shorter, weaker and with longer spaces between each feeble effort.

'Blink?' says Isobel, a question.

The hurly-burly of a working hospital abandons our awareness and the lights of the city outside the ward window darken to illuminate nothing.

There are no ambulance sirens, there is no metallic *ching* of medical charts lifted from and then replaced on the steel rails at the ends of other patients' beds.

Neither is there the sound of staff chatting, carts being wheeled, public address messages nor nurse-call buttons being pressed by patients wanting their pillows fluffed, painkillers or just some kind of attention.

There is no hint of the presence of people, who have dragged themselves half-asleep and dressed in whatever they grabbed first, only to sit for hours in the waiting room, confused and afraid and desperate for news, filling the time by drinking the scalding, piss-weak tea from the vending machine.

No wail of children crying over stomach-aches or fighting for breath against asthma or croup. No drunks with gashed heads talking gibberish. No one walking across to the night receptionist and asking timidly, 'Will the doctor be much longer, dear?'

All trace of such things vanishes and there is only this family. The world has shrunk to us.

When the end comes, Blink looks strong. He sits up and the drip catches on something, pulling away from his arm to dangle uselessly over the bedrail, pulsing its clear fluid onto the tiled floor.

'Blink?' says Isobel.

But she isn't there, nor are any of us, not even me.

For Blink, it is a long time ago and he is young and well and tending a garden.

The reddest of roses catches his eye and as he walks towards it he sees another young man. The two of them smile and embrace, the smaller man's neck against the taller man's shoulder.

Together they walk, out of the garden and up towards a hill where a windmill is turning.

Blink falls back on the pillows, dead before he sinks into their plumpness, and he lies there with one eye shut, one eye and his mouth open.

That one open eye is as clear and as blue as the sky on a Tasmanian spring morning.

Michael Jacobson was born in Launceston, Tasmania, in 1961.

He has been a journalist since 1980, having worked in Launceston, Hobart, Sydney and now the Gold Coast, where he has lived for the past thirteen years.

He is a book reviewer, magazine editor and chief feature writer for the *Gold Coast Bulletin* and is married with two children.